DEATH OF A
CAVE DWELLER

DEATH OF A
CAVE DWELLER

Sally Spencer

This first world edition published in Great Britain 2000 by
SEVERN HOUSE PUBLISHERS LTD of
9–15 High Street, Sutton, Surrey SM1 1DF.
This first world edition published in the U.S.A. 2000 by
SEVERN HOUSE PUBLISHERS INC of
595 Madison Avenue, New York, N.Y. 10022.

British Library Cataloguing in Publication Data

Spencer, Sally
    Death of a cave dweller. - (A Chief Inspector Woodend novel)
    1. Detective and mystery stories
    I. Title
    823.9'14 [F]

ISBN 0-7278-5543-3

Typeset by Palimpsest Book Production Ltd.
Polmont, Stirlingshire, Scotland.
Printed and bound in Great Britain by
MPG Books Ltd, Bodmin, Cornwall.

For Andy Jack, who still holds the torch high
so long after so many others have laid it down.

And for Connie, a tiny cat with the heart of a lion and the
spirit of an explorer. Wherever you are, Little One, I hope
you're happy.

Author's Note

Anyone lucky enough to have been familiar with the music
scene in Liverpool in those thrilling days of the early sixties
– as I was myself – will instantly recognise the fact that the
Cellar Club is based very heavily on the Cavern, and that
the *Mersey Sound* bears more than a passing resemblance to
Mersey Beat. The characters I have chosen to fill these two
venerable institutions with, however, have never done more
than live in my imagination.

"Remember all you cave dwellers, the Cavern is the best of cellars."

Bob Wooler, the Cavern's disc jockey

One

No one even suspected there was going to be a murder.
But then why would they? Murders took place in dark
alleys and on vast empty commons. They were essentially
private acts, shared only by the victim and the killer – not a
spectator sport for nearly three hundred people. And it seemed
somehow wrong that anyone should lose his life between the
hours of noon and one, which nature had decreed was the time
when all respectable people should be eating their dinner.

The girls, unaware that anything as horrific as homicide was
about to happen, were queuing patiently outside an unprepossessing wooden door on a cobbled street which was just wide
enough to allow two small lorries to pass one another at a
slow speed. Most of the girls were wearing the kind of
high-heeled shoes which their mothers disapproved of, and
had their lacquered hair piled high on their heads, in what the
newspapers were calling the 'beehive' look. They were typists
and shop assistants, junior shipping clerks and hairdressers.
After work, many of them returned to homes where their
fathers' word was still law; but now, in the middle of the day,
they were about to experience true freedom. Though the rest of
the world was still ignorant of the musical explosion which was
soon to hit it, *they* knew the revolution had already happened,
and that for the payment of just one shilling, they could shimmy
and shake to the liberating rhythms of rock'n'roll.

Ron Clarke, the Cellar Club's resident disc jockey and a
grand old man of nearly thirty-five, was sorting through his

1

collection of records and only half listening to the conversation which was going on behind him in the bricked-off alcove at the edge of the stage, generously called 'the dressing room'.

"Now remember, boys," said a voice Clarke recognised as belonging to Jack Towers, the group's manager, "this isn't just any old performance. It's *never* any old performance. This could be the day somebody really important comes into the club, and catches your act – so no messing about."

Ron Clarke shook his head and clicked his tongue. Would Jack Towers never learn? Hadn't he been the Seagulls' manager long enough to know that this kind of approach would never work with a lad like Steve Walker?

"You know somethin', Jack?" Walker asked. "Listenin' to you is just like bein' back at school." He slipped effortlessly into a middle-class accent. "'Are you *chewing*, Walker? You should be listening to me, not doodling, Walker. You'll never get anywhere in life with your attitude, Walker.' So what will *you* do if I misbehave, Jack?" he continued in his normal voice. "Give me the cane? Or just make me write out 'I must learn not to be a naughty little rhythm guitarist' a hundred times?"

The disc jockey turned slightly to watch the rest of the little drama between the manager and the guitarist play itself out, though why he was interested he couldn't really say, since he'd seen variations on the same theme at least a dozen times.

Central to the drama – for the moment at least – was Jack Towers. He was tall and gangly, and always looked to Ron Clarke like a scarecrow who had at last saved up enough for a decent suit, but remained a scarecrow nonetheless. He was standing awkwardly in front of the group, who were lounging with studied cool in four battered armchairs.

Towers lit a fresh cigarette from the stub of the one he'd just been smoking, and shifted his position slightly.

A wiser man would leave things as they were, Clarke thought, but not Jack. The problem with him is, he just doesn't know when to keep his gob shut.

"What you don't seem to realise, Steve, is you don't get

to be successful just because your music's good," Towers said. "Presentation counts too." He ran his eyes over the blue jeans, black sweaters and brown boots which the Seagulls wore almost as a uniform. "Now if you'd just tone down your act a bit, and wear nice matching suits like the Shadows do—"

"Dang, dang, dang, dangderang, dang . . ." Steve Walker interrupted, imitating a twanging guitar.

"Listen, Steve—"

Walker sprang to his feet so suddenly that for a moment Ron thought the boy was going to take a swing at his manager. But it soon became plain that the reason he'd stood up was to imitate the synchronised steps the Shadows used in their stage act as he continued to 'dang dang', drowning out whatever it was Jack Towers had wanted to say.

Steve had a reputation as a hard bugger, Ron Clarke reminded himself, and he looked the part with his solid muscular body and his face which was all angles – pointed nose, sharp cheekbones and a jaw which looked like it could open tin cans. Even his dark eyes seemed to have a cutting edge to them, especially on occasions like this, when he was starting to get angry.

Walker had finished his performance, and flopped back on to the couch again. "Do you really call that kind of rubbish *music*, Jack?" he demanded.

"The Shadows are very popular," Jack Towers said in a long-suffering voice. "They're one of the top acts in the country – and they look good on television."

"An' in twelve months' time, everybody will be wonderin' what the fuss was all about," Steve Walker said. "They're nothin' but a novelty act. But we're *real*, and we're goin' to be bigger than they could ever be – twice as big. So don't talk about the Shadows to me – we'll be *leavin'* them in the shadows. Only we're goin' to do it our own way." He turned to the pale, thin-faced boy sitting next to him. "Isn't that right, Eddie?"

Eddie Barnes had huge eyes which were so intense they

could look either haunted or haunting, depending on his mood, but now, as he turned them on Steve Walker, they were full of hero worship. "That's right, Steve," the young lead guitarist said.

Walker should have left it there, Ron thought, but just like Jack Towers, he didn't know when to shut up.

"You tell him, Billie," he said to the group's drummer, managing to make it sound almost like an order. "You tell him we're goin' to be massive."

Billie Simmons, the only member of the group to favour a cowlick curl over the quiffs the rest wore, let a slight smile play on his rubbery lips. "We're goin' to be massive," he said, but in such a deadpan drawl that it was impossible to say whether or not he believed it – or even if he cared one way or the other.

"So that's almost unanimous, isn't it?" Steve Walker said, looking pointedly at Pete Foster, the bass player and the fourth member of the group.

Ron Clarke saw the hesitant expression fill Foster's boyish face. He doesn't like arguments, this one, the DJ thought. He prefers to pretend that things are going absolutely fine, even when it's perfectly obvious to everybody else that they aren't.

"Well?" Steve Walker asked.

"There's no point in bein' a good group if nobody outside Liverpool ever hears us," Pete Foster argued. "An' there's no point in you an' Eddie writin' all those songs if we're the only ones who ever sing them."

Steve Walker's dark eyes became almost black. "Is that you talkin', Pete – or is it your mum?" he said, with a dangerous edge creeping into his voice.

"Leave my mum out of it," Pete Foster answered, for once seeming on the verge of getting angry himself.

"All right, I'll leave her out of it," Steve said curtly. "An' I'll leave you out of it an' all, if you like. You understand what I'm sayin', our kid? Any time you're not happy with the way the group's goin', you know where the door is." He

4

turned his attention to their manager. "An' that goes for you as well, Jack."

Jack Towers looked crushed. "I only want what's best for you," he said helplessly. "You know that. I only want the group to do well."

His words – or perhaps their tone of desolation – seemed to soften Steve Walker. The coiled-up tension left his body, and he leaned forward to pat the manager on the arm.

"You're a good lad, Jack," he said, "but you've got to learn that we're the musicians around here – an' we're the ones who make the decisions about the act." He put his hand in his trouser pocket, and rattled his change. "Must be at least two bob in there," he guessed. "How about we set up the gear, then nip across to the Grapes for a quick half?"

The other members of the group nodded their agreement. Jack Towers nodded too, and said, with some relief in his voice, "That's a good idea, but I'm buying, so you'll all have pints."

The argument had ended just as he'd thought it would, Ron Clarke told himself – which was to say it had ended not with anything being settled, but simply because Steve Walker had decided he'd had enough.

The drums were already on stage, but the rest of the equipment had been stacked at the far end of the dressing room. Clarke watched the Seagulls pick up their guitars and amplifiers. The guitars were not the best that money could buy, but they were adequate for the job. The amplifiers, on the other hand, were a disaster. They had been cobbled together from pieces of other amps which had long ago given up the ghost, and if they could be relied on to do anything, they could be relied on to break down. Which was a pity, Ron Clarke thought, because the Seagulls were a talented group and really did deserve better.

The group, guitars and amps in their hands, squeezed through the narrow space between the DJ and the wall. As they passed him, Ron Clarke caught a distinct whiff of aftershave. It came as a surprise to him, as he knew the Seagulls had always considered such things effeminate – and though he could not swear to it, he was almost sure that the person who was wearing it was Eddie Barnes.

The big red-haired man opened the door, and the girls began to stream in through the gap. Balanced precariously on their high heels, they clacked and clattered their way carefully down the twenty steep stone steps which led to the club.

The place was, in fact, no more than three parallel interconnected tunnels, each supported by a series of brick archways. The first tunnel could have best been described as a reception area – it was there that the money was paid and the coats deposited. The furthest tunnel, which was shorter than the other two because of the bricked-off dressing room, served as a dance area. But it was the middle tunnel which, inevitably, was the centre of attention. At one end of it stood the snack bar, which served milk, Coke, pies and sandwiches. At the other end was the concrete-floored stage. And between the two were row after row of hard wooden seats.

The stage itself was not much to speak of. Even with the minimal equipment they carried around with them, the groups who played on it found very little room for manoeuvre, often banging into the ancient upright piano which stood at one side of it, or almost falling through the gap in the wall which led to the dressing room on the other.

The cellar had minimal ventilation and once a group had been playing for a while, moisture would drip down the walls, sometimes fusing the crude amplifiers. As the lunchtime session progressed, the place would grow hotter and hotter, clothes would become little more than wet rags, and the atmosphere would be thick with the smell of sweat and cheap perfume. Nor were the cellar's acoustics much to write home about. Almost anywhere – even a rickety village hall used for a boy scouts' meeting one day and a Women's Institute tea

6

party the next – would have allowed a cleaner, clearer sound than was possible in the brick vault.

Noisy, suffocating, muffled. None of that mattered. The echoes of the drumbeats might bounce off the walls, drowning the vocals, but the audience knew, with an absolute certainty, that they were in the most exciting place in the world, and experiencing something they would remember for the rest of their lives.

For a few minutes the girls wandered around aimlessly, patting their helmet-like hairdos, lighting a fresh cigarette or ordering a meat-and-potato pie at the bar. Then a sound like the hiss of an angry snake filled the air – a sign that the disc jockey, crouched in front of a cupboard in the dressing room, had switched on his equipment – and a ripple of anticipation ran through the room.

Ron Clarke spoke, using just the words they'd known he would. "Hi, all you cave dwellers – welcome to the best of cellars." And before even the first few beats of the pulsating R&B assaulted their ears, some of the girls were already dancing.

At a quarter past twelve, Ron Clarke put a fresh record on the turntable, then stuck his head out on to the stage to see if there was any sign of the Seagulls. They were just arriving back from the pub, making their way past the hard wooden seats towards the stage. Not that it was an uninterrupted journey, Clarke noted, but then he'd never thought it would be. The Seagulls were local heroes, and it was only natural that some of the people who had come to see them – especially the girls – would want a few words with them before they went on stage.

He watched the way the four of them dealt with their admirers, and decided that in this, as in so many other ways, they were four very distinct personalities. Steve Walker just stood there, soaking up this show of minor adoration as if it were no more than his due. Billie Simmons, his long nose and thick lips twisted in a comical expression, was making the girls around him giggle. Pete Foster had an uncertain half-smile on his face – a smile which said that while he was loving all this, there was a part of him which was already worrying about how long his popularity would last. And Eddie Barnes? Eddie was trying to be polite to the girls who had surrounded him, but it was plain that he saw listening to them as nothing more than a distraction from his real purpose, which was to play his guitar.

They were all good lads, Ron thought. Steve could be a little abrasive, but he had a heart of gold. Pete was insecure – and with a mother like his, who wouldn't be? – which sometimes caused him to be less than honest, but he'd probably grow out of that. It was impossible not to like Billie, with his droll approach to life. But it was Eddie Barnes, Ron decided, who he had the softest spot for. Eddie was so serious and so gentle. He hardly ever said a word, yet the DJ sensed that it was he, rather than one of the others, that people would go to when they were in trouble.

The four young men climbed up on to the stage. Ron Clarke nodded to them, then retreated into the dressing room. Billie Simmons got behind his drum kit, and the rest of the group picked up their instruments.

The record which had been playing came to an end. There was a click as the needle navigated its way through the empty groove, then another hiss from the tannoy system. The uncomfortable seats were all occupied, and most of the girls who'd been dancing in the third tunnel now stood in the archways, craning their necks to get a good view of the stage.

From the cramped space in front of his record player, Ron Clarke made his announcement. "Put your hands together, boys and girls, and give a big welcome to one of Liverpool's greatest groups – the Seagulls!"

The young men just stood there while the applause filled the air. *"Never start playing until the clapping's begun to fade,"*

Jack Towers had told them more than once – and in this matter, at least, Steve Walker was prepared to follow the manager's instructions.

It was perhaps a minute before the applause did start to die down. Steve Walker and Pete Foster quickly stepped forward, but it was Steve who won the race to the microphone.

"Are you feelin' good?" he asked his audience.

A couple of hundred voices screamed back that they were.

Walker stamped his left foot on the ground, then dragged his heel a few inches, so that the metal studs imbedded in it threw up sparks. Make a show, they'd been told in Germany. Well, didn't he always? And with the lads behind him, there was none better.

"I mean, are you feelin' *really* good?" he yelled at the girls.

The screaming got louder.

Behind him, Steve could sense Pete's growing resentment that he was hogging the limelight. "This first number we'd like to do for you is one written by our lead guitarist, Eddie," he said. "It's called 'Lime Street Rock'."

He took a couple of steps backwards, to allow the pale young guitarist to take the central stage. Over his shoulder, he heard Billie Simmons start the introductory beat. Eddie lifted his pick to play the opening chords.

Instead of the frenetic explosion of sound which had been expected, there was nothing more than a weak 'plink'. Eddie shrugged his shoulders in disgust, then stepped back, turned, and bent over the crude amplifier, as he had done so often in the past. This time, however, it was different. This time, the moment his slim fingers touched the bass control, he began to writhe like a maniac. The fans turned to look at each other – puzzled expressions on their faces. They were used to Steve and Pete playing the wild man during the act – but Eddie was always the intense one, concentrating on the music as if each note was a huge effort. Later, of course, when those same fans were recounting the incident to friends who hadn't been there,

9

they would say that they'd known something was wrong right from the start. Some of them would even claim that they'd been able to smell the burning flesh.

Two

The murder of Eddie Barnes had been splashed across the front page of the *Liverpool Echo* in screaming headlines, but even before the paper came out, news of the young guitarist's tragic death had spread across the city by word of mouth. A small crowd had gathered outside the Cellar Club within a couple of hours, and had not dispersed until late in the evening. Another crowd – though perhaps not the same people – had appeared the following morning, and by eight thirty there were more than fifty onlookers standing in the street.

Not that there was much for them to see. True, five police cars were parked near the club door, making it almost impossible for lorries to make their deliveries to the warehouses. And true, behind the heavy wood and metal police barriers which sealed off the club were half a dozen uniformed constables who frowned at anyone who seemed likely to put even a foot inside the restricted area. But the spectators could only guess at the atmosphere inside the club itself. Still, when they did eventually begin to drift away, it was with the feeling that however far the investigation had progressed, it was at least steaming ahead purposefully.

There was very little sense of purpose in the two men who stood on the stage of the club, looking aimlessly into the cramped dressing room.

The elder of the two, a superintendent, glanced down at his watch. "It's now just over twenty hours since this Eddie Barnes kid got himself fried," he said. "An' what do we know now

11

that we didn't know at the start of this case, Frank? I'll tell you. Absolutely bugger all!"

"It's early days yet, guv," said his sergeant.

"An' furthermore, I don't see how we're *ever* goin' to find out anythin'," the superintendent continued, as if his bagman hadn't spoken the reassuring words which bagmen are always supposed to speak. "Look at the case usin' the standard procedural guidelines – means, motive and opportunity." He held out three fingers. "Means," he touched the first finger with his other hand. "Anybody who knew a little bit about electrical wirin' had that. Opportunity," he struck the second finger. "A lot of fellers had the opportunity – a bloody sight *too* many for my likin'. An' motive?" He brushed the third finger. "There *isn't* one! Eddie Barnes, accordin' to everybody we've spoken to, was a little saint. An' if all that's not enough to make you despair, there's the fact that the murderer didn't even have to be here when Barnes died."

"Point taken, sir," the sergeant said. "It's goin' to be a very tough case to crack."

"Tough!" the superintendent repeated scornfully. "It's goin' to be more than tough – it's goin' to be bloody impossible."

"So what are you goin' to do, sir?" the sergeant asked, picking his words carefully. "I mean, we can't just give up on it, can we?"

"I already have. That's why I'm goin' to tell the Chief Constable that we need outside help."

"Scotland Yard? You're callin' in Scotland Yard!"

"Who else?" The superintendent gave his sergeant a piercing stare. "You don't seem very keen on the idea, Frank."

"I'm not," the sergeant admitted. "To tell you the truth, I don't like the thought of somebody from London invadin' our patch – an' neither will most of the rest of the lads on the case."

"I'm not over the moon about it either," the superintendent told him. "But look at it this way. We've got two choices. We can fail to solve the murder ourselves, or we can let the Yard fail to solve it. If we do the second, then the moment they've gone back to London with their tails between their legs, we can start droppin' hints to the local press that without fancy detectives from London buggerin' it up, we'd have had the case cracked within the week."

"An' if they do crack it?"

"Then we let the local reporters know that we did most of the work. Either way, we can't lose."

"Even so . . ." the sergeant said dubiously.

"You talk about them invadin' our patch, but they won't be," the superintendent argued. "They'll be dealin' with a liaison officer who I'll have hand-picked. They'll be usin' my lads for their footwork, and they'll be workin' out of the local nick. Bloody hell, Frank, we'll have them under our thumb from the moment they get here."

"That might be true of most of them, sir," the sergeant said, with doubt still evident in his voice. "But what if they send us Mr Woodend? An' it's very likely that they will, because from what I've heard, the top brass at the Yard are never happier than when he's workin' a couple of hundred miles away from them."

The superintendent grinned. "You're right, they'll use pretty much any excuse to get him out of their hair," he agreed. "But I'm not a complete idiot, Frank. As soon as I got the idea of callin' in the Yard, I was on the phone to a mate of mine in administration. I asked exactly where Woodend was at the moment, an' it turns out that Cloggin'-it Charlie is up to his neck in a double murder in Birmingham. My mate doesn't think he'll be able to untangle himself from that mess until much before this side of Christmas."

Detective Sergeant Bob Rutter lay on his back in bed, smoking a cigarette and listening to his wife's slow, careful footsteps as she made her way up the stairs. She would be carrying a cup of tea in one hand, he thought – a cup of tea it had taken her at least ten minutes to produce.

He could picture her making that tea; counting slowly after she'd turned on the tap, so she knew when the kettle was full enough; positioning the tea pot in exactly the right spot on the work surface, so that when she poured the boiling water it wouldn't spill everywhere; feeling around with her left hand because the sugar bowl wasn't quite where she remembered leaving it . . .

He had watched her go through the same motions on hundreds of occasions in the previous few months, and sometimes it almost broke his heart. Yet even though he always longed to offer his help, he forced himself to keep quiet because he knew that his offer would at best cause resentment, and at worst, rage.

And who could blame her for that? he asked himself. Who could wonder that she felt the need to demonstrate her independence after the terrible tragedy which had befallen her?

The bedroom door opened, and Maria stepped into the room. As usual, her appearance caused Rutter's heart to give a little flutter. As usual, he was mildly surprised that he seemed to have forgotten just how stunning her dark Spanish beauty was.

Maria walked over to the bedside table, and placed the cup on it. It was almost as if she could see again, Rutter thought. But she couldn't. It was simply that she had practised this movement, just as she had practised her walk down the aisle in the church where they had been married.

"So you finally have a day off," Maria said, with just the slightest trace of a foreign accent in her voice. "What are you going to do with it?"

"Haven't really given it much thought," Rutter told her.

It was quite true. He'd expected to be stuck in Birmingham for at least a couple more weeks, but then his boss, Chief Inspector Woodend, had made one of his famous – some said *infamous* – imaginative leaps, and the case had been wrapped up at breakneck speed.

"It's nice to be home again," he continued. "Maybe I'll just potter round the house today."

"You don't have to stay in," Maria said, almost defensively. "I have plenty to keep me occupied."

"I thought I might help you."

"There's no one here to help me when you're out on a case," Maria reminded him. "And I manage perfectly well then."

"Perhaps I *want* to stay in," Rutter said, a defensiveness now creeping into his own voice.

"You used to play tennis nearly every day," Maria said, "but it's months since you even picked up a racket."

I used to play tennis with *you*, Rutter thought. Can't you see how painful it is for me now to play against someone else?

"I will not be treated like a child," Maria complained.

Rutter reached out, and gently pulled her on to the bed beside him. "Is that how I treat you?" he asked. "Like a child?"

"Sometimes."

He brushed his lips against hers. "Am I treating you like an adult now?" he asked.

"You're starting to," she admitted.

He reached up and caressed her right breast. "And now?"

"Your tea will go cold," she warned him.

"To hell with my tea," he said, starting to unbutton her housecoat.

Billie Simmons and Pete Foster sat opposite each other in the Casablanca Coffee Bar, just off Cook Street. In front of them were two untouched cups of cappuccino, which had been steaming when they'd first got them, but now were lukewarm. Neither the slightly plump bass guitarist nor the normally placid drummer looked at all happy.

"This thing with Eddie couldn't have happened at a worse time," Pete Foster said, lighting up a Woodbine.

"Oh, so there's a good time to be electrocuted on stage, is there?" Billie Simmons asked.

Pete jerked his head, as if he'd suddenly received a slight electric shock himself. "No, of course there isn't," he said hurriedly. He held his hands out, palms upwards. "Look, I'm as sorry about Eddie's death as the rest of you. I mean, he was my mate as well."

"He was *Steve's* mate," Billie corrected him. "As far as Eddie was concerned, you an' me were just the other fellers in the group."

"The point is," Pete persisted, "Eddie's death leaves a big gap in the band – my mum was sayin' the same thing just this mornin' – an' that's just what we can't afford right now."

"Why right now?" Billie asked, picking up on the last two words. "Do you know somethin' I don't?"

"How could I?" Pete asked, avoiding the question. "All I meant was, after all the work we've put in we're finally startin' to make a name for ourselves, and losin' Eddie is a big setback."

He was lying, Billie decided. Pete and Jack Towers were as thick as two thieves, and if the manager had any news to give them, Pete always got it first. But whatever the secret was that he was hiding, there was no way it could pried out of him now.

"When you asked me to come out for a coffee, you said you were worried about two things," the drummer said. "So what's the other?"

Pete Foster puffed nervously on his cigarette. "I'm scared, Billie," he admitted. "*Really* scared."

"Of what?"

"Of what?" Pete repeated. "Isn't it bloody obvious? I mean, it's not as if Eddie's death came completely out of the blue, is it? There's been all the other stuff – like the dead rat."

"That didn't have anythin' to do with Eddie gettin' killed," Billie said dismissively.

"Didn't it?" Pete replied, a hysterical edge creeping into his voice. "How can you be so sure of that? Are you an expert on murders, all of a sudden?"

"There's a big difference between bein' willin' to play a few dirty tricks an' bein' willin' to take somebody's life," Billie

16

argued. "The joker an' the killer just have to be two different people."

"When I was a kid, there was an old feller lived on his own at the end of our street," Pete said. "He was a right loonie – always shoutin' at us, an' wavin' his fist. Well, we began playin' this game with his front door. When it first started, the rule was that all you had to do was run up to the door an' touch it. But after a bit, that got borin'. So we said that from then on, you had to knock on the door as loud as you could. Finally, you had to knock on the door, an' actually wait there until he started to open it."

"What's your point?"

"That's what this feels like to me," Pete said. "First there were the phone calls, then the rat, now Eddie. Whoever's doin' this is gettin' more an' more extreme every time."

"You can't get more extreme than murder," Billie pointed out.

"Can't you?" Pete asked, nervously lighting a new cigarette from the stub of his old one. "Well, what about *two* murders?"

"You've got a screw loose," the drummer told him.

"I don't think I have," Pete countered. "It seems to me that somebody's got it in for the Seagulls – an' I don't want to be the next one to end up dead."

Rutter lay back contentedly, his wife's head buried in his chest. There were a few difficulties in their situation, he thought. More than a few. But not for a second did he regret marrying his beautiful, blind wife.

The nagging ring of the telephone in the hall cut into his thoughts. "Damn!" he said.

"You don't have to answer it," Maria murmured sleepily.

"If I don't, he'll only ring back in five minutes."

"You can't be sure it's Mr Woodend."

"Oh yes I can. I don't know how he does it, but nobody can

17

make the telephone bell ring like Cloggin'-it Charlie."

Maria sighed, and shifted her position so that Rutter could swing his body off the bed. Perhaps he was right. The telephone did seem to have a more insistent ring whenever the caller was Charlie Woodend.

Rutter made his way quickly down the stairs. They'd get a phone extension put in the bedroom, he decided. That way, when Maria was upstairs when it rang, she'd have time to answer the phone herself – before the caller hung up in exasperation.

He lifted the receiver. "Hello, sir."

The man on the other end of the line chuckled. "We'll make a detective of you yet," he said.

The voice sounded like the man himself, Rutter thought. Big and square and dependable. He remembered the first time he had met Woodend, on Euston railway station, and how shocked he'd been that a chief inspector should be dressed in a hairy sports coat, cavalry twill trousers and scuffed suede shoes. With the arrogance of youth, he'd assumed that Woodend's wife was to blame for his scruffy appearance. Now he knew better. Joan Woodend had tried for years to smarten her husband up, but though she could usually bend most people to her will, she'd had no success with her Charlie.

"Got any plans for your unexpected day off?" the chief inspector asked.

"Not really."

"Very wise," Woodend said. "A bobby should never count on havin' any free time."

"Where are we being sent?"

"Nowhere yet. But from what I've just read in the papers, I shouldn't be surprised if we get a call to say we're wanted in Liverpool."

Rutter nodded at himself in the mirror. If there were a case in Liverpool, it would almost definitely be theirs. "So what's the job?" he asked. "Does it sound interesting?"

18

Woodend chuckled again. "Oh, it sounds interestin' enough," he said. "An' it should be right up your street, an' all."

"Right up my street?" Rutter repeated, mystified.

"Aye, it's what you might call a rock'n'roll murder. Maybe the first one there's ever been."

Three

The ferry chugged stoically across the grey-blue water towards Liverpool's Pier Head. It was a mild morning in early April. The sun shone down benevolently on the docks – those same docks which had made Liverpool rich during the height of the slave trade, and had been the target for so much of the German Luftwaffe's fury during the war. Overhead, sea birds glided on the air currents and cawed incessantly. Underfoot, the boat's engine sent vibrations throbbing through the deck floorboards. An hour earlier, the ferry had been packed with commuters, but now the two men on the upper deck pretty much had it to themselves.

"We didn't need to take the train to Birkenhead, you know, sir," Bob Rutter said. "I checked up in the timetable. There was a direct connection from Euston to Liverpool Lime Street."

"So I believe," Woodend replied. "But if we'd gone direct, we wouldn't have had the pleasure of arrivin' in the 'Pool in style, would we?"

Rutter permitted himself a grin. He supposed he should be grateful that the ferry trip was putting his boss in such a good mood, because the journey up from London had been by diesel train, and Woodend – who thought that the only manly way to travel was under steam power – had been distinctly grumpy about it.

Woodend reached into one of the voluminous pockets of his hairy sports jacket and pulled out a package carefully wrapped in greaseproof paper. Rutter made a private bet with himself it contained corned-beef sandwiches, with the bread cut doorstep thick, and when his boss had unwrapped it, he saw that he was right.

"Dickens used to like comin' to Liverpool, you know," Woodend said, before taking a generous bite out of his sandwich.

"Did he, sir?"

"Aye, he did that. He said that it was his next favourite town after London. He used to take the ferry across the Mersey regularly. Claimed it helped him to clear his head."

Rutter shook his own head, wonderingly. Charlie Woodend and his Charles Dickens. The chief inspector was fond of saying that his favourite author should be used as part of the police training course, and though there were other officers who thought he was only joking, his own sergeant knew that he was deadly serious.

"I've got some old friends in Liverpool," Woodend said. He paused. "Some old enemies, an' all, if it comes to that."

Rutter simply nodded. That was how things were with his boss, he'd learned – either people liked him so much they'd climb a tree for him, or else they felt much happier when he was out of the way.

The chief inspector examined the dock front. Cranes were busy unloading cargoes from ships weighed down with fruit fresh from Africa. Liners, heading for American and Australia, bobbed quietly in the water and waited for the right tide. Even from a distance, he could sense the bustle.

"Bein' a southerner, you'll not have been here before, will you, Bob?" he asked, somehow making Rutter's unfamiliarity with the town sound like a character defect.

"No, sir, I haven't," the sergeant replied, deadpan.

"It's a grand place," Woodend told him. "There's a lot of life – a lot of excitement – in it. Do you know, I'm rather lookin' forward to workin' on this case."

"Are you indeed," Rutter said, raising a surprised eyebrow.

"An' what's that supposed to mean? Is it some clever

grammar-school way of takin' the piss?" Woodend asked, without rancour.

Rutter grinned again. It was not the first time that Woodend had brought up his grammar-school education, and he was sure it would be far from the last.

"It's just that I thought a country boy like you would be much happier working in a village," he explained.

The chief inspector sighed – a clear indication that he thought his sergeant had missed a fundamental point.

"You can't just define villages by geography," he said. He tapped his forehead. "Villages are up here – in your noggin."

"Would you care to explain that, sir?" Rutter asked, knowing his boss would, whether he wanted him to or not.

"Nobody lives in a city," Woodend said. "It's too big for the mind to take in. No, what people do is they build up their own little world which is bounded by their house, the pub they drink in, the place they work, an' their corner shop. They might venture out into the rest of the city now an' again, but when they do, they're only *visitin'*."

He was probably right, Rutter decided, thinking of his own childhood in north London.

"An' then there's the other kind of village," Woodend continued. "The village that is made up by havin' shared interests. It could be an amateur dramatic society, or a pigeon-fanciers' association, but when all those people who share that interest get together, what you have is a community."

"I see your point, sir," Rutter said, but what he was thinking was, 'Read your Dickens, Sergeant. You'll find it all there in Dickens.'

"Read your Dickens, Sergeant," Woodend told him. "You'll find it all there in Dickens."

He had finished his sandwich and now reached into another of his pockets, and pulled out a packet of Capstan Full Strength cigarettes. He did not offer one to Rutter, having long ago accepted that his sergeant – for some strange reason of his own – preferred to smoke fags with an American cork tip.

"You've been on the blower to the Liverpool bobbies, haven't you, lad?" he asked, striking a match and lighting up.

"Yes, sir. Just before we left London."

"So what did they have to tell you?"

"The dead man . . ." Rutter began. "Well, the dead *boy*, really – he was only just twenty—"

"A bit younger than you, then," Woodend interrupted, a look of amusement flashing briefly across his face. "Carry on, lad."

"The dead boy belonged to a band called the Seagulls."

"Should I have heard of them?" Woodend asked. "Are they famous, like this Buddy Ivy you're always listenin' to?"

"Buddy *Holly*," Rutter corrected him. "No, sir, they're not. Most of the famous groups are either American, or are based in the London area. Coming from the North is a little . . ." He groped for the right word.

"Unfashionable?" Woodend provided.

"I suppose so."

"Aye, your lot from down south never did give my lot much credit," the chief inspector said. "So, you were tellin' me all about these singin' sea birds."

"According to the local sergeant I talked to, they're very popular around the Liverpool area," Rutter said. "They've played in Germany, too. Hamburg, I think. Anyway, they were booked to appear at in a place called the Cellar Club the day before yesterday. They started playing, but the lead guitarist's amplifier wasn't working properly. He bent down to adjust the bass control, and was electrocuted. Someone had wrapped a live wire around the spindle. The Liverpool Police are convinced the re-wiring was done with malice aforethought."

"What I still don't understand is why it should have killed him," Woodend said. "I got a shock from the mains once, an' I'm still here."

Rutter looked a little embarrassed. "It's a bit technical, sir."

"You're a bright lad. You should be able to explain it even to a stone-age bobby like me," Woodend said.

"All right. Where were you when you got your shock?" Rutter asked.

"Upstairs. In the front bedroom."

"Eddie Barnes was in a cellar, much closer to the ground. Were your hands wet when you got the shock?"

"No, I don't think so."

"There's apparently very little ventilation at the club. Even if he'd only been there for a few minutes, Barnes would already have been sweating – and electrical current loves to travel through moisture. What were you wearing on your feet?"

"Carpet slippers."

"With rubber soles. Good insulation. Eddie Barnes was wearing leather boots with metal studs in them."

"I still don't see it," Woodend admitted.

"Think of electricity as water and you and Eddies Barnes as dams. The current wants to get through you and out again on the other side, but because you're well insulated – because there's no crack in your dam – it can't. Eddie's a different matter. The electricity finds a number of gaps in his dam, and it gushes through destroying everything in its path. Do you get it now, sir?"

"Aye, I think so," Woodend said. "So somebody wanted him dead, an' re-wired his amp. Does anybody have any idea when this re-wirin' might have been done?"

Rutter shrugged. "Sometime between the last time he used the equipment and the moment it killed him."

"That's not much help," Woodend mused. "Witnesses?"

"Round about three hundred of them actually saw the murder, but the police haven't managed to turn up anyone who saw the murderer tampering with the equipment."

The chief inspector threw his cigarette end over the side of the boat, and watched it fly through the air current until it crash-landed in the grey-blue river.

"Nasty things – murders by remote control," he said. "The

killer's got no problems with an alibi, has he? He could have been right in the room when the poor lad got himself electrocuted. On the other hand, he could have been miles away, havin' a coffee with his mates."

Rutter smiled in a way which alerted his boss to the fact that he thought he was about to score a point.

"It's not like you to be prejudiced, sir," he said.

"Prejudiced?" Woodend repeated. "What are you talkin' about?"

Rutter's smile broadened. "You keep saying 'he'. Does that mean you've ruled out the possibility that the murderer's a woman?"

"I can't say I've even thought about rulin' it out *consciously*," Woodend admitted. "But now you mention it, I suppose I have."

"Because of the murder method?"

It was rare to see the chief inspector look uncomfortable, but he did at that moment.

"Well, you know,' he said awkwardly. "Women and electricity. They don't really mix, do they?"

Rutter laughed. "You're behind the times, sir," he said. "Girls brought up since the war have a different attitude to ones you would have gone out with when you were young. Why, Maria wired her whole study herself. Of course, that was before her accident."

Her accident. Woodend marvelled at the calm, controlled way his sergeant could say the words, but he knew it was taking Bob Rutter a considerable about of effort to maintain that calm.

"I don't often ask about Maria," he said. "The way I see it, if you want to tell me anythin' about her, then you will. But I'm always thinkin' about her – worryin' about her."

"I know you are, sir," Rutter said gratefully. "But you shouldn't worry. She's treating the whole business of finding her way around as a challenge – almost an adventure."

"She always was a kid with spirit," Woodend said admiringly. "You're a lucky man."

"You don't need to tell me that," Rutter replied.

They had almost reached Pier Head, and could see a uniformed police inspector standing on the pier and gazing up at the boat.

"That'll be our reception committee," Woodend said. "Wonder how long it's goin' to take me to get him house-trained?"

Near the stage of the Cellar Club, the two old women who supplemented their state pensions with a cleaning job were mopping the floor. Standing by the snack bar, and half watching them, were a man and a woman. The woman was Alice Pollard, the owner of the club, a brassy blonde who would never see the right side of forty again. The man was much younger, perhaps no more than twenty-three or twenty-four, and had muscles which threatened to burst his shirt buttons every time he breathed out. His name was Rick Johnson, and for the last six months he had been employed as Alice Pollard's doorman.

Alice looked down longingly at the whisky bottle which was resting on the counter. It was a bit early in the day for her first drink, but what with the murder and everything, she reckoned she deserved one. She poured herself a generous measure, and knocked it back in one gulp.

"I'd go bit easier on that if I was you, Alice," Rick Johnson advised her.

Ignoring the warning, the woman poured herself a second shot.

"It said in the paper that the local bluebottles have given up trying to solve the case themselves and have called in Scotland Yard," she said.

"You don't have to tell me that," Johnson replied irritably. "I can *read*, you know."

"Course you can," Alice Pollard said in a soothing voice. "The thing is, it's obvious that these fellers from London are

26

going to be a lot more thorough than the bobbies we've had to deal with so far."

"What's that supposed to mean?" Johnson demanded.

"You know what it means. It means they'll be taking a much closer look at you than the Liverpool Police did."

"An' what if they do? I had no reason to kill Eddie Barnes," Johnson protested.

Alice Pollard sighed loudly. "They won't see it like that, and you know it," she said.

"Then to hell with them!"

"It's not that easy, luv. I only wish it was. They've got to arrest somebody for this murder, and the way things are looking you're a pretty good candidate."

"What do you want me to do?" Rick Johnson asked, more sulky than annoyed now.

"Just keep your head down for a while. Don't go charging around like a bull in a china shop like you usually do. If they talk to you, try smiling at them now and again, instead of looking like you'd like to catch them alone down a dark alley." She reached across and put her hand on his arm. "I'm only saying this because I care about you. I care about you very much."

"I know you do, Alice. An' I care about you an' all."

"So you'll follow my advice, will you?"

"Yes, I'll follow your advice," Johnson said, without much conviction.

Babysitting the men from London had not been a job anyone else had wanted, Inspector Brian Hopgood thought, as he watched the Birkenhead-to-Liverpool ferry docking – but that only showed what a lack of foresight his colleagues had.

Woodend's reputation had put the others off, and prevented them from seeing the fact that this investigation presented a tremendous opportunity. At the very least, the officer who worked with the men from Scotland Yard would get some of the kudos if the case were solved. And that *was* the very least. At best, if all went according to plan, Hopgood could take Woodend's findings, add his own local knowledge, and make the arrest himself.

He could imagine the newspaper headline – '**Local inspector succeeds where Scotland Yard fails**'! Oh yes, this was the chance he'd been looking for ever since he'd joined the force, and he wasn't about to blow it just because a few of the spineless bastards back at the station had been muttering about just how difficult Cloggin'-it Charlie Woodend could be.

The ferry mooring ropes had been tied firmly around the capstan, and now, slowly and creakingly, the gangplank was being lowered. Hopgood lit up a Player's Navy Cut, and steeled himself to meet the ogre whom lesser men stood in dread of.

His first sight of Woodend was reassuring. Certainly he was a big feller, as ogres are supposed to be, but from the way he was looking around him with obvious – almost naïve – interest, he seemed more like a rustic on his first visit to a large city than he did a hotshot up from New Scotland Yard.

The inspector stepped forward and held out his hand. "Brian Hopgood, sir," he said in the firm but reassuring tone he'd spent long hours perfecting. "I'll be your liaison with the Liverpool Police."

Woodend shook the hand, and ran his eyes quickly up and down the local flatfoot. Hopgood was in his mid-thirties, the chief inspector guessed. He had probably only just made the height qualification, had thin pointed features and the sort of eyes which suggested craftiness rather than intelligence. He probably wasn't a bad bobby in his own way, but he was certainly not one Woodend wanted to let anywhere near a murder investigation.

The chief inspector cocked his head in the general direction of Rutter.

"This is my sergeant," he said. "Bob Rutter. He was a grammar-school boy, you know, which means that he probably has more brains in that head of his than you an' me have between us. Which is another way of sayin' that he's got my complete an' utter confidence, so if he asks for anythin', there's no need to check back with me if he should have it. Understood?"

So much for the pleasantries, Inspector Hopgood thought. "Yes, sir, it's understood," he said.

"Right," Woodend continued. "Have you booked us in at a bed an' breakfast or summat?"

"We've got you rooms at the Adelphi, sir."

Woodend raised an eyebrow in mock astonishment.

"The Adelphi!" he repeated. "My, but we are grand. We'd better make this case last as long as possible, then, Sergeant."

"Sir?" Rutter asked quizzically.

"The Adelphi is probably the best hotel in Liverpool," Woodend told him. "You'll not be stayin' in its like again – not on a bobby's wages, you won't – so like I say, we better make the investigation last."

A look of concern appeared on Inspector Hopgood's face.

"That's just Mr Woodend's little joke," Rutter explained.

Hopgood turned his attention to the chief inspector, as if looking for confirmation.

"Aye, I'm a great one for makin' little jokes," Woodend assured him. His eyes narrowed. "I sincerely hope, Inspector, that the Adelphi Hotel – as grand as it is – isn't too far from the scene of the crime. Because if it is too far, it's no bloody good to me."

"How far *is* too far, sir?" Hopgood asked.

"If I can walk it from one place to the other in fifteen minutes, that'll be good enough for me."

"You won't need to walk, sir," Hopgood pointed out. "You'll have a car and driver at your disposal."

"An' sometimes I might actually use them," Woodend countered. "But you don't solve murders by lookin' out through the windows of a police Bentley. You have to clog it around. Get a taste of the place. Feel the pulse of it through the soles of your feet. So I'll ask you again, Inspector. Can I get from the hotel to the scene of the crime in fifteen minutes?"

"I should think so," said Hopgood, who had pretty much given up walking anywhere since he'd been promoted out of foot patrol.

"It'll do champion then," Woodend said. "Have our suitcases sent up there, will you?"

"Won't you be going there yourself, sir?" Hopgood asked.

"I've never really felt comfortable in posh hotel bars."

"I beg your pardon, sir?"

"It's thirsty work, travellin'," Woodend told him. "So where's the nearest ordinary, decent pub?"

Four

Inspector Hopgood – who didn't approve of drinking in the middle of the day, but in the few short minutes he'd known Woodend had already learned better than to protest – tried to steer the London men into the lounge of the Chandler's Arms, only to find that he himself was being skilfully manoeuvred into the public bar by the big detective in the hairy sports coat.

"I don't like pub lounges," Woodend said, running his eyes approvingly over the sawdust-covered floor of the bar. "Somehow the ale doesn't taste the same when the room's carpeted."

It was all Hopgood could do to avoid shaking his head bemusedly. Senior policemen, in his experience, didn't mix with the riff-raff when they went for a drink, and he couldn't quite work out what game Woodend was playing.

He cleared his throat. "Uh . . . what are you having, sir?"

Woodend patted him on the shoulder. "Nay, lad," he said. "I'm the one on the big wage. I'll get 'em in. You go an' sit over there, an' get to know my sergeant a little bit better."

The arrival of two men in suits, accompanied by another in a police uniform, had unsettled the other customers in the bar, who were mainly merchant seamen and dockers. Woodend had already noticed several hands being shoved into pockets as shady deals were rapidly postponed. He grinned to himself, and wondered how many stolen watches, illicit bottles of whisky and contraband cigarettes he could find in this pub if he really tried.

He bought the beer, and took it over to a cast-iron table in the corner of the bar where Hopgood and Rutter were sitting.

"So the murder victim's a teenager," he said, as he made himself comfortable on the cracked leather settle. "There were no such things as teenagers when I was growin' up. You were either a kid or you were an adult." He clicked his fingers. "The change happened just like that. You went straight from short pants an' comics to dressin' an' thinkin' just like your dad."

"Times change, sir," said Hopgood, who had little patience with anything which smelled of philosophical musing.

"Aye, times do change," Woodend agreed. "An' it's a damn good thing, in my opinion. I think teenagers are a fine idea. You might as well have your fun while you're young, because there's no bloody time for it later on." He took a sip of his pint, and smacked his lips with satisfaction. "Course, there are always some little pleasures left, however long in the tooth you're gettin'."

Faced with the choice of disagreeing with the Scotland Yard man or changing the subject, Inspector Hopgood reached into his briefcase and pulled out a typewritten sheet of paper.

"This is a list of all the people who had access to Eddie Barnes's amplifier between the last time he used it and the moment he was killed," he said crisply. "It includes their names, full addresses and – where applicable – their telephone numbers."

Woodend scanned the list. There seemed to be at least twenty names on it. He folded it roughly, and stuck it in the pocket of his sports jacket.

"Well, that'll give us plenty to go at," he said. "Now why don't you tell me a little bit about the band Eddie Barnes belonged to – the Albatrosses, isn't it?"

Hopgood frowned. "I think you mean, the Seagulls, sir."

"That's right," Woodend admitted, winking surreptitiously at his sergeant. "I suppose I do."

The inspector's frown deepened as perplexity set in. Why

32

the bloody hell should Woodend want to know about the band? How would that help him get to bottom of the murder?

"What exactly would you like to know, sir?" he asked.

"Anythin' and everythin' would be a good start."

Suppressing his own view that the Seagulls – like all the other bands of scruffy youths who made jungle music – should be banned from playing in public for ever, and possibly locked up, Hopgood searched his mind for some scrap of information which might keep Woodend happy.

"I believe they're quite a popular band," he said finally, "but they haven't got half the following of the Beatles."

"The Beetles?" Woodend repeated. "As in Colorado beetles – the marrow grower's worst nightmare, the Ghenghis Khans of the cabbage patch?"

If there was a joke in there somewhere Hopgood couldn't see it, and merely shook his head.

"Not beetles like that, sir," he said. "Beatles – with an 'a'. They're the real stars around Liverpool, but they're away performing somewhere in Germany at the moment."

Woodend turned to his sergeant. "Should I have heard of these Beatles, Bob?" he asked.

Rutter shrugged. "Probably not, sir. It's certainly a new name to me."

Woodend took another sip of his drink. "Is this club . . . this Cellar place . . . open again now?" he asked Hopgood.

"Yes, sir. Forensics gave it the all clear yesterday."

"Then I think I'll go have a look at it."

Hopgood glanced down at his wristwatch. "It'd be better to leave it for an hour or two, sir."

"Why's that?"

"It's dinnertime. The place'll be full of kids right now."

"Then I'd say right now is *exactly* the right time to pay it a visit," Woodend told him.

Looking up, Woodend could see the tops of the grim Victorian warehouses, their brickwork blackened by a hundred years of industrial soot, their iron pulleys hanging from upper-storey doors like sinister gibbets. Looking down he could see the cobbles, worn smooth and shiny, first by horses' hooves, and then by pneumatic tyres. This street would have looked exactly the same in Charles Dickens' time, he thought, and maybe the great man had actually walked along it while the plot for one of his magnificent novels was still buzzing around in his head. It made the chief inspector shiver just to think about it.

Outside the door he was heading for stood a young man in a cheap suit. He was around twenty-four, Woodend guessed. He had the body of a weightlifter, and the look of a man who would never knowingly walk away from a fight. He showed no interest in the chief inspector until it became obvious that Woodend was intending to enter the club, then he took two steps to the left to bar the way.

"This is a private club," Rick Johnson said. He sneered. "Anyway, it wouldn't be of any interest to an old feller like you. I mean, there aren't any strippers or mucky goin's on."

Always nice to get off on the right foot with somebody, Woodend thought. He put his hand in his pocket, and pulled out his warrant card.

Johnson examined it suspiciously. "You don't look like a chief inspector," he said.

"An' you don't look like the kind of door keeper you'd usually find outside a nice little dance club like this," Woodend countered. "Have a lot of trouble in there, do you?"

"Nah," Johnson said dismissively. "I have to tell somebody to leave once in a while, but it never gets as far as throwin' punches. Most of the customers are girls anyway, an' what lads we do get are pencil pushers from the shippin' companies, an' couldn't fight their way out of a paper bag."

"So why you?" Woodend asked.

"You what?"

"Why employ a heavy when one isn't needed?"

The question seemed to embarrass Rick Johnson, and for a

few seconds he groped for an answer. Then he said, "I asked Mrs Pollard for the job, an' she gave it to me."

"An' what were you doin' before that?"

"You ask a lot of questions," Johnson said aggressively.

"I know," Woodend agreed. "It's what I get paid for." He pulled out his packet of Capstan Full Strength, and offered one to Johnson, who refused. "If you were to ask me to take a guess," he continued, "I'd say you'd been in one of Her Majesty's rent-free boardin' houses."

"Yeah, I was inside," Johnson admitted. "What of it?"

"GBH?" Woodend asked.

"Look, I got into a fight," Johnson said. "I didn't start it, but the old fool of a judge wouldn't believe that, so while the other feller got off scot-free, I served eighteen months."

"So when Mrs Pollard was lookin' for a nice, diplomatic lad to stand on the door, you must have seemed like a gift from heaven," Woodend mused. "It's been nice talkin' to you, Mr . . .?"

"Rick Johnson."

" . . . Mr Johnson, but if you don't mind, I'd like to go inside now."

"Would it really matter if I did mind?" Johnson asked, stepping aside.

"Probably not," Woodend told him. "But I like to get the co-operation of the general public whenever possible."

He stepped through the doorway, and began to descend the steep stairs into the Cellar Club. Even at street level, the noise of the music was almost deafening, but by the time he had reached the cellar floor he felt as if his eardrums were about to explode. He began to notice the heat, too, and to regret the fact that he was wearing his heavy sports jacket.

There was a rickety table at the bottom of the stairs, and the old man sitting at it had a wooden bowl of coins in front of him. Woodend produced his warrant card again.

"We've been expectin' you," the old man said, "only I'd have thought you'd have come at a quieter time."

"The murder doesn't seem to have done business any harm," Woodend bawled over the noise of the music.

"Where else would they go at dinnertime if they didn't come here?" the old man shouted back.

"Got a register of guests, have you?"

The old man slid a cardboard ledger across to him. Woodend scanned the list of signatures. 'Les Bee-Anne', 'Michael Mouse', 'Elvis Presley' . . .

"You're not too particular who you let in, are you?" he asked.

"They're only kids," the old man answered. "There's no harm in any of 'em."

Maybe not, Woodend thought. Then again, maybe one of the people in the club right at that moment was a cold-blooded killer.

"How the hell do you manage to sit through this din for hours at a stretch?" he shouted.

The old man grinned. "I turn my deaf-aid off, don't I?"

Woodend made his way to the back of the tunnel. On the tiny stage were three young guitarists and a drummer, just as there had been at the same time a couple of days earlier. But this was not the Seagulls. According to the crayoned sign which had been hanging outside the club, this particular bunch called themselves Mickey Finn and the Knockouts.

A few of the girls standing in the far tunnel had noticed him, and were nudging each other, pointing to him and giggling. He couldn't blame them, he supposed. He didn't consider himself old – he was still a few months off fifty – but to them he must have seemed like a dinosaur.

He stripped off his jacket, loosened his tie, and wished he hadn't put on his string vest that morning. Suddenly aware of the fact that his mouth was parched, he made his way over to the small snack bar.

"Could I have a cup of tea, please?" he mouthed at the young girl behind the counter.

The girl gave him an odd look – but no odder than the others he'd been getting – then shrugged and went over to the large enamel teapot which was resting on a portable hotplate.

Woodend turned around again to face the stage. The singer – presumably Mickey Finn himself – was lamenting the fact that his baby had left him and never said a word. Woodend tried to tune his mind into the song. It wasn't anything like jazz, he decided. There was none the subtlety of a King Oliver, or the professional musicianship of a Jack Teagarten. Yet it had *something* – there was a raw energy and enthusiasm to the music which was not to be lightly dismissed.

"Yer tea!" shouted a thin voice just behind him. "That'll be fourpence ha'penny, please."

Woodend paid the money and took a sip of his tea. It was hot and wet – but that was all that could be said for it. On stage, the group reached the end of the number, and the audience applauded.

"Mickey an' the fellers will be back in a few minutes," the DJ said over the tannoy. "In the meantime, let's listen to a bit of good old rock'n'roll from Johnny Kidd and the Pirates. It's a little song they had a hit with a while back, an' it's called, 'Shakin' All Over'."

The record was a little less noisy than the live group had been, and Woodend was now fairly sure that the buzzing in his ears would go away eventually. He kept his eyes on the stage. The drummer and the two guitarists ducked under an archway at the side and disappeared from sight, but the lead singer, a tall, slim boy with blond hair which spilled well over his collar, climbed down the steps and was heading through the tunnel towards the snack bar.

The boy looked at him at him with the same surprise as everyone else in the club had. "Bit old for this, aren't you, grandad?" he said.

Well, at least he didn't ask me if I was expectin' to see a stripper, Woodend thought.

"I suppose I am a bit old for it," he admitted, "but I liked your set, anyway. Would you like a drink?"

Suspicion flared up in the boy's eyes. "You're not a poof out on pick-up, are you?" he demanded.

"No," Woodend said, pulling out his warrant card for the third time. "I'm a bobby."

The boy did not examine the card closely, as Rick Johnson had done. Instead he simply said, "You're here lookin' for Eddie Barnes's murderer, are you?"

"That's right, I am," Woodend agreed. "That drink's still on offer if you want it."

"I'll have a Coke," the boy said.

A Coke! Woodend thought. Whatever happened to good old-fashioned lemonade? Was there suddenly something wrong with dandelion and burdock?

"You must be Mickey Finn," he said, laying some coins on the counter. "Is that your real name?"

"I was christened Michael Finn," the boy said. "Most of the lads I knock around with call me Mike."

"Did you know Eddie Barnes well, Mike?"

Finn shrugged. "Depends what you mean by well. He wasn't a close wacker of mine, if that's what you're askin', but I did know him. Most of the lads who are in groups know each other. We're always performin' in the same places, you see. We help each other out. We cadge lifts in each other's vans. An' we lend each other guitarists or drummers when the feller who's supposed to be playin' has got to work late, or has been kept in by his dad."

Woodend forced himself to suppress a smile. Kept in by their dads! You saw these big lads strutting about on the stage and you got the illusion they were grown up. But they weren't. Come Friday night, they'd be handing their pay packets over to their mums and getting pocket money back in return. And as for having their own keys to the front door – well, that would have to wait until they turned twenty-one!

"Did Eddie Barnes ever play with the Knockouts?" Woodend asked the young singer.

"A couple of times."

"An' was he any good?"

"Not as good as our regular lead guitarist," Finn said proprietarily, and this time Woodend did grin.

Finn's band had re-emerged from the dressing room, and were picking up their instruments.

"I think you're wanted on stage," the chief inspector said.

"Yeah, I'd better go," Finn agreed. "Mrs Pollard likes to get value for her money."

Woodend watched the young man weave his way back through the audience. Mike Finn had seemed quite open, and what he had said could possibly turn out to be useful. Yet the chief inspector couldn't suppress a feeling that, if the singer had known there was a policeman standing at the bar, he would have stayed well away from it.

A man wearing a cord jacket and grey flannel trousers emerged from the dressing room, dismounted the steps, and made his way towards the snack bar. He had thinning brown hair and a totally unprepossessing appearance. He was, Woodend guessed, around thirty-five – which probably made him the third-oldest person in the club.

The man reached the bar. "Give me a glass of cold milk as quick as you like, Doreen," he said in a squeaky voice to the girl behind the counter. "I'm so dry I'm spittin' feathers."

He knocked back half the milk in a single gulp, then turned to Woodend. "You'll be a policeman, will you?"

"That's right," Woodend agreed. "And you'd be . . .?"

"I'm Ron Clarke, the resident DJ."

"Is that right?" Woodend asked, finding it hard to reconcile the washed-out little man standing next to him with the powerful, excited voice which had blasted its way out of the tannoy.

Clarke read his thoughts, and grinned. "I'm a different person with a mike in front of me gob," he said. "So how's the investigation goin'?"

"As far as I'm concerned, it's only just startin'," Woodend told him. "You must have known Eddie Barnes quite well, workin' at the club."

Clarke nodded. "Oh, I knew Eddie all right."

"An' what did you make of him?"

"Make of him?" Clarke took a reflective sip of his milk. "Serious," he said finally. "Very serious."

"About his music?"

"About life, really. He wasn't like the other Seagulls. You'd see the four of them in the pub when they had money – all gettin' pissed – but you could tell just by lookin' at him that Eddie would rather have been at home watchin' the telly if he'd had any choice."

"'If he'd had any choice'?" Woodend repeated. "You mean someone was forcin' him to be there?"

"Maybe I'm puttin' it badly," Clarke admitted. "It wasn't really a question of force. He was there because Steve Walker *wanted* him to be there."

"And what Steve Walker says, goes, as far as the rest of the Seagulls are concerned?"

"Not for all of them – Billie an' Pete can be quite independent when they want to be – but it did as far as Eddie Barnes was concerned. Anyway, that's how it looked to me."

"An' there was never any sign of the worm turnin'?"

"What do you mean by that?"

"You never got the impression that Eddie resented bein' bossed around by Steve?"

Ron Clarke shook his head firmly. "I really must be makin' a mess of explainin' myself," he said. "It wasn't like Steve was the boss an' Eddie was his slave. It was more like Steve was Eddie's big brother. Steve's a couple of years older than Eddie is . . . was. I think that made a difference."

"So Steve Walker must be really cut up about Eddie's death?" Woodend suggested.

"That's puttin' it mildly," Clarke replied. "He's devastated – totally devastated. I think, if he'd been given the choice, he'd have preferred it to be him what got electrocuted."

Mickey Finn was singing about some other guy who'd taken his girl away from him. Woodend glanced down at his watch, and wondered whether he should stay until the end of the show. On reflection, he didn't think he would. He'd probably learned as much as he could from one session, and besides, the heat in the place was making his armpits itch.

Five

Rick Johnson was no longer maintaining a lonely vigil at the club door. He had been joined by a slim pretty girl, with long dark hair. She reminded Woodend of his own daughter, Annie, who, at that time of day, would be in school. He wondered why this girl wasn't sitting at her desk, too.

"So you've seen enough of the club already, have you?" Johnson said aggressively.

Woodend gave the girl a friendly smile, then turned his attention back on the doorman.

"Is this one of those difficult customers that Mrs Pollard pays you to keep out?" he asked.

"She's my wife!" Johnson said, scowling.

Jesus Christ, Woodend thought. His wife!

She had to be older than she looked, but even so, she could barely be of marriageable age. The chief inspector found himself wondering exactly what set of circumstances would make a sweet little kid like her end up married to a bruiser like Rick Johnson.

"How do you do, Mrs Johnson? I'm very pleased to meet you," he said.

Instead of answering, the girl looked down at the ground. Her long dark hair now obscured her face, but Woodend would have been prepared to bet that she was blushing.

"My wife doesn't talk to strangers," Rick Johnson said, as if she weren't really there at all.

"Very wise," Woodend said. "An' you should tell her not

42

to take toffees from them, either. That's what I've always told my little girl."

Without waiting for a reply, he turned on his heel, and strode across the road. Whatever had made her marry Johnson, a man with a criminal record? he asked himself for a second time.

It was only a few short steps to the Grapes, the pub where he had told Rutter and Inspector Hopgood to wait for him. Woodend pushed open the door, stepped inside and took a look around him. The bar had a wooden floor and scrubbed wooden tables. Many of the customers seemed to be off-duty postmen, but there was also a smattering of young lads, some of them with guitar cases propped up next to them. So this place was the watering hole of the kids who played in the Cellar Club, the chief inspector thought. That was a very useful thing to know.

The two policemen were sitting at a table by the window. Both looked as if they had run out of things to say to each other long ago. Woodend bought a pint of best bitter at the bar, then walked over to them and eased his large frame into a free chair.

"I've been telling your sergeant here that I've fixed you up with a nice big office back at the station, sir," Hopgood said.

"That's very kind of you, Inspector," Woodend replied, "an' I'll make sure that word of how helpful you've been to us gets back to your bosses." He paused for a second. "But there's no point in wastin' much space on us, because we'll hardly ever be there."

"I'm afraid I don't quite follow you, sir," Hopgood said. "If you're going to conduct a murder inquiry, you'll surely need—"

"While I get some ale down me, why don't you explain to the inspector how we work, Sergeant," Woodend interrupted.

Rutter sighed softly to himself. Breaking in the new help was always a tedious business, which was why the chief inspector was leaving it up to him. Still, he supposed that was what a bagman was for – to do the tedious business.

"Mr Woodend doesn't like to get too far away from the scene of the crime," he said.

"Meaning what, exactly?" Hopgood asked.

"Meaning he doesn't have much use for police stations."

Doesn't have much use for police stations? The idea of not basing things at the local nick was inconceivable to Hopgood.

"So where exactly *will* he be conducting his investigation from?" the inspector asked.

Rutter looked across at Woodend questioningly.

"Where would *you* guess I'll be conductin' my investigations from, Bob?" the chief inspector asked.

It wasn't very hard to work out the answer, Rutter thought – not when you knew Woodend as well as he did.

"You'll probably be running it from inside the club itself, won't you, sir?" he asked.

"Spot on," Woodend agreed.

"But . . . but at midday and during the evening, it's full of teenagers," Hopgood pointed out.

Woodend grinned. "Quite right. An' by some happy coincidence, those are just the times that this hostelry – which you can see for yourself is so convenient for the crime scene – is open."

"You can't run an murder investigation from a pub," Hopgood said, clearly outraged.

"Not only could I, but I have done on a number of occasions, Inspector," Woodend replied mildly. "You can learn a hell of a sight more sittin' in a pub – right in the middle of things – than you ever would behind the closed doors of the local cop shop."

"But that's just not the way things are done in Liverpool, sir," Hopgood protested.

"Maybe it isn't – but it's the way I do 'em."

Hopgood took a deep breath. "You're here as guests of the Liverpool Police," he said, "and I'm afraid that my superiors are going to insist that you observe the proper form."

Woodend sighed, not softly as his sergeant had earlier, but with all the exasperation of a man who has obviously played this same scene through dozens of times before.

"How many murders do you reckon we've worked on together, Bob?" he asked Rutter.

"Six," the sergeant replied. "Starting with the case of that young girl in Salton and—"

"Forget the details," Woodend said airily. "An' of those six, how many times have we caught the killer?"

"Six," Rutter said, doing his best to hide his smile.

"Six out of six," Woodend said musingly. "Not a bad record, all in all." He took another sip of his pint of bitter. "Am I makin' my point clearly enough for you, Inspector?"

Hopgood flushed. "Your methods are unorthodox, but you usually get results?"

"Nearly right," Woodend agreed. "My methods are unorthodox, and since I've had this bright grammar-school lad workin' with me, I've *always* got results. So you can just relax, Inspector. Leave us to do things our way, an' we'll find your killer for you."

Hopgood stood up. "If you'll excuse me, sir, I have to go and make a phone call," he said.

"I'm sure you do," Woodend agreed. "An' while you're talkin' to your boss, tell him that if he's not happy with the way I'm conductin' my inquiries, I'm more than willin' to catch the next train back to London. My roses'll appreciate me gettin' back, even if no bugger else does."

Rutter grinned as he watched the inspector make his way hurriedly towards the pay phone in the corridor next to the toilets.

"You don't have any roses, sir," he pointed out.

"No, I don't. But then again, they're not goin' to send us back to London, either."

"You're sure of that?"

"Oh yes. They need somebody to take the blame for not

45

comin' up with a murderer, an' we're the lucky devils who've drawn the short straw."

Rutter frowned. "So you're not really as confident as you sounded a few minutes ago?"

"Well, of course I'm not sure," Woodend replied. "Detection's hardly a science at the best of times. It's not like workin' in a laboratory, when the only thing the rats are interested in is food, an' there's only two or three ways they can get it. Murderers' minds are much more complicated than that. So I'm never confident I'm goin' to get a result. An' when I say that, I'm talkin' about a result in the straightforward cases – which this one obviously isn't. But one thing I am sure of – we'll have more chance doin' it my way than if we behaved like the good little bobbies Inspector Hopgood wants us to be."

"So what line do you think we should be taking?"

"I won't know until I've had a root around an' stirred things up a bit," Woodend admitted, "but if you're askin' me to put my money on anythin', I'd say we should start by lookin' for a motive."

Inspector Hopgood returned, still looking flushed. "I've spoken to my Chief Super, sir," he said, "and he says the last thing he wants to do is inhibit your investigation."

"I'm pleased to hear it," Woodend said. "Now would you like to tell me what strings are attached?"

"No strings, sir," the inspector replied unconvincingly. "But the boss did mention in passing that he would appreciate it if you'd keep him up to date with developments."

"A very reasonable request," Woodend said easily. "Tell him to rest assured that as soon as they *are* any developments to be reported, he'll be the first to know about them." He checked his watch. "The club should be just about closin' now. Time for us to make a move."

"You're going back to the Cellar?" Hopgood asked.

"I am if my sergeant made the phone call I asked him to make. Did you, Sergeant?"

"Yes, sir," Rutter replied, deadpan.

Hopgood was slowly piecing things together. The quiet conversation the sergeant and the chief inspector had had in the doorway of the Grapes before Woodend went off to the club. The fact that Rutter had excused himself, saying he wanted a pee, and had been gone for nearly five minutes.

This wasn't how it was supposed to be at all! If anybody was to keep anything from anybody else, it should be him keeping vital facts from Woodend and Rutter, so he could conduct his own investigation. Yet despite the fact that the Scotland Yard men had been in Liverpool for only a couple of hours, they were already blind-siding him.

"So you made the call, Sergeant, but you didn't think to tell Inspector Hopgood about it?" Woodend asked innocently.

"Must have slipped my mind, sir," Rutter confessed.

Woodend shook his head. "These young lads we have to work with," he said to Hopgood. "They've no idea how to a proper job, have they? I blame it on the army. You used to go in a boy an' come out a man, but they seem to handle the conscripts with kid gloves these days."

Hopgood wasn't fooled for a second – but then he suspected that Woodend hadn't wanted him to be.

"Would you like to tell me about the phone call *now*, sir?" he asked through gritted teeth.

"Oh aye. That list you gave us down at the Chandler's Arms is already provin' very useful. I asked the sergeant to phone the Seagulls' manager at work, an' tell him to round up his lads an' meet us in the club as soon as it was closed for the afternoon. Did you succeed in that mission, Sergeant?"

"Yes, sir."

"So that's what we're doin', Inspector. We're goin' back to the club to talk to the Seagulls."

He should never have given them the bloody list, Hopgood thought. He should have made them come to him for every name and every address that they required. But how could he have known that the stories they told about Woodend in the canteen were only a pale imitation of the real thing?

"I suppose I'd better come with you and make the introductions," the inspector said, trying to sound casual.

Woodend drained the last few drops of his pint. "Thanks, but that won't be necessary," he said.

"It's no trouble."

"I'm sure it isn't," Woodend agreed. "But I'm equally sure that a hard-workin' bobby like you can find better things do with his time than tag around behind me. Besides, bein' questioned by two policeman is intimidatin' enough for most people – even if one of them is no more than a lad. There's no point in completely overwhelmin' 'em with three."

"As you wish, sir," Hopgood said, ungraciously.

"Thank you, Inspector," Woodend replied. He turned to Rutter. "Before we leave Liverpool, you really must remind me to have a word with the Chief Super about how co-operative Mr Hopgood's been."

Hopgood watched the two Scotland Yard men leave the pub. They had won this particular round, he told himself, but if he had anything to do with it, the hand raised in victory at the end of the contest would be his.

Six

The typists and shop assistants who had been gyrating to the beat of Mickey Finn and the Knockouts had drifted back to their desks in the typing pools and their positions behind department-store counters, and without them to fill up the space, the brick-vaulted Cellar Club seemed achingly empty. Not that it had been entirely abandoned. Rick Johnson and his wife were sitting on a couple of the hard chairs facing the stage, talking in low and urgent tones, and four young men were standing by the snack bar, looking very ill at ease.

"We'll be with you in a couple of minutes," Woodend called to the men at the bar. He turned to his sergeant. "We'll go an' have a look the murder scene first, shall we?"

They walked up the side of the middle tunnel, their footsteps echoing off the arched ceiling. Once they had mounted the small stage, Woodend swung around to face the back of the club.

This was almost the last thing Eddie Barnes ever saw, he thought – a cramped, sweaty cave of a place, full of adoring female fans.

There was no door separating the dressing room from the stage, just a jagged gap in the wall, where the bricks had been knocked out.

Woodend sighed. The fellers who had built this place, back in Charles Dickens' day, had taken pride in their work, even though they knew that it was only going to be used for storage. The ones who had modified it – to make it into a place for people – hadn't been bothered to make more

49

than a botched job of it. And they said progress was *always* a good thing.

Bending his head to avoid banging it, Woodend stepped through the gap. The dressing room itself was longer than it was wide, and was illuminated by a single, naked light bulb hanging from the ceiling. Near the door was a cupboard which contained the disc jockey's turntable and records. Beyond that were several rickety chairs and an equally rickety table. The whole place stank of sweat and stale cigarette smoke.

"Ah, the glamour an' magic of show business," Woodend said, almost to himself.

He picked his way between the chairs to a small, stained sink. It didn't take a detective to work out that the lads who played in the groups used this more as a toilet than for washing – the smell of urine provided all the evidence anyone would need.

Guitars and amplifiers were heaped up in a pile next to the sink, and beyond them was a curtained-off area. Woodend drew the curtain back, and found himself looking down at a battered couch.

"Looks like they have all the comforts of home in here," Rutter said, over his shoulder.

"Aye, a real little palace all right," Woodend replied.

The two policemen climbed down the steps again, and Woodend walked over to Rick Johnson and his wife.

"Why don't you slip out and have a cup of coffee?" he suggested. "Half an hour should be long enough."

Johnson jumped slightly, as though he'd been so wrapped up in his conversation he hadn't even heard the chief inspector's approach.

"If we want coffee, we can get it here," he said.

Woodend shook his head disbelievingly. "Don't play thick with me, lad. You know what I meant. I want you out of here, so I can have a private conversation with the Seagulls."

"I'm not supposed to leave the club unless the door's locked behind me," Johnson said.

"What? Worried about burglars when you're leavin' two bobbies inside?" Woodend asked. "Trust me, lad, the place'll be safe enough."

"I've got my instructions," Johnson said stubbornly.

"I think we'd better go, Rick," his wife told him. "After all, if this policeman wants to—"

"Keep your trap shut, Lucy!" Johnson said angrily.

The woman – the girl! Woodend couldn't think of her as a woman, even if she was married – looked down at her hands, which were clasped tightly together on her lap. Her brown hair, which curled in to cover her cheeks, shifted slightly, and the chief inspector saw the bruise under her right eye.

Woodend thought of his own daughter again, and felt a sudden anger rising from the pit of his stomach.

"Have you been knockin' your wife about, Mr Johnson?" he demanded roughly.

"What's that got to do with you?" Rick Johnson said, jumping to his feet and thrusting out his chin aggressively.

"Go on, take a swing at me," Woodend said softly. "I'd really like you to do that."

"Why? So you can summons me for assault?"

Woodend shook his head. "No. Because it'll give me just the excuse I'm lookin' for to knock you flat on your arse."

"You an' whose army?" Johnson sneered.

"Sir . . ." Rutter said, putting his hand on Woodend's arm.

The chief inspector brushed the hand away. "You stay out of this, Bob," he warned. "This is between him an' me." He turned his attention back to the doorman. "I'll tell you somethin' for nothin', Johnson. You might get the better of me, but you won't find it as easy as beatin' up a kid like her."

The two men stood glaring at each other, Johnson with his fists bunched, Woodend watchful and tensed. It seemed as if they would be like that for ever – until, perhaps, they had turned into stone – then Lucy Johnson said, "Rick didn't hit me. I walked into a door."

Woodend was struck by how vulnerable her voice sounded.

It was almost, he thought, like the cry of an injured kitten.

"You heard her!" Rick Johnson said. "I didn't hit her. She walked into a door."

"Well, you'd better make sure she doesn't walk into any more," Woodend told him. He forced his body to relax. "But to get back to the other matter, I'm goin' to have to insist you leave the club now. I'll square it with Mrs Pollard."

Johnson looked down at his wife, then put his hand on her arm and half-assisted, half-pulled her to her feet.

"Half an hour," he grunted. "That's how long we've got to be out of the club, isn't it?"

"Half an hour," Woodend agreed.

He watched them head for the stairs, Johnson with his arm around his wife's shoulders, then he and his sergeant made their way across to the snack bar. The four people waiting for them there were the three surviving members of the Seagulls and their manager, Jack Towers. The manager was wearing a blue suit, but the group members, he noted, were all dressed in black turtle-necked sweaters, imported American bluejeans – and brown boots with metal studs in the heels.

"It was good of you all to make the time to see me at such short notice," Woodend said.

One of the Seagulls, the one with the sharp features and quick, intelligent eyes, snorted.

"I don't know how things work down in London, but up here in Liverpool, when you're told the filth want to see you, you always manage to find the time," he said. "Unless, of course, you talk with a posh accent or live in one of them big houses in Blundellsands. Then, for some strange reason, the police don't seem to bother you at all."

"Aye, they do say posh people can get away with murder, don't they?" Woodend replied. "But it's not true. Nobody gets away with murder. Not if I can help it."

"Well, I'm sure that's a great comfort to us all. But it won't bring Eddie back, will it?"

52

The young man was angry, Woodend thought, but beneath that anger lay a deeper pain. "I don't think I caught your name," he said.

"That's probably because I never told it to you."

"Would you like to tell me now?" asked the chief inspector, refusing to be rattled.

"It's Walker. Steve Walker."

The one who called the shots, Woodend reminded himself – the one who'd taken young Eddie Barnes out drinking with him whether the dead guitarist had wanted to go or not.

"Would the rest of you mind telling me who you are?" the chief inspector asked.

"I'm Jack Towers, the manager," said the man in the suit.

He was maybe twenty-five or twenty-six, Woodend decided. He was tall and skinny, wore heavy horn-rimmed glasses, and had pale sensitive features. He probably found the abrasive Steve Walker very hard to handle at times.

"You're a shippin' clerk, aren't you, Mr Towers?" he asked.

"Yes," Jack Towers agreed reluctantly, almost as though he considered working in a shipping office some kind of crime. "But that's only temporary. As soon as the boys take off . . ."

"So were you workin' at your desk at the time that Eddie Barnes was murdered?"

"No," the manager said. "I was right here. I always try to catch the boys' performances."

"Jack thinks if he's not there to watch over us, we'll fall apart," Steve Walker sneered.

"We need Jack," said another member of the group, a boy who was probably the same age as Walker, but had not yet quite lost his puppy fat. "He stops us from goin' off the deep end."

Towers rewarded the young man's support with a short, nervous smile. "Thank you, Pete."

This was Pete Foster, then, which meant that the third

member of the group, who had a dour expression which was almost comical, had to be Billie Simmons, the drummer.

"There's two things I'd really like to know," Woodend said. "The first is why Eddie didn't get a shock the second he plugged his amplifier in."

Steve Walker shook his head almost despairingly. "The only thing that was live was the bass control," he said. "An' Eddie had no need to touch that until somethin' went wrong, did he?"

"Didn't he?"

"Of course not. It was already set at the right level."

"All right, I can see that now," Woodend said. "So let's go on to my second question – when could the amplifier have been tampered with?"

"This is a waste of time. We've already told the local bluebottles everythin' we know," Steve Walker said.

"I'm sure you have," Woodend replied. "An' I'll be lookin' at their reports – when I get round to it. But me, I'm the sort of feller who likes to get everythin' straight from the horse's mouth. I expect that you're a bit that way inclined yourself, Mr Walker."

Steve Walker did not deny it. Instead, he lit a Woodbine, took a deep drag on it, and said, "The equipment was workin' perfectly when we played our gig the night before."

"And where did you play this gig?"

"Here. In the Cellar Club. It was what Mrs Pollard calls 'The Battle of the Bands Night'."

"The Battle of the Bands Night," Woodend repeated. "So you weren't the only ones performin'?"

Walker shook his head. "No. There were three other groups on with us – Len Tooley an' the Aces, The Fantastics, an' Mickey Finn an' the Knockouts," he said. "We were the ones who closed the show," he added, with just a hint of pride.

That would explain all the people down on Inspector Hopgood's list, Woodend thought. Four groups. That meant at least sixteen people who had access to the dressing room. But

54

wait! Eddie Barnes's equipment couldn't have been tampered with until after he played the last set, and if the other groups had already buggered off by then . . .

"Did you all leave the club at the same time?" he asked.

"More or less. Apart from Rick an' Lucy Johnson. They stayed behind to lock up."

"An' what time would that be?"

"About half-past one."

Woodend whistled softly. "Clubs in Liverpool do seem to keep pretty late hours."

"The *club* closed at eleven," Steve Walker said disdainfully, as if he thought Woodend should already have known that. "But that wasn't your question, was it? You asked what time we left, an' I told you that was around half one."

"What were you doin' in those two an' a half hours?"

Steve Walker shrugged. "Messin' around with the other groups, like we always do on Battle of the Bands Night."

Damn, Woodend thought. "So the other groups stayed on when they'd finished their sets?" he said.

"I would have thought that was pretty obvious, even to you," Steve Walker replied.

"Would you care to be a little more specific about what you mean by messin' around?" Woodend asked, ignoring Walker's tone.

"We chewed the fat for a while, told a few jokes, then a few of us had a jam session."

"Was Eddie Barnes part of the jam session?"

"Not that night."

"But on other nights?"

"Eddie used to join in," Pete Foster said, "but for the last couple of weeks he's been . . ."

"Been what?"

"It's hard to say exactly. He was still serious about his music, but he didn't seem to be enjoyin' it as much."

Now that *was* interesting, Woodend thought, filing it in his mind as something to come back to later.

"Let me get this straight," he said. "The equipment couldn't have been tampered with until after you finished playin' at eleven, so the murderer had to get at it either before you left the club at half-past one or in the mornin'. Who's here in the mornin's?"

"Wouldn't know about that – you see I'm usually in bed until about eleven thirty," Steve Walker said, with a grin which showed another side of his character. "You'd better ask Rick."

Yes, Woodend thought. There were a number of things he'd like to ask Mr Rick Johnson about, when he got the chance.

"Do you know if anyone had threatened Eddie Barnes?" he asked.

The four young men exchanged rapid, uneasy glances. "Not exactly threatened *him*, as such," said Jack Towers, regaining the initiative which he had earlier lost to Steve.

"What do you mean by that?"

"Well, a few nasty things have been happening recently, but they've been directed against the whole group, rather than just Eddie."

"Such as?"

Towers took a packet of cigarettes out of his pocket and handed them around. His hand was trembling, Woodend noted.

"It was just annoying little things, really," the manager said, as if he now wished he'd never brought the matter up. "Somebody – and we've no idea who it was – rang one of the venues I'd booked, pretended to be me, and said we couldn't make it that night. When we turned up, we'd already been replaced by another group. Another night we came out of a club in Birkenhead and found all the tyres on the van had been slashed."

"Tell him about the rat," Steve Walker said.

Towers sighed. "A few days ago, Eddie found a dead rat in his guitar case," he admitted reluctantly.

"But it wasn't *just* dead, was it?" Walker persisted.

"No, it wasn't just dead," Towers admitted. "It had a string noose tied around its neck."

"A noose!" Woodend repeated. "And what do you think was the point of that?"

"I don't really know," Towers said. "Somebody's idea of a sick joke? An attempt at revenge?"

"Revenge for what?"

From the unhappy expression on his face, it was obviously a question Towers would rather not have answered.

"The lads are . . . er . . . very popular in Liverpool, especially with the girls," he said. "I suppose it's possible that one of those girls' boyfriends might have misunderstood the situation."

"Or understood it only too well," Walker said, and the other two Seagulls sniggered.

"So Eddie Barnes was a bit of a one for chasin' the girls, was he?" Woodend asked.

"No, he wasn't," Steve Walker said hotly. "The rest of us will poke anythin' that's willin', but Eddie wasn't like that. He was a romantic. He believed in true love, an' he was waitin' for the right girl to come along. A lot of good it did him! At least when I die, I won't go out a virgin."

"Is that what Eddie did?" Woodend asked. "Go out as a virgin? Are you sure?"

Walker's anger, which seemed never to be very far below the surface, burst forth again. "Of course I'm bloody sure," he said. "He was my best mate. We didn't have any secrets from each other."

"Steve's right," said Pete Foster, who Woodend had already marked down as the peacemaker of the group. "If Eddie had been goin' out with any girls, we'd have known about it."

The interview was somehow losing its momentum, Woodend thought. It was time to put the cat among the pigeons and see who flew where.

"So what happens now?" he asked innocently.

"Now?" Towers repeated, as if he had no idea what the chief inspector was talking about.

"With the group," Woodend explained. "I mean, you're goin' to need a new lead guitarist, aren't you?"

Billie Simmons and Pete Foster exchanged another hurried glance, but, Woodend noticed, Steve Walker had his eyes fixed, firmly and intently, on their manager.

Towers shifted awkwardly. "I've . . . I've already put an advertisement in the newspaper," he admitted.

"You've done what?" Steve Walker demanded, his voice so high that he was almost screaming.

The manager held out his hands in what was either a gesture of supplication or helplessness.

"It had to be done," he said feebly. "The group has to have a lead guitarist, Steve."

"I know we need a new lead guitarist," Steve Walker said. "But we don't have to have one *yet*. Not before Eddie's even cold in his grave. Don't you have any respect?"

Jack Towers puffed nervously on his cigarette. "I'm sorry that Eddie's dead," he said. "Really sorry. But we have to be practical. We've been cancelling gigs all over the place. Everybody understands us doing that for a few days, but it can't go on indefinitely, or all we've worked for will have gone down the drain."

It was evident from the look on Steve Walker's face that that had been the wrong thing to say.

"All *we've* worked for!" he repeated. "What have *you* done? We're the ones who've written the songs. We're the ones who get up on the stage night after night – singin' till we're hoarse, playin' our instruments till we've got blisters on our fingers. All you have to do as our manager, Jack, is pick up the phone an' make a few calls."

"You're not bein' fair to the man, Steve," Pete Foster said.

Another bad move, Woodend thought. But with Walker in the mood he evidently was in, was there any such thing as a good move?

"So, you think I'm not bein' fair, do you?" Walker ranted. "Well, let me tell you somethin', Pete – it's not a fair world. If it was, Eddie would be standin' with us right now."

"Look, Steve," Jack Towers said, "I was keeping it as a surprise, but I suppose you'd better know now – I've managed to get you an audition with a record company in London, two weeks from today."

Woodend quickly glanced from face to face. Billie Simmons' expression told him that the announcement came as news to the drummer, but Pete Foster's look said that he had known about the audition for a while.

As for Steve Walker, his face was still blazing with anger. "How long have you known about this?" he demanded.

Towers shrugged. "A few days."

"And why the bloody hell didn't you tell *me* about it?"

"I was going to – but what with Eddie dying like that . . ."

He'd been holding it back as a surprise, Woodend thought. Waiting for the right moment to produce it like a rabbit out of a hat – the right moment to show Steve Walker just what a good manager he really was. "Anyway, the fact is that you *have* an audition with a record company," Jack Towers continued. "*Now* do you see why we need a new guitarist as soon as possible?"

"There was a time when I'd have been over the moon to get news like that," Steve Walker told him. "An' do you know what it means to me now? Absolutely nothin'! Bugger all! In case you three have forgotten it, Eddie was our mate. We went through a lot together. An' now, even though he's only been dead a couple of days, you're all acting as if he never existed."

"We can't throw away the group's chances just because Eddie's dead," Pete Foster said quietly.

"Can't we?" Steve Walker screamed back at him. "Well, maybe you can't, Pete, but just watch me."

Elbowing his way between the others, he strode furiously across the room and disappeared through the archway. Those who remained were silent for some seconds, then Pete Foster said, "He'll be back."

"I'm not so sure of that," Jack Towers said worriedly.

"The Seagulls are the best chance any of us have of ever bein' famous," Pete told him. "Steve knows that as well as I do, an' he wants to be a success – perhaps more than any of us."

Woodend lit a cigarette, more to be doing something than because he needed a smoke. He knew that the scene he had just deliberately engineered would have been bound to happen sooner or later anyway, but now, looking at the expression of devastation on Jack Towers' face, he couldn't help but feel guilty.

Seven

The black police Humber, which was parked in the canyon between the two blocks of tall Victorian warehouses, seemed almost as if it had strayed into the area by mistake, but the uniformed inspector standing next to it – and watching Woodend's approach with something very much akin to suspicion – looked as if he were on familiar territory.

"Aye, an' that's the trouble – whatever else is wrong with him, he does know his patch," the chief inspector muttered to himself as he approached Hopgood. "An' though I don't want to use the bugger – it'd be like usin' a sledge hammer to crack a walnut – I may not have any choice."

With what looked like a considerable effort on his part, Hopgood forced a half-smile to his face. "Did you learn anything interesting from talking to the Seagulls, sir?" he asked.

"Oh, I learned a hell of a lot that was *interestin'*," the chief inspector told him. "I'm just not sure yet whether I've learned anythin' which might help me to solve this case."

"And now you want to go and see Eddie Barnes's parents?"

"That's right."

"Might I ask why, sir? They're not likely to have murdered him now, are they?"

Woodend sighed. How could he ever hope to explain the way he worked to this stolid, unimaginative bobby?

"I want to understand the dead lad better," he said. "I want to find out what made him tick."

"I see," Hopgood said – though it was plain that he didn't. "Shall I come with you?"

61

"I don't think so," Woodend said. "I prefer to be alone when I'm dealin' with grievin' parents."

"Please yourself, sir."

Hopgood tapped on the window of the Humber, and beckoned. The door opened, and a tall, thin constable with sandy hair got out.

"This is Constable Bates," Hopgood said. "He'll take you wherever you want to go."

"Right then, Bates, let's get started," Woodend said.

The constable moved smartly round to the back of the car, and opened the door.

"You've got long arms, son, but I think even you'll have trouble drivin' from the back seat," Woodend said.

"I . . . er . . . thought you'd want to sit in the back, sir," Bates said. "Most senior officers do."

"Nay, lad, I'll ride in the front with you – like a real grown-up," Woodend told him.

He heard Hopgood's loud snort, and realised he had just managed to offend the inspector's sense of what was right and proper again. Well, stuff the officious bugger.

Liverpool was nothing like the size of London, and the police Humber had soon left the city centre and was heading out into the suburbs. Woodend watched a seemingly endless stream of semi-detached houses fly past the window, each with its own small, but tidy front garden.

The men who owned these houses were probably train drivers and electricians, plumbers and assistant shop managers – fellers who had, in all likelihood, been brought up in back-to-back terraced houses and were probably immensely proud of what they'd managed to provide for their own families. And why the bloody hell shouldn't they be proud? Woodend asked himself.

Constable Bates slowed, and finally came to a halt in front of one of the semis. "This is the place, sir," he said.

Woodend sighed. This was a part of the job which, however

often he did it, he'd never been quite able to come to terms with.

"Did somebody think to ring the parents up to tell them that I was makin' a visit?" he asked.

"They haven't got a phone, sir," the constable replied.

No, of course they wouldn't have a phone, Woodend thought. Nobody on this estate would have a phone – unless their jobs required it.

"So I'll be goin' in cold, will I?" he asked.

"Oh no, sir," the driver replied. "I got one of our fellers to pop round on his beat an' say you'd be comin'."

Woodend smiled gratefully. "Good lad," he said. "I expect your boss has told you to stick to me like glue, hasn't he?"

Constable Bates coloured slightly. "I was . . . er . . . told to offer you all possible assistance, sir."

Woodend chuckled. "You're wasted in the police force, son. The diplomatic service is the place for you. Does this 'all possible assistance' include comin' into the house with me?"

"Not as far as I know, sir. I think that I'm just expected to wait outside for you."

"I'm not familiar with this area, but I imagine there must be a cafe somewhere near here," Woodend mused.

"There is, sir. A bloody good one."

"Hmm," Woodend said. "I expect to be in that house for half an hour. Now we both know you're not supposed to go away, but we also both know that if you did, I'd be unlikely to find out about it."

The driver smiled. "Thanks, sir."

"What for?" Woodend asked innocently.

He made his way up a crazy-paving path bordered with flowers, and lifted the highly polished brass knocker on the front door. The man who answered his knock was probably around forty-five years old, but he looked considerably older.

"You'll be that detective from London," the man said.

"That's right, Mr Barnes," Woodend agreed.

"You'd better come in then."

A woman was hovering in the hallway. As with her husband, the strain of the recent days clearly showed in the lines on her face, but she did her best to look welcoming as she introduced herself.

The grieving parents took Woodend into a front parlour which was probably only ever used for entertaining guests.

"Would you like a cup of tea?" Mrs Barnes asked.

"That's most kind of you," Woodend told her, more because he knew it would help to put her at ease than because he actually wanted a drink.

Mrs Barnes disappeared through the door, and after a few awkward seconds, her husband muttered something about helping her, and excused himself.

Left to his own devices, the chief inspector examined the room. The fitted carpet was patterned with red and yellow swirls. There was a piano up against the wall which faced the window, and a fan made of wallpaper in the empty fireplace. Large plaster spaniels gazed at him from the hearth, and souvenir ornaments from Blackpool stood proudly on the mantelpiece. Three plaster ducks of differing sizes – and in full flight – occupied one part of wall opposite the fireplace, and a stylised, sentimental print of a small child with huge eyes filled much of the rest. The place reminded Woodend of his own front room.

The couple returned, Mr Barnes carrying the tea tray, as if he doubted his wife's ability to lift it.

"Do sit down. Please," he said, as he laid the tray carefully down on the coffee table.

Woodend lowered himself into one of the imitation-leather armchairs, and Mr Barnes plopped down heavily on the sofa opposite him. The tension in the room was so thick it could have been cut up and used to make bricks.

Mrs Barnes bent down over the coffee table. "Milk and sugar?" she asked Woodend.

"Yes, please," the chief inspector replied. "I'm sorry about your son. I've got a kid of my own, not that much younger than your Eddie was, an' if anythin' happened to her, I don't know what I'd do." He paused. "But I'd like to think that if I did lose her, I could handle the situation with the same courage you're showin'."

Mrs Barnes nodded gratefully. "Eddie worked so hard at that guitar of his," she said, as she ladled the sugar into Woodend's cup. "Hours an' hours he'd be up in his room, practisin'. Sometimes he'd get so frustrated he was almost in tears, but he'd never ever think about givin' up."

"He was a real tryer," Mr Barnes said solemnly. "Always had been. I remember when he was just a little kid an' he had these buildin' blocks. Every time he tried to build a wall with them, they'd tumble over, but he kept at it till he'd got what he wanted."

"Would you like to see a picture of him?" Mrs Barnes asked, as she handed Woodend his tea.

"Aye, I would."

Mrs Barnes went over to the sideboard, and returned with a photograph in a silver frame. Woodend took it in his free hand, and examined it. Two young men were standing side by side in front of the Mersey ferry, their arms over each other's shoulders. Woodend immediately recognised one as Steve Walker; the other had to be the dead guitarist.

Eddie Barnes had been a thin young man, with pale, intense features and eyes almost as large as those of the child in the picture on the wall. A sensitive kid, Woodend guessed – a kid with a big heart.

The chief inspector felt himself in the grip of a familiar sensation – one he always tried to resist, despite acknowledging the fact that it made him a better policeman. He was starting to get personally involved.

He handed the photograph back to Mrs Barnes. "Tell me about Eddie's relationship with Steve Walker," he said.

The woman sat down on the sofa next to her husband. She was holding the photograph tightly, as if she were afraid it

65

would slip out of her fingers. A sad smile came to her face. "Eddie an' Steve were best mates."

"So I've been told," Woodend said, returning her smile. "I never met your son, but I have recently met Steve Walker, an' I find it hard to picture them gettin' on. Seems to me they were as different as chalk an' cheese."

"A lot of people have got Steve all wrong," Mrs Barnes told him. "They say he's a hard case, an' . . . well, I suppose it's true he's been in a few fights in his time. But deep down, he's as gentle as a lamb."

"You're obviously very fond of him."

"He's two years older than our Eddie is . . ." Mrs Barnes gulped. "Than our Eddie *was*. By rights, they shouldn't have been mates at all, but they were. Eddie's . . . Eddie was always a bit of a gentle soul, you see, an' you know how other kids react to that. He didn't have things easy in the primary school, but he was bullied somethin' terrible durin' his first couple of weeks at the secondary. Then Steve stepped in, an' the bullyin' stopped."

"We were grateful for what he did for our Eddie," Mr Barnes said, "but that isn't the only reason we're fond of him."

"You're quite right, Father," his wife agreed. "Like I said before, there are hidden depths to Steve."

"Did you see quite a lot of him?" Woodend asked.

"He was always round here, wasn't he?" Mrs Barnes replied. "To tell you the truth . . . well, I don't want to gossip, but I don't think he's had a very happy home life."

"In what way?"

"His dad's a drunken brute, by all accounts," Mr Barnes said. "When he was younger, Steve used to have bruises which I'm sure didn't come from fightin' with other kids."

"An' as for that mother of his, you could see she couldn't be bothered to turn him out properly in the mornin'," his wife added. "I doubt if he knows the meanin' of the words 'hot breakfast'."

"We'd never have let Eddie go to Hamburg if Steve hadn't been goin' too," Mr Barnes told Woodend.

"Indeed we wouldn't," his wife concurred. "But we knew that Steve wouldn't let any harm come to him. He was more like a big brother than a friend."

Which was pretty much what Ron Clarke had said, Woodend thought.

"Did Eddie have any other friends?" he asked.

"Well, I suppose you might say Pete an' Billie were his friends, in a sort of way."

"I mean, outside the group?"

Mrs Barnes shook her head. "He didn't really seem to need anybody apart from Steve."

"Girlfriends?" Woodend asked.

"Definitely not," Mr Barnes said.

But the chief inspector noted the briefest flicker of doubt cross the woman's eyes.

"You don't seem quite as sure as your husband about that, Mrs Barnes," he said.

Eddie's mother twisted one of the buttons on her cardigan round, until it looked like she'd twist it off.

"I'm not so sure," she admitted. "I couldn't say anythin' definite, but I have noticed some changes in him recently."

"Like what?"

"Well, for a start, he bought some expensive aftershave, an' hid it at the back of his wardrobe."

"But you still found it, did you?" Woodend asked, resisting the temptation to smile.

"It's not as if I was lookin' for it," Mrs Barnes said defensively. "I was only tidyin' up. But I did think it was strange. Why should he need to go usin' aftershave when all he'd got on his chin was a bit of bum-fluff?"

"Anything else?"

"There were days in the last few weeks when I knew the group wasn't playin', but he'd go out anyway. An' that was unusual – he always stayed at home when he wasn't with Steve.

Very mysterious he was about it, too. When I asked him where he'd been, he'd just change the subject. But if he did have a girlfriend, I don't see why he didn't tell us about her."

Perhaps because she wasn't the type of girl he could have taken home to meet his mum and dad, Woodend thought. Because maybe she was more the sort of girl the other members of the group had talked sniggeringly about – the fans who were prepared to go the whole way with one of them, just because the Seagulls had a bit of local fame.

"I'm sorry, but there's one more question I simply have to ask," he said. "Did your son have any enemies?"

"Enemies?" his father repeated. "No, not our Eddie. I don't think he ever upset anybody in his entire life."

Then who the bloody hell had risked getting a long prison sentence just for the satisfaction of seeing him dead? Woodend wondered.

On the way back to the centre of Liverpool, Woodend neither said much to Constable Bates, nor paid any attention to the view. Instead, he was thinking about what he had learned about Eddie Barnes – especially his mother's suspicions that he might be seeing a girl.

If Eddie *had* been seeing someone, he would surely have told his best friend Steve Walker, he argued to himself. Or perhaps not. Perhaps there were some things Eddie would have wanted to keep even from him.

He pictured Eddie falling for one of the girls who hung around the club, and telling Steve about it.

He could imagine the conversation.

"You've done what?" Walker would say, incredulously.

"I've fallen in love."

"Not with that girl you were talkin' to last night."

"That's right."

"She's nothin' but a slag. She's probably been to bed with half the guitarists in Liverpool."

"She isn't like that," Eddie would protest.

68

"They're all like that."

Yes, that was the way it would have gone. Because, like the big brother he almost was, Steve would be overprotective. Because Steve really *did* see girls as nothing but an opportunity for a one-night stand. And because, possibly, Steve couldn't bear the thought of Eddie caring more for a girl than he cared for him.

Eddie definitely wouldn't have told Steve if he'd had a girlfriend, Woodend decided. But even if he had had one, did that have anything to do with the murder? Could it, for instance, be a spurned boyfriend who had killed Eddie? Would kids really go to that extreme to get their revenge?

He suddenly felt out of his depth – unable to really understand the people he was having to deal with. In his own day, the jilted boyfriend would have challenged his successor to a fight on the nearest piece of waste ground, so even if he didn't get the girl back, he would at least keep his honour intact. That was how things had been settled in the thirties. But so much had changed since the war. The old certainties were gone, the codes of behaviour no longer universally agreed on. Life was so different now that he sometimes felt as if he were living in a foreign country.

The chief inspector sighed and lit up a Capstan Full Strength. "You're gettin' philosophical, Charlie," he told himself, "an' the last thing this case needs is a philosophical bobby in charge of it."

Eight

It was early evening. The postmen had gone home in anticipation of an early start the next day, and members of the
various groups were, presumably, already sitting in back of
ancient Bedford vans, jammed between amplifiers as they made
their way to gigs in village halls and working men's clubs. Now,
most of the customers drinking in the Grapes were young men
with short hair, wearing suits.

Office workers, Woodend thought. Bank tellers and shipping
clerks. He might have ended up as one of them himself, if
it hadn't been for the war. Certainly it had always been his
mother's deepest ambition to see him go out to work each
morning dressed in a suit.

He imagined what she would say if she could have seen him
now. *Why don't you follow the example of that nice young
sergeant of yours, Charlie, an' smarten yourself up a bit?*

He chuckled at the thought, then turned to the nice young
sergeant in question. "What's our next move, lad?" he asked.

Rutter, who always matched his boss's pints with his own
halves, lit up one of the cork-tipped cigarettes Woodend was
always pulling his leg about.

"We know the Seagulls were the last group to perform the
night before the murder, so it stands to reason that the amplifier
was all right at that point," the sergeant said.

"Agreed."

"So the first logical step would be to question everyone who
had an opportunity to meddle with the thing between then and
the moment it killed Eddie Barnes."

70

Woodend tilted his head to one side, and looked at his sergeant quizzically. "You might talk about questionin' everybody who was there, but you've already got a suspect in mind, haven't you, lad?"

Rutter spluttered into his beer. "How on earth did you know that, sir?"

"Because I know *you*," the chief inspector said. "So come on, sunshine, spit it out."

Rutter hesitated for a second, then said, "Rick Johnson."

"Why him?" Woodend asked. "I'll admit he must have got a refund for the course he took at charm school, an' believe me, there's nothin' I'd like better than to see the wife-beatin' bugger locked up for a good long time – but that still doesn't make him a murderer."

"Look, it probably didn't take too long to switch round the wiring on the amp, but the murderer still needed *some* time on his own to do it," Rutter argued. "Now we know there were four groups playing that night, so how likely is it that the murderer – if he was one of them – would have got even a minute alone?"

"Not *very* likely," Woodend admitted.

"So, the party breaks up at around one thirty, and everyone goes home. Everyone, that is, apart from Rick Johnson and his wife. And that's when the re-wiring is done."

Woodend stroked his chin thoughtfully. "Does Johnson look thick to you?" he asked.

"I wouldn't bet on him to win Brain of Britain, but he doesn't strike me as stupid."

"I agree with you there," Woodend said. "So the question we have to ask ourselves is this – if he'd really wanted to kill Eddie Barnes, would he have chosen that method, knowin' that somebody was bound to reach the same conclusion as you just have?"

"It could be a big bluff. Johnson could have calculated that we'd never think he did it because he's such an obvious suspect," Rutter countered, but without much conviction.

"Aye, an' maybe Eddie's death was no more than an elaborate suicide," Woodend said dryly, "but it doesn't seem likely, does it?"

"No," Rutter agreed. "But it didn't seem likely that a country vicar in Hampshire would have two bodies buried in the back garden of his rectory, either. Yet that's what we found, isn't it?" He checked his watch. "Mind if I go and make a phone call, sir?"

"Maria?"

Rutter nodded. "I like to ring her at about the same time every day. It gives her some kind of structure to work around."

"Then you'd better not be late," Woodend told him.

The chief inspector watched his sergeant head towards the public phone next to the toilets. He worried about Bob – worried rather more than he'd be prepared to admit. It was hard enough making your way in the police force, without needing to deal with the extra complication of having a blind wife. Yet the sergeant seemed to be handling it well enough – at least for the moment.

A tingling sensation at the back of his neck told him that someone was watching him. He turned round, and saw Steve Walker was standing at the bar. Woodend raised his index finger, and beckoned to the young guitarist. For a moment, Walker just stood there, looking sullen, then he made his way slowly across to the table.

"Yeah? What do you want?" he demanded.

"Just a talk," Woodend said.

"What about?"

The chief inspector smiled. "Well, if you don't sit down, you'll never know, will you?"

Not without a show of reluctance, Walker lowered himself on to the stool opposite Woodend's.

"That was some kind of stroke that you pulled back in the Cellar Club," he said.

"Some kind of stroke? I don't know what you're talkin' about," Woodend replied.

"'You're goin' to need a new guitarist, aren't you?'" Steve Walker said, in a fair imitation of Woodend's Lancashire accent. "You knew just what shit you were goin' to stir up, didn't you?"

"No," Woodend replied honestly. "But I had a pretty good idea that I'd be stirrin' somethin' up."

A grin appeared out of nowhere, filling Walker's face and blunting the aggression of his thin features.

"I suppose I can't blame you for it," he said. "In your place, I might have done the same thing."

Woodend signalled the waiter for two more pints. "You seem to have calmed down a lot since the last time I saw you," he said.

The grin acquired a sheepish edge. "Yeah, well, when all's said an' done, Jack was right. We *are* goin' to need a new lead guitarist. An' we're goin' to need him soon. Eddie wouldn't have wanted the group to die with him. He cared almost as much about it as I do."

"Do you mind if I ask you a question?" Woodend said.

"Seems to me you slipped in a couple of questions already. But go ahead. Ask me another."

"Why do you call yourselves the Seagulls?"

That was clearly not one of the questions Steve Walker had been anticipating. "Why do you want to know that?"

"Just by the nature of his job, a bobby has to be curious," Woodend told him. "But I was curious before I was a bobby. So indulge me."

"The kind of music we play started in America," Steve Walker said earnestly. "But we're not just copyin' the Yanks. The songs we write have a lot of us in them, an' a good part of what we are is Liverpudlian. If you listen to our songs – I mean really listen to them, get right below the surface – you'll hear the clankin' of the tram cars, the swish of the river, the hooters on the docks, an', most of all, you'll hear the screech of the seagulls, because they were here long before there ever was a Liverpool."

"You're a bit of a poet on the quiet, aren't you?" Woodend said, an amused smile playing on his lips.

"I'm a rock'n'roller," Steve Walker replied. "An' one day soon I'm goin' to be famous."

"Well, you don't lack confidence, I'd say that much for you," Woodend told him.

"Would you?" Walker countered. "I play my music because I think I'm good. I wouldn't do it if I didn't. Would you be able to do your job if you didn't think you'd catch the murderers?"

"Good point," Woodend agreed. "Why don't you tell me a little bit about your manager."

"Why would you want to know about him?" Walker asked, some of his aggression and suspicion returning.

"Truthfully, I want to know about him because, of the four of you, he's the one I really haven't got figured out."

Steve Walker laughed scornfully. "You've talked to us once, and you think you know us, do you?"

"Let's just say I can sketch in the broad outlines."

"Go on, then," Walker challenged him.

Woodend took a sip of his pint. "Billie Simmons is an easy-goin' sort of feller. He might like playin' his drums, but he'd be just as happy drivin' a bus. Pete Foster's a different case altogether. He's not very sure of himself, is he?"

"Neither would you be if you had a mother like his."

"What's that supposed to mean?"

"Nothin'. Forget I ever spoke."

"Pete doesn't like trouble, because he's never quite convinced he'll come out on top," Woodend continued. "An' he needs to get approval – you've only got to see the way he acts around your manager to realise that." He paused. "How am I doin' so far?"

"Not bad," Steve Walker admitted grudgingly. "What can you tell me about me?"

"I think you're drawn to victims," Woodend said. "Eddie Barnes may have become your best mate, but the main reason you got to know him in the first place was because he needed

74

your help. An' I'm willin' to bet that he's not the only one you've protected over the years."

Steve Walker was beginning to look distinctly uncomfortable. "You're makin' me sound like a saint," he said awkwardly.

"No, not a saint," Woodend replied. "Just a lad who needed help himself at one time – and didn't get any."

Walker gave him a hard, assessing stare. "You're not stupid, are you?"

"Sometimes I do manage to get things right," Woodend agreed. "So, now that we've finished dissectin' the Seagulls, why don't you tell me a little bit about Jack Towers?"

Rutter had a finger in the ear which was not pressed against the telephone receiver, but with all the noise in the pub, hearing what his wife had to say was still not an easy business.

"So how are you feeling?" he asked.

"I'm fine," Maria replied. "Joan Woodend came to see me this afternoon, and we went for a walk in the park. It was lovely. When you can't see, you notice sounds and smells so much more."

Her words would probably have fooled anyone else, but Rutter picked up a false note in them.

"You're sure you're OK," he persisted.

"Yes."

"We had this agreement," Rutter reminded her. "We said, right from the beginning, that if anything was bothering one of us, we wouldn't keep it a secret from the other."

There was a pause, then Maria said, "I think I've had a touch of 'flu, but I'm over it now."

"'Flu?" Rutter repeated. "What were the symptoms?"

"The usual ones. Giddiness. A nagging headache. But like I said, I'm over it now."

Rutter had suddenly developed a pounding headache himself. "I'll catch the next train back to London," he told his wife.

75

"And what good would that do?" Maria asked, a hint of anger creeping into her voice.

"I . . . I could look after you, until you feel better."

"Don't you ever listen?" Maria demanded. "I'm already feeling better! Tell me the truth, Bob – would there have been any talk of catching the next train back if I wasn't blind?"

"I suppose not," Rutter admitted guiltily.

"We had another agreement," Maria said. "Before I accepted your proposal, I made you promise that we'd lead as close a life as we could to any other married couple. Do you remember that?"

"I remember."

"Keep that promise," Maria urged him. "Stop being so protective all the time. I can't breathe because of it."

"I only want to—"

"You want to treat me like a helpless kitten," Maria cut in. "Well, I'm too old to be a kitten, and I'm far from helpless." She paused. "I love you, Bob. I always will. But unless things change, I can't see this marriage of ours lasting."

"So you want to know about Jack, do you?" Steve Walker asked Woodend. "Anythin' in particular you'd like to hear?"

The chief inspector shook his head. "Just say what comes naturally. The details aren't important. I just want to build up a picture of the man."

"The first time I noticed him was in the Cellar Club," Walker said. "He was standin' at the back of the room, near the coffee bar, watchin' us. Understand what I'm sayin'? He wasn't boppin' to the music like everybody else in the place. He was just watchin'."

"I think I'm gettin' the idea."

"He'd gone by the time we finished our set, an' I never expected to see him again. But he was waitin' in the street when we slipped out to the pub, like he'd known that was just what we were goin' to do – so maybe he already knew

76

more about us than we realised. Anyroad, he asked us if he could buy us a drink."

"An' you, of course, said yes?"

Walker's grin was back in place. "We had enough money for four halves, an' he looked like he was willin' to shell out on pints. What would you have done in our place?"

"I'd probably have said yes."

"Once we were in the pub, he made small talk for a while, sayin' how much he liked the music we played, an' how he thought that we had real talent. Then he started to feed us this line of crap about how he had all kinds of contacts in the record business an' how he was a mate of a couple of the big promoters. You should have seen the look on Pete's face. He was over the moon."

"But you weren't?"

Walker shook his head. "You've met Jack, haven't you? Would you ever mistake him for somebody with important connections in the music world? I didn't know he was a shippin' clerk back then, but I knew he had to have some kind of minor clerical job."

"So why did you take him on?" Woodend asked, offering Walker a Capstan Full Strength. "Because it was what the others wanted?"

Walker puffed on his cigarette, and shook his head again. "Things don't happen in the Seagulls unless *I* want them to happen."

"Well then, what did make you agree?"

"Jack has his uses. He does make bookings for us, even if it's only in crappy little clubs in back streets. He always drives the van, so the rest of us can get pissed after a gig. And whenever we're short of a few bob, we can rely on him to put his hand in his wallet."

Woodend shook his head disbelievingly. "That's just not good enough," he said.

Anger flashed briefly in Walker's eyes. "What do you mean by that?" he demanded.

"I mean, you're not convincin' me. If you're as good as you claim you are, you shouldn't have any trouble getting a better-connected manager than a young shippin' clerk."

Walker grinned again, and this time there was a definite rueful edge to it. "If I tell you the real reason, will you keep it to yourself?"

"Might it have anythin' to do with the investigation?"

"No."

"Then I won't tell a soul."

Walker took another deep drag on his cigarette. "If you thought I was being a bit hard on Jack back in the Cellar, you were dead right," he said. "I can't help myself sometimes. The feller gets up my nose so much that I just have to lash out. But deep down, I like him."

"Go on," Woodend said encouragingly.

"There's a lot of people who could probably manage us better than he does, but there's no one in the whole of Liverpool who *wants* to manage us as much as Jack. I saw that the moment I met him. It was desperately important to him. An' I didn't have the heart to say no."

"So you put your careers on the line just to make someone you'd only just met a little bit happier?"

Walker shrugged. "It's more than a little bit happier. He's on top of the world. Anyway, the way I see it, we'd make it if we had a monkey as a manager. It just might take a bit longer, that's all."

Woodend remembered the scene back in the club. How Towers had looked so stressed when bringing up the issue of a new guitarist to replace Eddie Barnes. How he'd thought then that such scenes could not be uncommon when dealing with a volatile personality like Steve Walker.

"What's in it for him?" he asked.

"Who? Jack?" Walker asked evasively.

"That is who we're talkin' about, isn't it?"

"What's in it for any manager?" Walker countered, still evasive.

Woodend sighed. "Look, from what you've said, he doesn't seem to be particularly interested in the music. An' bein' your manager is costin' him both money an' effort. So why's he doin' it?"

Another shrug. "Jack's got a lot of free time on his hands since his wife left him."

"When did this happen?"

"A few weeks before he met us. She ran off with the coal man. That's like the end of a bad joke, isn't it?"

"How did he take it?"

"Like I said, it happened before we met him, so I've no idea what he was like before."

"I still don't see why he should decide to manage a group," Woodend mused. "If he wanted somethin' to keep him occupied, why didn't he just join some kind of social club?"

"Don't ask me," Steve Walker said, with the hint of evasion back in his voice. "I've given up mind-readin' for Lent."

"There's somethin' you're not tellin' me, isn't there, lad?" Woodend asked.

"There's a lot of things I'm not tellin' you," Walker replied, "an' the reason for that is they're none of your bloody business."

Bob Rutter returned to the table, looking considerably more tense than he had when he'd left it, and carrying a large scotch in his hand.

A bad sign, Woodend thought, but aloud he just said, "Mr Walker and me have just been havin' a very interestin' little talk while you were away phonin' home, Sergeant."

"About anything in particular?" Rutter asked, sitting down.

Steve Walker shot the chief inspector a worried look, as if, having exposed what he probably thought of as his weaknesses to Woodend, he was eager not to have knowledge of it spread any further.

"We talked about music, mainly," Woodend lied. "Who do you like, Sergeant, apart from this Buddy Mistletoe feller of yours?"

Rutter sighed indulgently. "Holly, sir," he said. "The man's name is Buddy *Holly*."

Woodend turned to Walker. "I'm a slow learner, as you'll probably have gathered by now," he said. "But I usually get it right in the end. So who *do* you listen to, Bob?"

"I like the Everly Brothers," Rutter said. "And I'm a big fan of the Drifters and Ricky Valance."

Steve Walker stubbed his cigarette out in the ashtray, and snorted in what could only have been disgust.

"I get the impression Mr Walker's not too impressed with your taste in music," Woodend said, with some amusement in his voice.

"You're dead right there," Walker told him. "The Everly Brothers! The Drifters! It's all so bloody tame. It's like the corporation bogs when the council's been down there with their disinfectant. It's all so . . . so . . ."

"Sanitised?" Woodend suggested.

"Yeah, that's the word," Walker agreed. "Groups like the Drifters take somethin' with real life in it, an' scrub away at it until there's nothin' left that's any good."

"How do you feel about Huddie Leadbetter?" Woodend asked, completely out of the blue.

Walker nearly dropped his pint. "Leadbelly!" he said. "*You've* heard of Leadbelly?"

"Aye, that surprised you, didn't it? In point of fact, I've done more than just heard of him – I've got some of his music on old seventy-eights."

"An' you really do like him?" Steve Walker asked, as if he suspected that Woodend was playing some kind of game.

"Aye, I do. My main interest's New Orleans jazz, but I appreciate a bit of blues now an' again." Woodend took another swig of his pint. "Who do you think killed Eddie Barnes, Mr Walker?" he asked, suddenly changing tack.

"I've no idea," Steve Walker said.

Woodend shook his head again. "Don't come that with me. You're far too smart a lad not to have thought it over. An' once you *had* given it some thought, you're too smart not to have come up with some conclusion on the matter. Shall I tell you what I think?"

The young guitarist shrugged. "You might as well."

"I think you take Eddie's death personally . . ."

"Well, of course I take it bloody personally. He was my best mate."

" . . . an' it's crossed your mind that if anybody's goin' to punish the killer, it should be you."

Walker hurriedly knocked back the rest of his drink, and stood up. "I'd better be goin'," he said.

"Interestin' feller, Huddie Leadbetter," Woodend said, looking up at him. "He was jailed for murder, you know. Not just once, but twice. An' both times he got a free pardon because he was considered such a unique musician that it seemed a crime to keep him in gaol."

"What's your point?" Steve Walker asked.

"Isn't it obvious? You're not Leadbelly, an' this isn't the American Deep South in the 1930s. So bearin' all that in mind, I'd go very carefully if I was you, Mr Walker."

The temperature had dropped as night had fallen, and standing in the hallway of his small terraced house, the telephone receiver in his hand, Jack Towers felt a shiver run through him.

He wondered how long the man on the other end of the line had been keeping him waiting. Two minutes? Three? Possibly even longer than that. But he knew that he had no choice but to hang on and wait until the all-powerful club owner was ready to speak to him.

"You still there?" a voice from the receiver crackled.

"Yes, I'm still here."

"Might have a slot for your lads next Saturday. Course, they'll only be the openin' act, so I can't pay them more than a fiver."

"A fiver!" Towers repeated. "A fiver's peanuts. It'll barely cover the cost of the petrol."

81

"That's really not my problem, Mr Towers," the club owner said. "If the Seagulls aren't willin' to do the gig for that money, then all I can tell you is, there's plenty of other groups that will."

Towers pictured himself having to tell Steve Walker that he'd only managed to negotiate a five-pound fee for a Saturday night. He could already see the look of derision on the young guitarist's face – could already hear Walker's hurtful words buzzing in his ears:

Five quid! You expect us to play our guts out for one pound five shillin's each? What kind of manager are you, Jack? Our cat could get us a better deal than that.

"The group's got an audition with a record company in London in less than two weeks' time," Towers argued, trying his best not to sound desperate. "The man in charge has already heard a demo, and he thinks that they're going to be the next big thing."

"Well, when they are the next big thing, ring me up again an' I'll probably be willin' to pay them more," the club owner said tartly. "But for the moment, a fiver's as high as I'm prepared to go. Do you want the bookin' or what?"

If he could scrape together five pounds of his own, he could tell Steve Walker that they were getting paid ten pounds for the gig, Towers thought.

"Yes, we want the booking," he said wearily.

"Right. I'll see you on the night."

Towers replaced the receiver on its cradle. Even for ten pounds Steve was not going to be happy about playing in yet another seedy club, he told himself. But a seedy club was better than no club at all. Besides, it would give the group the opportunity to practice with their new guitarist in front of a live audience. And practice was what they needed. If the truth be told, he was terrified that the lads wouldn't be well enough prepared for the audition, and so would blow the one real chance they were ever likely to get. And what Steve Walker say then? Who would he blame for their failure?

The answer was so obvious that it brought Towers out in a cold sweat.

He heard a soft plop behind him. He turned round towards the front door and saw that someone had pushed an envelope through his letterbox. He bent down to pick it up, noting as he did that the envelope was not the classy kind like Basildon Bond – which was what he always used for all Seagulls business – but instead was tatty, and so thin that it was almost transparent.

He held the envelope up to the light. There was no address written on it, but that was hardly surprising, since it was far too late for it to have delivered by a postman. He slit the envelope open, and took out the single piece of paper which lay nestled inside.

There was neither handwriting nor typing on the sheet. Instead, a number of words had been cut out of newspapers and magazines, then glued to the page.

It did not take him long to read the message, but even before he had finished it, he could feel the bile rising to his throat.

Who could have put together such a dreadful thing? he asked himself, as the hallway began to swim before his eyes.

A sudden thought hit him like a thunderbolt. Why was he just standing there like a bloody fool, he wondered, when whoever had put the letter together had probably also been the person who'd pushed it through his letterbox a minute or so earlier?

On legs which felt as if they were made of rubber, he staggered up the hall and flung open the front door.

There was a distinct chill edge to the air, but he didn't even notice it. He glanced frantically up and down the road. The street lamps were shining brightly – far too brightly, it seemed to him, for his eyes to take. A row of dustbins stood lined up, ready for an early-morning collection. Further down the street, a neighbour he vaguely recognised was putting her milk bottles out on the step, and from across the road a stray cat stared wildly at him, then made a dash for freedom. But of the author of the vile message, there was absolutely no sign.

Nine

Despite his intermittent nagging worries about his wife, Bob Rutter found he really enjoyed his first night's sleep in the Adelphi Hotel. Luxury, he decided, as he shaved in his *en suite* bathroom the following morning, was something he could very easily become accustomed to. And there was more luxury to come, he thought as he stepped out of the lift – a breakfast eaten off fine china plates, coffee poured from a silver-plated pot, crisp white tablecloths and napkins.

It was not to be. "You know what I really fancy for me breakfast?" Woodend asked him, when they met in the lobby. "An egg-an'-bacon buttie, smothered in thick brown sauce. An' since I reckon I've got as much chance of gettin' one of them in this poncy place as I have of bein' elected Pope, why don't we go an' find a decent, honest cafe?"

With a regretful sigh, Rutter followed his boss out on to the street. On the corner a newspaper vendor, wearing a cloth cap and a heavy muffler, was bawling out the day's headlines.

"Read all about it! Russians put the first man in space! Read all about it!"

Woodend stopped and bought a copy of the *Daily Sketch*. "So, the Comrades have got there first," he said. "Well, the Yanks won't like that – especially not that President Kennedy of theirs."

"It's a tremendous achievement, isn't it?" Rutter said enthusiastically, as they walked along the street.

"I suppose it is," Woodend replied, sounding unconvinced. "But where's it all leadin', that's what I want to know? They'll be wantin' to go to the moon next, though God only knows why – the place is about as desolate as a Butlin's holiday camp on a wet Thursday in March."

The chief inspector came to a halt right in front of a cafe which had its menu painted on the window. He sniffed the smells drifting out through the open door with gusto.

"This'll do champion," he announced.

There were already a number of customers inside, mopping up egg yolk with bits of fried bread and drinking strong tea out of large pot mugs. Bob Rutter sat down at one of the rickety Formica tables and thought once more of the starched linen tablecloths and discreet service he could have been enjoying in the Adelphi Hotel.

Woodend ordered the egg-and-bacon sandwich he'd been lusting after, and when it was plonked unceremoniously on the table in front of him, he attacked it with the enthusiasm of a man who hadn't eaten for days.

Rutter contented himself with buttered toast and, as he nibbled at it, he found himself wondering when would be the earliest time he could call his wife without it angering her.

"There's a murderer out there – probably not more than a mile from this very spot," Woodend said, when he'd finished eating. "He knows we're lookin' for him, an' he's scared."

"Or *she* knows we're looking for *her*, and *she's* scared," Bob Rutter countered.

"You're right," Woodend admitted. "My problem is, I'm still findin' it difficult to use 'woman' an' 'wirin'' in the same sentence. Anyway, do you mind if, for the present, I talk about him as if he was a man?"

"Go ahead."

"He's out there, an' he's scared. I can almost smell his fear. I've got absolutely no idea what he looks like, or why he killed poor Eddie Barnes, but I'll tell you somethin' for nothin', Bob – no matter how frightened he is, he'll kill again if he has to."

"What makes you say that? Instinct?"

"Aye, if you like."

85

"Which has been wrong before," Rutter pointed out.

"True," Woodend agreed. "But there's been plenty of times when it's been right an' all." He drained the last dregs of his large mug of tea. "It's time we were gettin' to work," he continued. "I'm goin' down to the Cellar Club to talk to this Mrs Pollard who owns it."

"And what do you want me to do, sir?"

"You take yourself down to the local nick an' have a look at this room which Inspector Hopgood's assigned us," Woodend said. "He'll probably ask you if you think it'll do, an' when he does you're to say that it's absolutely bloody perfect, that you'd never – not even in your wildest dreams – have thought they'd give us such a wonderful room."

Rutter grinned. "I'll probably tone that down a bit, sir."

"Aye, that might be wise," Woodend agreed.

"And once I've told them the room's satisfactory, what do you want me to do?"

"Scatter a few papers around the place, so it looks as if we're actually usin' it. Oh, an' have a look at their reports on the investigation they conducted before we arrived."

"Should I be looking for anything in particular?"

Woodend shook his head. "I don't expect you'll find anythin' of much use – if they'd had any real leads to follow, they wouldn't have called us in. Still, you never know your luck."

"Where will me meet up again?"

"How about in the Grapes, round about dinnertime?" Woodend suggested, standing up. "Take a taxi down to the nick at the long-sufferin' taxpayer's expense, if you feel like it."

"I think I'll walk, sir. 'Feel the rhythms of the place through the soles of my feet', as an old bobby I know I once said."

His sergeant was smiling, Woodend thought, but he could see that it was an effort. He wondered just what had been said during the phone call to Maria to make him tense up so much. But no doubt Rutter would tell him when he was good and ready.

*   *   *

86

Death of a Cave Dweller

The door to the Cellar Club was closed, but when Woodend turned the handle, it swung obligingly open. As the chief inspector made his way down the stairs, he could hear a number of voices coming up from below. Once at the bottom, he could see who had been making the noise. The three surviving members of the Seagulls were standing on the tiny stage, and sitting on the hard chairs in front of it were several young men holding guitars. The auditions to find a replacement for the murdered Eddie Barnes were already under way.

Steve Walker placed his mouth close to the microphone. "Right, let's hear the next one," he said, with weary resignation in his voice.

A boy wearing blue jeans and a leather jacket mounted the steps, and plugged his guitar into the amplifier.

"I'd like to do a song called 'Some Other Guy'," he said into the microphone. He turned his head in Steve Walker's direction. "That's all right, isn't it? You do know that one?"

"Do we know it?" Walker asked scornfully into his own mike. "Of course we bloody know it. Let's get this straight. We're not just some tinpot group of beginners. We're *real* musicians, kid. We've played the Star Club in Hamburg. When you've been on stage for eight hours a day, every day, like we have, you learn every song that's ever been written."

The young guitarist looked chastened. There'd been no need for that, Woodend thought – no need at all to broadcast to the whole club that he thought the lad was a prat even before he'd played the opening bars.

The chief inspector's glance took in the rest of the club. The pale, thin Jack Towers was standing at the far end of the tunnel, nervously sucking on a cigarette. He must somehow have managed to get a morning off work from the shipping office. Either that or he'd called in sick.

Just beyond the harassed manager, standing by the snack bar, were Rick Johnson and a middle-aged woman with hair which, even in the poor lighting, Woodend could see was a brassy blonde. The two had their heads close together, as if they were having a serious discussion, and for one brief moment the woman put her hand on Rick Johnson's arm.

The group had started the number. Even to Woodend's untutored ear, the hopeful guitarist seemed to be making a mess of it – but that was hardly surprising after the way Steve Walker had unsettled him.

As Woodend made his way across the back of the club, Jack Towers seemed to notice him for the first time, and stepped directly into his path. The manager's eyes were red, and there was stubble on his chin. He looked as if he had spent a very bad night indeed.

"We've got to have a talk, Chief Inspector," the manager said. "It's very important!"

It had not been part of Woodend's plan to speak to Towers again until he had more background information, but there was an urgency in the man's tone which suggested he was going to be very insistent.

"Give me half an hour," Woodend said. "As soon as I've had a chat with Mrs Pollard, I'll get back to you."

"This won't wait," Towers said.

Woodend sighed loudly. He was beginning to see what Steve Walker meant when he said that Towers sometimes got so far up his nose that he just felt he had to lash out.

"There are very few things in this world which take any harm for waitin' half an hour to be dealt with," the chief inspector said. "Listen to the audition, Mr Towers. That's what you're here for."

But then Towers wasn't really interested in the music, he reminded himself as he walked towards the snack bar. When the Seagulls had first noticed their soon-to-be-manager, he hadn't been swaying with the beat as everyone else had, but just standing there, stock-still.

Rick Johnson had noticed Woodend's approach and was about to beat a hasty retreat, but before he left, Mrs Pollard took the opportunity to touch his arm again. Woodend added that fact to the dossier on Johnson which he was already building up in his mind.

Close to, the owner of the Cellar Club did not look quite as brash as she had from a distance. True, she had the sort of hard features which said she would not stand for being messed about, but beneath that steely exterior Woodend guessed there lurked a soft heart.

"You'll be Mrs Pollard," he said.

"And you'll be Chief Inspector Woodend, all the way from London," she said. "Would you like a drink?"

"A cup of tea would hit the spot."

"I've got something a bit stronger than tea under the counter," the woman said, winking a heavily made-up eye.

"It's a bit early in the day for me," Woodend told her.

"It's a bit early in the day for me, too," Mrs Pollard replied, "but when you've had a murder in your own club, I think you're entitled to it."

She lifted the flap, stepped behind the counter, and filled the kettle.

The group had just reached the end of 'Some Other Guy'. "Right, let's have the next one up here," Steve Walker said.

His audition over – his chance blown – the guitarist in the leather jacket made his way down the steps, his head bowed.

"Give your name an' address to our manager," Pete Foster said into the mike. "He's standin' over there. We'll be in touch if we need you."

He was only trying to be kind, Woodend thought. But Pete Foster's kindness was very different to that shown by Steve Walker. Pete spread it thin, so that everyone got a share, while Steve lavished his – in huge dollops – on a few, carefully selected people.

Another young hopeful had already mounted the stage and was standing in front of the mike.

"What's yer name?" Steve Walker asked disinterestedly.

"Phil Rourke."

"An' what song do you want us to do?" Steve asked. "Better

make it somethin' easy," he continued, casting a brief, contemptuous look at the leather-jacketed youth who was giving his name to Jack Towers, "'cos it's well known we can only play a few tunes."

"I'd like to do 'Lime Street Rock'," Phil Rourke said.

The effect of the words on Steve Walker was instantaneous. He seemed to swell with rage, and for a moment Woodend feared that he would club the newcomer with his guitar.

"What's the matter?" Pete Foster asked.

"What's the matter?" Steve Walker repeated. "He wants to play 'Lime Street Rock' – that's what's the matter!"

"Well, why shouldn't he? It's a good song."

"It's *Eddie's* song. Eddie wrote it."

"I know Eddie wrote it, but it's no good to him now, is it?"

The two young men glared at each other across the stage. At this point, the manager should step in and take charge, Woodend thought, but Towers was staying where he was – probably afraid to cross Steve Walker when he had a mood on him.

"Listen, I can do 'Please Don't Tease' instead," Phil Rourke said, the expression on his face clearly showing that he suspected what everybody else already knew – that as far as Steve Walker was concerned, he had blown the audition before it even started.

"Yeah, do that one instead," Pete Foster told him, and before Steve Walker had time to say anything else, he began the count-in to the song. "One . . . two . . . three . . ."

"My husband had plans to turn this place into the smartest restaurant in Liverpool," said a voice behind Woodend, and he turned to see that Mrs Pollard had placed a cup of tea at his elbow.

"A restaurant," Woodend replied, noncommittally.

"A *smart* restaurant," Mrs Pollard emphasised. "Just look at the place! He must have wanted his bumps feeling for imagining, even for a minute, that the *crème de la crème* of Liverpool society would ever come all the way down here for their fish-and-chip suppers."

Woodend found himself liking the woman, and chuckled. "But you had other plans," he suggested.

"I had no plans at all until my Les went and got himself killed," the woman replied.

"I'm sorry. I didn't know."

Mrs Pollard shrugged. "No reason why you should. He tripped up, and banged his head on the kerb. Other men can fall off high buildings and live to tell the tale. My Les plunged five feet seven inches to his death."

"So what gave you the idea for startin' up the club?"

"I was stuck with a useless hole in the ground which I didn't know what to do with, and then I noticed that all the office and shop girls were spending most of their dinnertimes in the record shops. Put the two things together, and you've got the Cellar Club."

"You seem to have made a nice little business out of it, anyroad," Woodend said.

"Oh, I'm not complaining."

"Can I ask you about the night before the murder?"

"Be my guest," said Mrs Pollard, reaching under the counter and pulling out a bottle of Johnny Walker Red Label.

"Who went into the dressing room?"

Mrs Pollard was suddenly very cagey. "We gave the local bobbies a list," she said.

"I know. An' I've got it in my pocket. The question I've got to ask is, is it a complete list?"

"As far as I know," the club owner lied.

"Look, I'm here to find a murderer – an' for no other reason," Woodend said. "I'm not in the least concerned about the fact that you've got booze on unlicensed premises . . ."

"That's just for personal use," Mrs Pollard protested.

"They could still do you for it, luv," Woodend told her, "but like I said, it's not my concern. Nor am I goin' to worry my head with anythin' else the local bobbies might get upset about – like you runnin' a disorderly house. So why don't you tell me about the girls?"

"How did you know about them?" Mrs Pollard gasped.

"The couch," Woodend told her. "It was a dead give-away, especially with that curtain."

The club owner grinned ruefully. "When the boys asked if they could put it in there they said it was so they could grab a bit of shut-eye between sets, but I wasn't fooled for a minute. How the hell could anybody sleep with all the noise going on a few feet away from their lug-holes?"

"How many girls usually go backstage?"

"It depends. Some nights there's three or four, some nights only one, and other nights none at all."

"An' the night before the murder?"

"One, as far as I know."

"What's her name?"

"I don't know. She wasn't a regular, I'm sure of that. And I certainly haven't seen her since."

Woodend's next question was cut off by a loud, "Well, look what the cat's dragged in!" from Steve Walker, who was sounding happier than he'd done all morning.

Everyone in the club followed his gaze towards the back of the room, from where yet another young man carrying a guitar was just emerging.

"How are you, Steve, you big tosspot?" the new arrival asked, a grin spreading across his face.

"All the better for seein' you, you little toe-rag," Walker replied. "You know Terry Garner, don't you?" he asked the other two members of the group. "He'll be playin' next."

"There's others waitin' their turn," Pete Foster complained.

"Yeah, but the thing is, they've got all day, an' Terry has another appointment," Steve Walker said airily. "Come on up, our kid, and show us what you can do."

Woodend turned his attention back to Mrs Pollard. "Who could have got to the amplifier between the time the club finally closed down for the night an' the moment it killed Eddie Barnes . . ." He paused to give weight to his next few words. "Anybody apart from Rick Johnson, I mean?"

Mrs Pollard tried to fake shock at the suggestion that he might suspect Johnson – and didn't quite make it.

"Rick might be a bit rough – that's why I employ him – but he's no murderer," she said, with a mixture of anger and defensiveness.

"Oh dear, have I touched a nerve?" Woodend asked.

Mrs Pollard brushed a strand of brassy hair out of her right eye. "No," she said, unconvincingly. "Of course not. I just don't like hearing you make assumptions about Rick, that's all."

"Is that what I was doin'?"

"It's what it sounded like."

The Seagulls and Terry Garner were doing a number which seemed to be called 'The Hippy Hippy Shake'.

"Talkin' of sounds, do you know anythin' about this kind of music?" Woodend asked.

"I know enough to say whether it's good or bad," Mrs Pollard replied, obviously glad to get off the subject of Rick Johnson.

"So what's this new lad like?"

Mrs Pollard listened to the song for perhaps half a minute. "He's all right, but he's nowhere near as good as the kid who was on before him," she said. "Why are you asking?"

"Just curious," Woodend lied. "You were tellin' me who might have been able to nobble the amplifier after the groups had gone home."

"Well, there was me, for a start."

"Who else?"

"Rick, as you've already gone out of your way to mention. The two cleaners who come in first thing in the morning – but they're old dears, pensioners who probably couldn't even change their own light bulbs. And Ron Clarke, the disc jockey. That's about it."

The song had reached its final chord. "We'll do 'What do you want to make those eyes at me for?' next," Steve Walker announced.

"What do you mean 'next'?" Pete Foster demanded. "There's other people waitin' to come on."

93

"Well, it won't do them any harm to wait for another three minutes, will it?" Steve Walker asked.

Pete Foster strode furiously across the stage and clamped his hand over the microphone, so the rest of his conversation with Walker wouldn't be blasted across the club.

"Do they always go on at each other like that?" the chief inspector asked Mrs Pollard.

"There's always a bit of tension – a bit of rivalry as you might call it," the club owner replied. "But it doesn't often reach this level. I expect it's because Steve's still upset over Eddie's death."

"And Pete? Isn't he upset, too?"

"He didn't have as close a relationship with Eddie as Steve did. And I sometimes got the impression that he thought he'd work better with Steve if Eddie wasn't around." Mrs Pollard put her hand up to her mouth. "Oh my God! I didn't mean that to come out like it did."

Pete Foster had ended his argument with Steve Walker and had returned to his own microphone.

"From now on, we're goin' to let everybody who's auditionin' play two songs," he announced.

"A compromise seems to have been reached," Woodend remarked to Mrs Pollard.

"It usually is. They might fight, but they both know they're not half as good on their own as they are together. Listen, what I said about Pete and Eddie, I don't want you to . . ."

"I'd soon have found out from somebody else if I hadn't got it from you," Woodend told her. "Don't worry, I'm not goin' to put the cuffs on him the second he steps off the stage. For a start, I don't have any on me."

Mrs Pollard was obviously still shaken, but managed a weak smile. Behind them, Terry Garner and the Seagulls broke into 'What do you want to make those eyes at me for?'.

"D'you know what's one of the first things I do when I'm assigned to a case?" Woodend asked conversationally.

"No. How could I?"

"True enough," Woodend agreed. "Well, what I do is, I seek out a Wise Man."

Mrs Pollard giggled. "You mean an old man with a long white beard?" she asked.

"He doesn't have to be old at all," Woodend said seriously. "He can be quite young as long as he's got the knowledge. I'll give you an example. A couple of months ago, I was workin' on a case in Hampshire. Now the Wise Man in that investigation was a local poacher who couldn't have been more than twenty-five. He was suspicious of me at first, naturally, but once I'd persuaded him I wasn't goin' to run him in, he turned out to be very helpful – told me things about the area an' the people I'd never have found out myself in a thousand years. So what I'm lookin' for now is a Wise Man who knows about his way around here. Or should I say *her* way – because I think it might be you."

"I'm sure there are hundreds of people who know their way around Liverpool better than I do."

"I'm not talkin' about Liverpool in general. I'm talkin' about the rock'n'roll scene."

"I'm still not your woman," Mrs Pollard replied. "I know some of the groups, because they play here, but there's dozens of other clubs and hundreds of other bands. If you really want to find your Wise Man, then you should go and see Geoff Platt."

"Who's he when he's at home?"

"He runs a weekly newspaper called the *Mersey Sound*. He's got a mind like an encyclopaedia when it comes to music in the 'Pool."

"Where will I find him?"

"His office is just at the end of the road. Right on the corner of North John Street."

"An' when do you think would be a good time for me to pay this Mr Platt a call?"

"Doesn't really matter. The sign on the door says the office closes at five, but Geoff's the sort who works around the clock."

The song had come to an end. "This next one's called 'Too Much Monkey Business'," Steve Walker announced, as if he were performing before an audience instead of holding an audition.

Terry Garner played the opening bars, and Steve Walker came in with the accompaniment. It was perhaps ten or fifteen more seconds before Billie Simmons added a drumbeat, and a full half-minute before a furious-looking Pete Foster finally gave up and joined in.

"It's been nice talkin' to you, Mrs Pollard," Woodend said. "Now if you'll tell me how much I owe you for the tea . . ."

"On the house," the club owner told him.

Woodend nodded his thanks, and headed towards the door. It was not until Jack Towers loomed in front of him that he remembered his promise to spare the manager a few minutes of his time.

God, the man looked rough, Woodend thought. No wonder he hadn't made any attempt to sort out the argument between Steve Walker and Pete Foster – it seemed to be taking all his effort just to stand up.

"This came through my letterbox at around eleven o'clock last night," Towers said, as he thrust a cheap brown envelope into Woodend's hand. "I thought you'd better see it."

Woodend opened the envelope and read the short message.

WHICH one will **die** *Next*?

Maybe Steve Walker

Get out of **LIVERPOOL** while

You *STILL* **GOT** the chance

"'While you still *got* the chance'," Woodend read aloud. "Well, he's not much of a scholar, whoever put this together. Or maybe it's just that he wants us to think he isn't."

"Is it a serious threat?" Towers asked. "I mean, do you think it was actually sent by Eddie's murderer?"

"It could have been," Woodend conceded. "Then again, it could simply have been sent by somebody with a screw loose. Whenever there's a murder, any number of nutters come crawlin' out of the woodwork. You have no idea yourself who might have sent it?"

Towers shook his head. "I was in the hall at the time. I should have gone straight out on to the street the moment the letter landed on my mat," he said regretfully. "If I had done, I'd have been bound to see him. But I didn't think. I just didn't think."

"Don't blame yourself, sir," Woodend said. "You're not trained to handle this kind of situation."

"Bloody right I'm not," Jack Towers agreed, wiping his forehead with his handkerchief. "So now you've seen the letter, what are you going to do about it, Mr Woodend?"

"I'll ask Inspector Hopgood to send some of his lads round to question your neighbours," Woodend told him. "It was quite late when the letter was delivered – which isn't very helpful – but there's always a chance that somebody walkin' his dog or comin' back from the pub might have seen somethin' suspicious. An' if your neighbours are anythin' like mine, there's bound to be at least one nosy old bat who peeps from behind her curtains every time she hears a noise."

"What about protection?" Towers asked, as if tracking down the author of the letter was not his main concern.

"Protection?" the chief inspector repeated. "What exactly did you have in mind, sir?"

Towers shrugged helplessly. "You're the experts. But I should have thought that at a minimum you'd need to assign at least a couple of policemen to each of my boys."

If the manager hadn't been so obviously earnest about it, Woodend would have laughed out loud.

"A couple of policemen on each of your lads!" he repeated.

"You think that's too few?"

"I think it's far too bloody many. At three shifts a day, that'd take eighteen officers off the streets. How many bobbies do you think there are goin' spare in this city?"

97

"So many can we have?"

"That's up to the local Chief Super," Woodend told him. "But if you want my opinion, I'd be surprised if you get a single officer."

"Then just what are the boys expected to do?" Jack Towers demanded, aggrieved.

"Tell them to be extra careful," Woodend advised. "Make sure they always check their equipment carefully before they plug it in, and that they never go anywhere alone." He put his hand on the manager's bony shoulder. "Don't look so worried, Mr Towers. Like I said before, there's a very good chance this letter was written by a crank. Most of them are."

"It wasn't a crank who killed Eddie," Towers pointed out.

"No, it wasn't," Woodend agreed. "A lunatic, maybe, but not a crank." He placed the anonymous letter carefully in one of the pockets of his hairy sports jacket. "I'll get the fellers at the local police lab to give this a once-over," he continued. "Not that I expect they'll find anythin'. Whoever wrote it an' posted it through your letterbox was probably wearin' gloves. An' even if he wasn't, whatever prints he left will probably have been obscured by yours."

"'Get out of Liverpool while you got the chance'," Towers quoted, bitterly. "What have I been doing on all those trips down to record companies in London if it wasn't trying to get my boys out of Liverpool?"

Ten

Mugs, half full of cold coffee, perched precariously on stacks of poorly printed handbills. Paper clips, linked together in a chain, lay discarded beside broken pencils and blunt crayons. The notice board was covered with reminders of events long since past, and the two typewriters were – at the very least – pre-war. The office in which the *Mersey Sound* was put together was just about as chaotic as any office can be while still being classified as a workplace.

"I'm told you know more about local music than anybody else in Liverpool," Woodend said to the plump man with wild, curly hair who was sitting behind the battered desk.

"If I don't, then I shouldn't be running this newspaper," Geoff Platt replied with no attempt at false modesty.

"So paint me a picture of it."

Platt rested his interlocked hands on his ample belly. "A picture wouldn't do you any good at all," he said with a smile. "It'd be out of date almost before the paint was dry."

Woodend grinned. "You mean that things are changing very fast round here," he said.

Platt looked out of the window, which would have benefited from a good cleaning. "Put it like this," he said. "There are lads who are playin' together now who will be in rival groups by next month. Maybe even by next week."

As if to prove the truth of the statement, the phone on Platt's desk chose that moment to ring.

"Excuse me for a minute," he said, picking up the receiver. "Geoff Platt speaking . . .Who? . . .." He rummaged around the surface of the desk and finally managed to come with a scrap of paper and badly chewed pencil. "What are they planning to call themselves? . . . The Black Aces? So they'll be playing what kind of music? Mainly rhythm'n'blues?" He scribbled down a few names. "Thanks for the story, our kid. Next time I see you in the Grapes, remind me I owe you a couple of pints."

He replaced the phone on its cradle. "There are literally hundreds of groups playing all around the Liverpool area," he told Woodend. "Some of them only last a couple of weeks before they break up. On the other hand, there are groups that have been around for two or three years, maybe even longer than that. And there are some kids who play in more than one group. It's all very fluid. For instance, I know of one drummer who plays in five different groups. It's not that he's a particularly good musician, you understand, but he has got his own drum kit, and having a bad drummer backing you is a damn sight better than no drummer at all."

The phone rang again.

"Is it always like this?" Woodend asked.

"Yes, this is a pretty normal day," Platt told him, searching for another scrap of paper on which to write the details of the break-up of a group which called itself the Deluxes.

"So many young kids chasin' so few available dreams of fame an' fortune," Woodend said, almost wistfully.

Platt shook his head. "It's not really like that. There are a handful of groups who have a real chance of getting their music heard by a much wider audience, but for most of the kids being in a band is a laugh, and a way to earn a bit of pocket money." He winked. "And, of course, it's a hell of a way to pull the judies."

"Yes, I suppose it is," Woodend said, thinking of the girl who had been in the Cellar Club dressing room the night before Eddie Barnes had died.

"The majority of the groups don't really expect to make a record, or appear on television," Platt continued. "If they manage to get the third spot on the bill at a dance in the New

Brighton Tower Ballroom, they think they're the kings of the world. And they are – because for them the 'Pool *is* the world." He paused. "There's a lot of fans – especially the girls – who hope none of the groups they like ever get famous, because then they wouldn't just belong to the city, they'd belong to anybody with enough money to buy a record."

"But some of them are going to get famous eventually, aren't they?" Woodend asked.

"The Beatles will definitely make it sooner or later," Platt said with conviction. "And they won't just be one of these one-hit-wonder groups, either. It wouldn't surprise me if they managed to get five or six discs into the Top Ten before they're finished. They might even get around to making a long-playing record if they're very lucky."

"What about the Seagulls?"

"They're another talented bunch of kids, and they've got a good chance of making it too. But they're going to need a new lead guitarist first."

"They'll have one by the end of the mornin'," Woodend told him.

"How do you know that?" Platt asked, surprised.

"I've just seen them auditionin' for one down in the Cellar Club."

"Have you, by God?" Platt asked, reaching for yet another scrap of paper and making a note on it, this time with a yellow crayon.

"An' I shouldn't be at all surprised if their new guitarist's name is Terry Garner," Woodend said.

Geoff Platt frowned. "Are you sure you've got the name right?"

"What makes you ask that?"

"Terry's a nice enough lad, but I wouldn't have thought he was really up to the Seagulls' standard. When I was drawing up my own list of possible replacements last week—"

"Wait a minute," Woodend interrupted. "You were drawin' up a list of replacements *last* week?"

101

"That's right."

"Before the murder?"

"I suppose it was, now I think about it."

Woodend leaned forward in his chair. "Are you tellin' me that you knew in advance that Eddie Barnes was goin' to be killed?"

Platt looked thunderstruck. "No, of course I didn't! But I knew he was planning to leave the Seagulls."

"If that's true, why didn't any of the group mention it to me?" Woodend demanded.

"Probably because they didn't know."

"So where did you get your information from?"

An evasive look came to Geoff Platt's face. "I got it from what we journalists call a 'very reliable source'."

"And that would be?"

"I can't remember."

Woodend leant a little further, moving his own head a couple of inches closer to Platt's. "Do you really expect me to believe that?"

"It's the truth," the editor said. "Look, you've seen what it's like in here. People are calling me all the time. And what I write down is the information, not the source. Fellers come up to me in the pub and say I owe them a drink because they gave me this or that story, so I buy them a pint. But I couldn't swear to the fact that they were ones who gave it to me. So what I'm saying is, I remember being told Eddie was leaving the Seagulls, and I remember thinking that the person who told me knew the business, so it had to be kosher. But I can't actually come up with a name at the moment."

It was difficult to judge whether or not he was lying, Woodend thought, and more difficult still to decide whether or not Eddie Barnes's decision to leave the group – if he really had made such a decision – had anything to do with his death.

A new idea suddenly came to Woodend. "I'd like to buy some advertisin' space in your paper," he said.

Platt grinned. "Thinking of forming a group yourself, are you? Chief Inspector Woodend and the Rockin' Bobbies?"

"No, I'm not formin' a group," Woodend said seriously. "But I do want to talk to anybody who might have any information about Eddie Barnes's death, an' since he was a musician, it seems to me like the best way to reach them is through the *Mersey Sound*."

"In that case, you can have your space. A whole page if you want it. And it won't cost you a penny."

"That's very generous of you."

"If I hadn't liked Eddie – and I did – I'd still do anything I could to see his murderer caught."

"So you'll put it in this week's edition."

Platt shook his head. "Now that I can't do, however much I might want to help."

"Why not?" Woodend asked. "Your paper comes out on a Tuesday, doesn't it?"

"That's right."

"An' it's only Thursday now. That should leave you plenty of time to make the insertion."

"We work on a very tight budget here," Platt said apologetically, "which means that we have to cut corners wherever we can. Printing costs is one of the ways we do it."

"How do you mean?"

"The printers give us the best rates for the times when they're least busy. Which means that though the paper comes out on Tuesday, it's printed much earlier." He looked down at his watch. "They should already have gone to press by now, which means it's too late to make the next edition. But I'll make sure it appears in the edition after that."

"Jesus, I was hopin' to have the case wrapped up by then," Woodend told the editor.

"Really?" Platt said, with obvious surprise.

"In my experience, there are two kinds of case," Woodend said. "The first kind are the ones that drag on for months, or maybe even years, but eventually you get a result. Then there's

103

the other kind – the ones you either crack in the first few days on the job, or else or you never crack at all. I've got a feelin' that this case is goin' to be one of the latter."

"I hope you're right," Platt said. "I mean, right about getting an early result. We'll never be able to put Eddie's death entirely behind us as long as his killer's on the loose."

Woodend took out his cigarettes out of his pocket, and offered one to the editor.

"Make my job a bit easier for me, Mr Platt," he said, after he'd held a match under the other man's Capstan Full Strength. "Tell me who you think killed Eddie Barnes."

"I can honestly say I haven't got a clue," Platt said – and Woodend believed him. "Eddie was a really nice kid. Why should *anybody* want to hurt him?"

The door swung open, and a man of about twenty-seven entered the room without knocking. He seemed both surprised and confused to find that Geoff Platt was not alone.

"I . . . er . . . didn't know you had company, Geoff," he said. "I'll come back later."

Woodend examined the man more closely. Nice suit – off the rack, but probably middle price range. Tired eyes. Delicate hands. If he'd had to put money on it, he would have bet the new arrival was a doctor.

"No need for you to go, sir," the chief inspector said. "I was just on the point of leavin' myself."

But he made no move to rise from his seat, and after a few seconds' silence which embarrassed the other two men much more than they embarrassed Woodend, Geoff Platt finally said, "Chief Inspector Woodend, I'd like you to meet Doctor Trevor Atkinson."

Now Woodend *did* stand up, and held out his hand.

"*Doctor* Atkinson," he said. "Are you one of them doctors I should come to see if I want to know somethin' about Sumarian pottery in the third century BC, or one of them who can give me somethin' to get rid of the chinky rot I've got between my toes?"

Atkinson laughed – rather uneasily, Woodend thought. "I can get rid of your chinky rot in no time at all," he promised.

"Well, you should have a word with my GP," Woodend said. "He's been about as much use as a spare prick at a weddin'."

The doctor laughed a second time, and the note of unease was just as strong as it had been previously.

"If you'd like to give me the name of your doctor . . ." he suggested.

Woodend slapped him on the shoulder. "Only jokin', lad," he said. "I've not got chinky rot. You're not allowed to have anythin' wrong with you if you're in the police force. Didn't you know that? We're superhuman."

"I . . . er . . . you're joking again, aren't you?" the doctor said.

"You catch on quick, don't you," Woodend replied. "Aye, I was joking, lad. But maybe you have to come from Lancashire to really appreciate it." He turned his attention back to the editor. "Thank you for your time, Mr Platt. You've been a real help."

He opened the door, stepped out on to the stairs, and started to make his way down to the street. Why had the doctor seemed so nervous? he asked himself. Come to that, why had Atkinson been visiting the editor in the middle of the day? Was it a professional visit? Or a social one? As far as he could tell, there was nothing which even remotely tied Geoff Platt into the case, but Woodend still filed the encounter away in his mind for future use.

Rutter stood in a phone box on the corner of Cook Street, listening to his home telephone ring.

"There's no reply," the operator told him.

"Keep on ringing. She might be upstairs."

"If she was in the house, she should have had time to answer the phone by now."

"She's blind!" Rutter said, more aggressively than he'd

intended. "It takes her longer to reach the phone than it takes most people. All right?"

"Oh, I'm sorry," the operator said – and sounded it.

"No. *I'm* sorry," Rutter told her, feeling contrite. "There was no excuse for my snapping at you. It's . . . it's just everything's so much more difficult for her than it is for normal people."

"Of course," the operator said sympathetically.

But Rutter was already drowning in guilt. What was it that he had just said? *More difficult for her than a normal person*? But Maria *was* a normal person. She just happened to be a normal person who was blind.

The ringing continued, and Rutter suddenly had a nightmare vision of his wife tripping on a loose rail and tumbling all the way down the stairs.

He had to get a grip, he told himself. He had to learn to have confidence in Maria's ability to take care of herself.

The ringing stopped, and the voice he knew so well said, "This is Clapham seven-two-seven-one."

"It's me. Were you upstairs?"

"That's right."

"In the bathroom?"

"No," Maria admitted. "I . . . I was lying down."

"Have you been feeling ill again?"

"A little. But it's not as bad as it was the last time. I think I must be nearly over whatever bug I've caught."

"I could catch a late-night train down to London," Rutter suggested. "It wouldn't affect my work at all. I could be back in Liverpool in the morning, before Cloggin'-it Charlie even knew I'd gone."

"That really won't be necessary," Maria replied, with a warning edge to her voice.

"You're sure?"

"I'm sure."

"I love you," Rutter said.

"I know you do," his wife told him.

*   *   *

Window cleaners were cleaning windows, shop assistants were standing behind their counters and pickpockets – probably – were picking pockets. If putting a man into space really had changed the world for ever, as the papers were suggesting, then there was little evidence of it on the streets of Liverpool that day. Yet despite what he'd said to Bob Rutter on the way to breakfast, Woodend did feel as if the Russian cosmonaut's adventure had had an effect on him. It was all part of the feeling of vague unease that he'd had since he'd talked to Eddie Barnes's parents – a feeling that he was losing touch. Certainly, he had summed up the characters of the three surviving Seagulls well enough to impress Steve Walker, but knowing what they were like was a big step from knowing how they would act.

It was just after noon when he arrived at the Grapes, and already the place was filling up with postmen from the North John Street post office, knocking back pints of draught Guinness. Were these postmen troubled at how fast the world seemed to be moving? Did it bother them at all that although they had been born at a time when flying across the Atlantic Ocean was a novelty, they now found themselves living in an age when landing a man on the moon was more than a distinct possibility? Or were they just getting on with the life they had been given and enjoying their dinnertime pint? Probably the latter, Woodend thought. And maybe he would follow their example.

He was just ordering a pint of bitter when he noticed Billie Simmons sitting alone in the corner.

"Make that two pints," he told the barman.

He took the drinks over to Simmons' table, placed one of them in front of the drummer, and sat down.

Simmons looked at the glass for a couple of seconds, then said, "Is that for me?"

"I've not quite got to the stage of drinkin' my pints in doubles, so it must be," Woodend told him.

"It's the first time a copper's ever given me anythin' other than a clout round the head," Billie Simmons said, blunting the

107

harshness of his words with an ironic smile. He raised the glass in the chief inspector's general direction. "Cheers."

"Cheers," Woodend responded, raising his own glass. "So you're on your own then, are you?"

Billie Simmons made a great show of looking under the table. "Seems that way."

"Any particular reason?"

"Steve's gone off for a drink somewhere else with Terry, Pete's gone off in a sulk, an' Jack's stopped pretendin' he's a real manager an' gone back to the shippin' office."

"I take it that means that Terry Garner is goin' to be the Seagulls' new lead guitarist."

"Of course he is. He was at school with Steve, you see. One of his pals. An' now that Eddie's dead, he's found himself suddenly promoted to the position of Steve's best pal."

"Why do you always let Steve Walker get his own way over things?" Woodend asked.

Billie shrugged. "We need him. Pete might be the brains of the group, but Steve's the heart."

"And what about you?"

The ironic smile played on Simmons' lips again. "Me? Hasn't anyone told you? I'm just the drummer."

"Tell me about the girl who was in the dressin' room the night before Eddie Barnes died," Woodend said.

"Girl?" Simmons repeated. "What girl?"

"The one that somebody had a quick session with on the sofa behind the curtain."

Simmons' smile became a grin. "Oh, that girl," he said. "I think her name was Mavis."

"Had you seen her before?"

"A couple of times."

"But not since?"

"No."

"Who took her behind the curtain?"

"Steve."

"So he knew her, did he?"

Billie Simmons shook his head. "No."

"How can you be so sure?"

"He spotted her when were on stage. As were comin' off, he asked me if I knew what she was called."

Woodend pulled out his cigarettes, and offered Billie one. "Who do you remember bein' in the dressin' room after the club closed?" he asked.

Simmons put his hand over his eyes, as if that would aid his concentration. "Let me see. All the Seagulls were there, an' so were Mike Finn an' his band. A couple of the Fantastics stayed behind. They had their manager with them. Jack turned up just after midnight, an' hung about until we needed drivin' home – like he usually does. Oh, an' a couple of Pete's mates were there an' all."

"What were you all doin'?"

Simmons grinned again. "Apart from Steve, you mean?"

"Yes, apart from Steve."

"It's like we told you in the club. We were talkin', smokin', drinkin', messin' about playin' a few tunes. It's what Steve calls 'attendin' the University of Rock'n'Roll'."

He had a way with words, did Steve Walker, Woodend thought. "An' all your equipment was where, exactly?" he asked.

"At the end of the dressin' room. Next to the curtain."

"You know what I think?" Woodend asked. "I think that for anybody to have time to change the wirin' in Eddie's amplifier, somethin' must have happened to distract everybody else's attention. Can you think what that might have been?"

Billie Simmons blinked only once, but Woodend did not miss it. "Are you askin' me if anythin' unusual happened?" the young drummer asked. "Like a fire breakin' out in the waste-paper basket, or somethin' like that?"

"That's it," Woodend agreed. "Or somethin' like that."

"No, there was nothin' out of the ordinary," Simmons said, totally unconvincingly.

"Everybody says they want me to catch this murderer, but

nobody seems willing to do anythin' to help me," Woodend said impatiently. "If you know somethin', Mr Simmons, for God's sake spit it out."

A look of uncertainty crossed the drummer's face. "I'm an only child," he said. "My mum was nearly forty when she had me. My dad died when I was three. It wasn't easy for her, bringin' me up, but she always did the best she could, an' I love her to bits."

"I'm not sure I know where you're goin' with this," the chief inspector told him.

"The only thing Mum has always worried about is me keepin' my nose clean," Billie Simmons said. "I think it'd just about kill her if I got into any trouble with the police."

"Do you think you are in trouble with the police?"

"I could be."

"What for?"

The hesitancy and uncertainty were still there on Billie Simmons' face. "When we were in Hamburg, we had a pretty wild time," he said finally. "We were playin' in the club until the early hours of the mornin', an' then goin' on to parties after that. I never added it up, but we can't have got more than three or four hours' sleep a day, an' . . . ."

He stopped suddenly, and stared into the middle distance. Woodend turned around, and saw that Bob Rutter had just come through the door.

Billie Simmons drained the half of his pint which remained in one quick gulp. "Look at the time. I have to be goin'," he said.

"You were just about to get somethin' off your chest, weren't you, Billie?" Woodend asked.

Billie Simmons shook his head. "No. You've got it wrong. I was just talkin' about the good old days in Hamburg. That's all."

He rose to his feet and made a rapid exit.

Rutter slid into the chair the drummer had just vacated.

"Now that's what I call bloody good timin'," Woodend said grumpily.

"I beg your pardon, sir."

"That lad, Billie, was just about to tell his Uncle Charlie somethin' very interestin'."

"What about?"

"I've no idea, because he saw you with your smart suit an' neat haircut, an' he clammed up tighter than a duck's backside."

"I'm sorry, sir," Rutter said.

"Oh, it's not your fault," Woodend told him. "It was just unlucky you happened to come in at the moment you did." He took out his cigarettes and lit one up. "So how did things go down at the local nick?"

"Inspector Hopgood's a lot happier now that we've given him something positive to do," Bob Rutter said. "He's got half a dozen men out on the street asking Jack Towers' neighbours if they saw the man who pushed the poison-pen letter through the door."

"That's good," Woodend said. "Not only does it keep the bugger off our backs for a while, but he might actually find out somethin' useful."

Rutter smiled, and in that smile Woodend thought he detected the slightest hint of a look of self-congratulation.

"I may just have found out a couple of useful things myself, sir," the sergeant said.

"Oh aye? An' what exactly might these few interestin' things be, young Robert?"

"I've been checking on which of the people who might be involved in this case have criminal records."

"And which ones do?"

"Well, for a start, there's Mrs Pollard."

Woodend raised one eyebrow. "The brassy blonde? Really? What's she been up to?"

Rutter lit one of his cork-tipped cigarettes. "Recently, she's been up to nothing at all. But before she ever met her husband – which must have been back when Adam was a lad – she was on the game."

"Well, I'll go to the foot of our stairs!" Woodend said. But he was thinking: 'Back when Adam was a lad.' Bloody hell, he makes her sound ancient, and she's younger than I am.

"She was nicked a couple of times for soliciting outside Lime Street Station," Rutter continued, not noticing his boss's expression. "She's never actually done time, but she paid a few fines."

"An' now she's a successful club owner," Woodend mused.

"Leslie Pollard, her late husband, was a rag-and-bone merchant. Started with a horse and cart, but eventually bought his own lorry. According to an old bobby I talked to down at the station, most people who knew him thought he was a bit slow – especially when he decided to marry a woman who was well known to be a prostitute – but he can't have been that thick, can he, or he'd never have got enough money together to buy what eventually became the Cellar Club?"

"Are there any suspicious circumstances surroundin' his death?" the chief inspector asked.

Rutter shook his head. "He was coming out of the pub with some of his mates last thing one Saturday night. All the witnesses said he'd had a fair amount to drink, and he simply lost his balance. It was just hard luck for him that he hit the kerb badly. He had a brain haemorrhage and died on the way to hospital."

Woodend nodded. "You said you'd been lookin' at criminal records in the plural. Who else have you got somethin' on?"

"Rick Johnson."

"Ah, your favourite candidate for toppin' Eddie Barnes," Woodend said. "I already know about him. He's been inside for GBH, hasn't he? Eighteen months he got, if I remember correctly."

"That's right. Eighteen months," Rutter agreed. "Then, of course there's Steve Walker."

"Has *he* got a record?"

"He's never actually been charged with anything, but he's

no stranger to the police station. From what I could gather, he doesn't need much an excuse to start throwing punches."

"Yes. I'd already got the impression that young Steve has a bit of a temper on him."

Rutter's smile was now definitely self-congratulatory. "Do you know what's *really* interesting, sir?" he asked.

"No, I don't," the chief inspector said dryly. "Why don't you enlighten me, lad."

"The last time Rick Johnson was in any trouble with the police was about a month ago. He got into a fight with another man in a pub. According to eyewitnesses again, it could have turned quite nasty if a third chap hadn't appeared and broken it up. Anyway, the constable on the beat walked Johnson down the local nick, where they knew him well, and where he would have been charged right then and there – but for one thing."

Woodend sighed heavily. "I know you like to spin your stories out, lad," he said, "an' I'm sure you'd be a big hit on the music-hall circuit. But you have to admit, this is a bit long-winded even for you."

Rutter grinned, sheepishly. "Sorry, sir. The reason that Rick Johnson wasn't charged with the assault was that the victim went down the police station himself, said it was all his own fault, and insisted he'd give evidence to that effect if the case ever got to court."

"So?" Woodend asked.

"So the man Rick Johnson attacked – apparently for no reason – was Eddie Barnes . . ."

"Really?" Woodend said.

" . . . and the man who split them up before any real damage could be done was Steve Walker."

"Now that *is* interestin'," the chief inspector agreed.

Eleven

Woodend stood in the doorway of the Grapes, looking at the little drama which was unfolding just across the road in front of the Cellar Club. There were two participants. One of them was Rick Johnson. The other was a smaller man who was probably around the same age as the bouncer. He was wearing blue overalls, and from the oil stains on them it seemed likely that he was some kind of mechanic.

For someone who often thought with his fists, Rick Johnson seemed to go in for a lot of intense conversations, Woodend thought. First there had been the one with his wife on the hard seats in front of the Cellar Club stage; then the one with Mrs Pollard, during which she'd managed to touch his arm twice; and now here he was in deep discussion with a man who was a complete stranger to the chief inspector.

The smaller man was reaching forward, and poking Johnson in the chest. The doorman angrily brushed his arm aside. For a couple of seconds, it looked as if they would both start throwing punches. Then the smaller man turned and strode furiously away.

Woodend walked across the street, aware that Johnson's eyes were on him, feeling the other man's hostility even from a distance.

"That feller a mate of yours, is he?" he asked the doorman when he was close enough to speak without shouting.

"No, he isn't," Rick Johnson replied sulkily.

"But you're obviously acquainted with him."

"Yes, I know him. He's a troublemaker. That's why, when he asked if he could get into the club, I told him he couldn't."

"Funny that he should try to get into the club at all in overalls, isn't it?" Woodend asked. "Most of the lads wear suits."

"He said he only had an hour for dinner, an' he didn't have time to go home an' get changed," Rick Johnson told him. "An' said that I wouldn't have let him into the club whatever he'd been wearin'."

What were the chances that a man in overalls would even think of trying to get into a club like the Cellar? Woodend wondered. Very slight. Rick Johnson, Woodend decided, wasn't a very good liar – or, at least, he wasn't making a very good job of it on this particular occasion.

"There's a question I've been meanin' to ask you, Mr Johnson," the chief inspector said.

"Look," Johnson snarled, "I've told you until I'm sick of bloody tellin' you that I know bugger all about Eddie Barnes's murder."

"It's not Eddie's *murder* I want to know about. Tell me about the fight you had with him a month ago."

"What fight?"

Woodend sighed. "That bright young sergeant of mine has been down at the local nick an' had a good look at your sheet. It's all down there in black an' white. So why don't you co-operate, Mr Johnson? All I want to know is what the fight was about."

"We . . . er . . . well, we had a bit of a disagreement, you see," Johnson said reluctantly.

"Aye, people who end up in fights normally do," Woodend said dryly. "What I really want to know is who disagreed with who about what, an' which of you threw the first punch."

Rick Johnson looked down at the ground. "I can't remember now," he muttered.

"You've forgotten all about an incident which could have had you back inside?" Woodend asked incredulously. "An incident which happened only last month? Come on, lad, stop pullin' my leg."

Johnson's chin was set at a stubborn angle. "I've told you, I don't remember," he said.

"Do you know how it looks to me?" Woodend asked.

He allowed a short pause for Rick Johnson to speak, but the doorman was clearly set on saying nothing.

"It looks to me as if you had a pretty big grudge against Eddie Barnes," he continued. "At first, you thought you could settle it in your usual way – with your fists. But after the fight you found that whatever he'd done to make you upset was still eatin' away at you."

"I never—" Johnson interrupted.

"I haven't finished," Woodend told him. "It was then that you must have realised you were goin' to have to do somethin' more if you were ever to get rid of the achin' in your guts. So on the night before Eddie died, you waited until all the others had gone home, then you went into the dressin' room an' you re-wired Eddie's equipment."

"You don't really believe that," Rick Johnson said.

"You're right," Woodend admitted. "I don't. Even if you did hate Eddie badly enough to want to kill him, electrocution just wouldn't be your style. But I'm not the only bobby workin' on this case, you know, an' there's others who might take a completely different view to mine. So what you should be really doin', lad, is makin' every possible effort to clear your name. An' you could start by tellin' me about the fight."

Rick Johnson's gaze was still fixed firmly on the pavement. "I've got nothin' more to say," he grunted.

Woodend shrugged. "Well, I've given you your chance," he said. "If you don't choose to take it, then it's your own funeral."

The lunchtime session of the Cellar Club presented the chief inspector with no surprises. From half-way down the stairs he could see the army of beehive hairdos bobbing up and down in uneasy harmony with the rhythm which vibrated through the walls and the brick floor. At the bottom of the steps he passed a group of young men who were smoking, digging each other in the ribs, and assessing their chances of making a dinnertime pick-up.

If the lads really wanted to get off with the crumpet, Woodend thought as he made his way to the snack bar, they should learn to play an instrument and join a group.

"Tea?" mouthed the girl behind the counter, the actual word drowned out by the sound of Mickey Finn and the Knockouts' loud rendition of 'The Hippy Hippy Shake'.

"Tea," Woodend agreed.

There was no puzzled expression on the girl's face, as there'd been the first time she saw him, Woodend thought. Now she accepted him in just the same way as she probably accepted her own parents – an inevitable feature in her world, but not really of it.

He shook his head, and lit up a Capstan Full Strength. On none of his other cases had he ever felt so out of his depth, and it didn't exactly help to realise that Bob Rutter – who was supposed to be his *protégé* – was becoming more and more comfortable in this environment which he himself found so alien. He was still a few weeks short of his fiftieth birthday, he reminded himself, but already there were so many options which had closed to him, whether he liked it or not.

He couldn't go up in a rocket, because, unlike the Russian cosmonaut, Yuri Gagarin, he wasn't twenty-seven any more. His chances of playing professional football for Accrington Stanley were long since passed, too, as was the possibility that he might learn to play the trumpet and start his own jazz band. The only thing he had to look forward to was grandchildren – and if that wasn't an old man's thought, what was? Maybe it was time to stop the world and get off. Perhaps his best course would be to take whatever pension he was entitled to, and settle down in a nice cosy environment he would understand, like that of private security.

The group finished playing, and Mickey Finn made his way towards the snack bar. He was half-way down the tunnel when he noticed Woodend standing there, and the chief inspector was sure that, for the moment, the young singer was tempted to turn around. But he didn't, and by the time he reached the snack bar he had even managed to force a friendly smile on to his face.

"I've got a couple more questions that I'd like to ask you, Mr Finn," Woodend said.

"Oh yeah?" Finn replied cautiously.

"I want to know what happened in the dressing room the night before Eddie Barnes died."

"Happened?" Finn said, turning away. "What do you mean? Happened? I've no idea what you're talkin' about."

Woodend lit up another Capstan Full Strength from the butt of his first. "Somethin' occurred which distracted everybody's attention while the murderer re-wired the amp," he explained.

"You don't know that for a fact," Finn replied, still not looking at him. "It could have been done after we all left."

"I'll tell you something else," Woodend said, ignoring both the comment and the possibility. "I think that whatever caused the disturbance, it was connected in some way with Hamburg."

Even looking at him almost sideways on, the chief inspector could not miss the look of surprise – or maybe even shock – which crossed the young singer's face.

"Last time we spoke, didn't you tell me that you an' the Knockouts had played in Hamburg, Mr Finn?" Woodend continued.

"There's any number of groups from Liverpool who've played in Hamburg," Finn muttered.

"But how many of those groups were in this club that night?" Woodend countered.

"Only the Knockouts an' the Seagulls," Finn admitted.

"An' you're still denyin' that anythin' unusual happened?"

"Steve Walker had a girl with him on the sofa behind the curtain," Finn told him.

If he thinks he can distract me into talkin' about Steve

118

Walker's bit of fluff, Woodend told himself, he's got another think comin'.

"I know all about the girl," he said, "an' I'm not interested in her. Steve Walker's love-life is nobody's business but his own. All I want to do is catch myself a murderer."

"You're missin' the point," Mickey Finn said.

"An' just what point might that be?"

"You've been into the dressin' room, haven't you?"

"Yes."

"So you've seen for yourself how most of the equipment gets stacked up next to the curtain."

"Go on."

"When one of the lads is 'on the job', the rest of us move to the other end of the room, to give him a bit of privacy, like. An' the last thing we want to do is look towards the curtain. I mean, it'd be a bit embarrassin' really."

The chief inspector nodded. "Spell the rest of it out."

"I don't want to get anybody in trouble," Mike Finn told him, "but just how difficult do you think it would have been for Steve to slip his hand through the curtain an' do whatever he had to?"

"Let's review what we have so far," Woodend said, taking a sip of the pint of best that Rutter had just bought him. "One: Eddie Barnes was a nice quiet lad who only ever went out on the town when that was what Steve Walker wanted him to do. He may, or may not, have had a girlfriend. His mother says she thinks he did, both because of the aftershave and because of the way he'd started actin', but his best mate is adamant that he didn't."

"And which of them is more likely to know the truth of the matter?" Rutter pondered.

"Buggered if I know," Woodend confessed. "Two: the Seagulls – an' in particular Eddie Barnes – have been the victims of a series of unpleasant jokes, endin' up with an anonymous letter which was pushed through Jack Towers' letterbox, a few days after Eddie's death."

"Which could have been pasted together by the killer or might just be the work of a crank," Rutter pointed out.

"True," Woodend agreed. "Three: we have the editor of the *Mersey Sound* tellin' me that he's sure Eddie was plannin' to leave the group, but he can't remember where he got the information from. Now that raises a number of questions, doesn't it? *Was* he plannin' to leave the group, an' if he was, *why* was he? If he was goin' to leave, did Steve Walker know about it? An' if Walker did know, what action would he have been likely to take?"

"Are you saying that Steve Walker could have killed his best friend?" Rutter asked, astonished.

"It might sound incredible at first, but when love turns to hate, it's often the strongest hate of them all," Woodend said. "Anyroad, let's follow this thought through. Steve Walker finds out Eddie Barnes is goin' to leave without tellin' him, an' he sees it as the worst kind of betrayal. He decides that Eddie will have to pay the maximum price for his treachery."

"He'll have to die."

"Exactly. An' because Steve Walker's got a bit of a poetic nature, he decides to kill him on stage. Why not? Eddie's crime was wantin' to leave the group – well, he can, but not in the way he intended."

"If what you're guessing is true, Steve Walker's a bloody good actor," Rutter said.

"It wouldn't be the first time we've come up against bloody good actors, now would it?"

Rutter knocked back what was left of his half of bitter. "Does that mean we're going to target our investigation solely on Walker?"

Woodend shook his head. "We can't afford to do that, if only because even if Steve Walker is guilty, as things stand I've no idea how we're ever goin' to prove it. So what we're forced into is tryin' to approach the problem from a completely new angle."

"And what angle would that be, sir?"

"We have to *cherchez la femme*, as they say in the pictures."

"Which particular woman will we be looking for?"

"Two possibilities," Woodend said. "The first is this lass Steve Walker was behind the curtain with. She should be able to confirm whether or not Walker just took her there for a quick rattle, or whether he used her just as an excuse to get close to Eddie Barnes's amp. Enough people saw her for us to come up with a decent description. Have some identikit pictures drawn up, and give 'em to Inspector Hopgood's lads."

"Should I tell them why we're looking for her, sir?"

"Tell them she was in the club an' might be a witness. No harm in that. But skip the bit about the sofa – there's no point in gettin' Mrs Pollard in trouble with the local bobbies unnecessarily."

"Who's the second woman we're looking for?"

"That's a bit more difficult," Woodend conceded, "because we're not even sure that she exists. It's this lass of Eddie Barnes's. If she is real, she might be able to give us the answers to a lot of questions – like, for example, whether he was plannin' to leave the group or not."

"But how can we find her when we don't even know what she looks like?" Rutter asked.

"We know what Eddie Barnes looked like, don't we? We'll find her through him."

"You've lost me," Rutter confessed.

"They had to meet somewhere," Woodend explained. "Where would that somewhere be likely to have been?"

Rutter shrugged. "Cinemas. Coffee bars. Pubs. All the usual sort of places boys meet girls."

"Exactly. But they can't have been the cinemas, coffee bars and pubs that any of their mates used, or the rest of the Seagulls would have soon known about it, wouldn't they?"

"So the first thing to do is to find out where Eddie's mates hung out . . ." Rutter began.

121

"Hung out?" Woodend repeated, puzzled. "What does that mean?"

"Where they spent time with their chums," Rutter elucidated. "And once we know where they are, we can cross them off our list. Because if Eddie *was* seeing a girl, he'd never have taken her to any of those places."

"Now you're with me," Woodend said. "Which only leaves the places Eddie an' his mates *didn't* go to. An' in a city of this size, there can't be more than a few thousand of them."

"You wouldn't like Inspector Hopgood's lads to handle the footwork on this, would you?" Rutter asked hopefully.

"No, I bloody wouldn't," the chief inspector said. He smiled. "It's a bit more subtle than the other inquiry, an' I'd be much happier if it was handled by an ambitious young sergeant who knows the only way he's goin' to get promotion is through results."

Rutter smiled back. "They told me when I was assigned to you that you were a hard man," he said.

"I've put a lot of effort into buildin' up that reputation, lad," Woodend told him.

Maria Rutter made her way slowly along the street, counting her steps as she went and tapping the lampposts with her white stick to check she was still on track. She was aware of all the noises around her – the sound of footsteps, the buzz of the traffic, the occasional snatches of conversation. She could even tell when someone had stepped to the side to let her pass. But she had no idea of what any of these people who made way for her looked like, or how they were dressed.

She laughed – almost without bitterness – at the thought that there could be a crowd of thousands surrounding her, and as long as the people who made up that crowd held their breaths and kept perfectly still, she would know absolutely nothing about it.

She had reached the corner, and turned to the left. Her destination was five doors down the road, and she knew just how many measured steps it would take her to reach it.

It would have been easier to make this journey with Joan Woodend at her side, and she was sure that Joan would have been perfectly willing to accompany her, but she couldn't bear the thought of having someone else with her when she learned what she had set out to learn.

She clanked her white stick against the railings, and, having fixed her exact location, walked up to the door. Just to be certain – it was always best to be certain when you were blind – she reached up and felt for the number.

Five, her fingers read. That was right. She found the door handle, turned it, and carefully stepped over the threshold.

"Ah, Mrs Rutter, isn't it?" said a cheerful female voice from out of the darkness which permanently filled her world. "You're right on time. The doctor is expecting you."

Bob Rutter had gone off to compile the information he needed for his identikit picture of the girl who had been on the sofa with Steve Walker, but Woodend still had most of a pint left, so instead of wandering across the road himself, he lit another Capstan Full Strength.

It was as he took the first puff that he started to feel old again. Rutter had worked with him for a little under two years, but he was sure that when their partnership began he could match his sergeant's halves with his pints, drink for drink. Now he was falling behind. He'd be starting to go bald next, he thought gloomily.

It was his training which made him notice the woman standing at the bar – or perhaps it was the fact that she was the only woman in this all-male preserve. Not that that seemed to bother her, he thought. She seemed perfectly at home surrounded by postmen and warehouse workers. But something was bothering her – and from the way she kept glancing in his direction, he rather suspected that that something was him.

He took a closer look at her. She was around forty-five, he

guessed, with bright red hair and deep green eyes. Judging from her build, she was probably the sort of woman who had a tendency to put on weight, but if that were the case, she was fighting the tendency very successfully. Certainly from where he was sitting, she seemed to have all the right curves in all the right places. A very attractive woman, Woodend thought, even as he admitted to himself that Bob Rutter would, at best, see her as nothing more than a mother figure. And though he was sure he'd never seen her before, there was definitely something familiar about her.

The woman knocked back the gin and tonic she ordered, swivelled round, and headed in his direction. When she reached his table, she sat down uninvited and said, "I don't want you messin' up my son's career."

"Now why would I want to do that, Mrs Foster?" Woodend asked – because up close it was obvious that she was Pete Foster's mother.

"Why should you want to?" the woman repeated. "Because that's just the sort of thing that people like you do."

He was getting tired of being classified by nearly everyone he met. First of all there'd been the kids in the club – and, to a certain extent, his own sergeant – seeing him as something of a dinosaur. Now there was this mother who automatically assumed that he embodied the qualities of every insensitive flatfoot she'd ever met.

"You sound like you're speakin' from bitter personal experience, Mrs Foster," he said.

"I am," the woman replied. "I used to be a singer in a jazz band. The Tom Hartington Quintet, featuring Ellie Thompson, the Duchess of the Blues. That was me," she added, unnecessarily. "Ellie Thompson."

"You know, I think I might have seen you once," Woodend said. "Did you ever play Accrington Working Men's Club?"

The comment seemed to knock the woman off her stride, but only for a second.

"We played in a lot of working men's clubs," she said, "but we'd almost put all that behind us when it happened."

"When what happened?"

"When one of your bloody lot put his size-nine boot in, an' messed it all up for us."

"One of the band got into trouble with the police, did he?" the chief inspector asked.

"We were just about to hit the big time when they arrested Tom," Ellie Foster said. "They claimed he was dealin' in stolen property."

"An' was he?"

Ellie Foster shrugged. "Everybody in the country was on the fiddle just before the war."

"I wasn't," Woodend said.

"You would say that," Mrs Foster retorted tartly. "Anyway, whatever Tom was doin', he was doin' for the good of the band – just to keep us goin'. But did the judge see that? Did he hell as like! He sent Tom down for two years. Well, that was it. The band split up, an' I never got the chance to make a name for myself again. Now let me tell you, Mr Policeman, I'm not about to stand aside an' let the same thing happen to my son."

"Are you suggestin' that Pete had somethin' to do with Eddie Barnes's death?" Woodend asked.

The woman snorted. "Of course I'm not, you bloody fool! But that's not the same as sayin' you won't find a way to bugger up this record contract, one way or another."

"They haven't got it yet," Woodend pointed out, mildly.

"But they will get it – I know they will – if you'll just leave them alone," Mrs Foster said.

Woodend took a sip of his pint. "You don't really care whether we find Eddie Barnes's killer or not, do you?" he asked.

"I liked Eddie – even if he did sometimes stir up trouble between Pete an' Steve – an' I'm sorry he's dead," Mrs Foster said.

"You've no idea how many people have started a sentence

like that," Woodend told her. "The thing is, there's always a
'but' on the end."

"But my Pete's worked damned hard to get where he is
today," Ellie Foster said. "We've *both* worked damned hard.
An' I'm not about to see it thrown away now."

"That sounds just a little bit like a hooded threat to me,"
Woodend said.

"Take it any way you like," Mrs Foster said indifferently.
"All I will say is this. I know quite a lot of senior officers on
the Liverpool force, an' there's a few of them who've not been
shy in lettin' me know that they'd like to spend more time with
me. If I was nice to them – an' I can be very nice when I want to
be – I'm sure they'd help me any way they could. Which
means they could make life very difficult for you."

"Suppose I was to ask you out for a few drinks," Woodend
said. "Would you say no?"

Mrs Foster tilted her head to one side, in a coquettish manner.
"I don't know," she said. "I might say yes – just to see how we
got on together. Why? Are you about to invite me out?"

Woodend shook his head. "Nay, lass," he said. "I've never
been much of what you might call a philanderer, an' even if I
was, I think I might be a bit more particular than to go out with
somebody like you."

For a moment, it looked as if she were about to strike him,
then she took a deep breath and said, "You've no idea what it's
like to feel something's almost in your grasp, then to watch it
slip away."

"What's gone is gone," Woodend told her. "You can't
make your dreams come true by livin' them out through
someone else."

Ellie Foster stood up. "Maybe you can't," she hissed. "But
it's better than nothin'."

She turned, and strode towards the door.

Well, that encounter had answered a couple of questions,
Woodend told himself. He knew now where Pete Foster got his
ambition from. And he also knew why the young guitarist was

anxious, at all costs, to avoid conflict – brought up by a mother like that, who wouldn't be? What he still didn't know was the extent to which Pete would go to please his mother. Would he, for example, go as far as killing Eddie Barnes because he feared that if Eddie left the group, Steve Walker might go as well?

The cigarette in his mouth suddenly tasted like dried camel dung. The longer he was involved with this case, the more suspects he threw up – and the more confused he got. He felt like he was sure Maria Rutter must feel – groping around in a world of darkness, trying to build random sounds and sensations into a pattern which would so easily form into a complete picture if only he could see. If only he was young enough to see.

Twelve

Only a little under an hour and a half ago, the club had been full of frantic girls, bopping to the music of Mickey Finn and the Knockouts. Now the stage was empty, and the only people in the place were a chief inspector from Scotland Yard and the group members and hangers-on who had also been there the night before Eddie Barnes died.

Woodend was sitting next to the snack bar, behind the rickety old table which normally served as the entrance desk. From there, he had a good view of his suspects – and that was what they were, he reminded himself, because any one of them could have killed Eddie – who sat on the hard seats facing the stage.

He switched his attention from the tunnel to the young man who was seated directly opposite him. Steve Walker's face was a complete blank, but, as always, Woodend detected that just below the surface lurked both anger and a willingness to be amused.

"The last time we talked you forgot to mention the fact that you were with a girl that night," the chief inspector said.

"I didn't forget," Walker contradicted him. "I just couldn't be bothered to tell you about it."

"*Why* couldn't you be bothered?"

A shrug. "There didn't seem to be any point. She was just a judy, like dozens of other judies. I don't even remember her name – if I ever knew it."

"What a very convenient memory you do have," Woodend said. "You don't remember her name, even though you must have been introduced – or at least introduced yourself."

Steve Walker laughed loudly, with what sounded like genuine amusement.

"Introduced!" he repeated. "Who do you think me an' the judy are? Lord an' Lady Muck? I'm not the sort of feller who goes up to a girl an' says, 'Good evening, my name is Steven Ponsonby Walker. May have the pleasure of this foxtrot?' An' she wasn't the kind of girl to expect me to, either."

Woodend sighed. "So how did it happen?"

"I'd seen her in here a few times before, maybe even talked to her once or twice. I don't remember. Anyway, that night, when I was standin' at the snack bar, she came up to me an' asked if I could show her what it was like backstage. Well, I knew just what she was after – an' that suited me, too – so I said yes. We had a quick screw behind the curtain, an' that was all there was to it. It's got nothin' to do with Eddie's murder."

"Hasn't it?" Woodend asked. "When you were on the sofa, you were very close to Eddie's amplifier."

Steve Walker chuckled. "What are you suggestin' now? That she only let me poke her because it would give her a chance to fiddle with the amp?"

"That's one possibility," Woodend said noncommittally.

"You've been readin' too many cheap detective books," Steve Walker told him. Then a look of sudden shocked realisation came to his face. "Or are you suggestin' that *I* used *her* as an excuse to get near the amp?"

"That's another possibility," Woodend admitted.

"Yesterday you were warnin' me off tryin' to find out who killed my best mate, an' today you're accusin' me of doin' it myself!" Walker said angrily. "What's made you change your mind about me?"

"I haven't necessarily," Woodend replied. "But there's a lot of things I know now that I didn't know yesterday."

"Like what, for instance?"

"I didn't know about the fight in the pub about a month ago, for one thing. An' I still don't know what it was that made

129

Rick Johnson attack Eddie Barnes. Maybe you can help me out there."

"I would if I could, but I don't know myself," Steve Walker said, regaining a little of his self-control. "An' that's the honest truth."

"Did they have an argument before Rick Johnson started throwin' his punches?"

"If they did, it was a very short argument. Listen, here's how it went. Eddie an' me were in the pub together. I wanted a piss, so I went to the bogs. I couldn't have been gone more than a couple of minutes – three minutes at most – but when I came back Rick was already layin' into Eddie."

"An' Eddie didn't tell you why it had happened?"

"He said he didn't want to talk about it."

Woodend shook his head. "You were his best mate, an' he still wouldn't tell you. I find that very hard to credit."

Walker's eyes were moist, and Woodend thought he was probably doing his best to hold back the tears.

"Most people think Eddie was a weak-willed sort of feller," he said. "But he wasn't like that at all. He was a gentle kid, there's no arguin' with that, but he could be as stubborn as buggery when he wanted to be."

"He could keep a secret, too," Woodend said. "Did you know he was plannin' to leave the group?"

Walker looked even more astounded than he had when Woodend had all but accused him of murder.

"That can't be true," he said. "I just won't believe that's true. He'd never have deserted me."

Emotive words, Woodend thought, and said with real conviction. But, as Bob Rutter had pointed out, it was always possible that Steve Walker was just a very good actor.

"Maybe I got it wrong," the chief inspector said mildly. "Maybe it was some other group I heard about that was losin' one of its members." He offered Walker one of his Capstan Full Strengths. "How are the Seagulls gettin' on without Eddie, anyway?"

130

"What can I say without it soundin' all wrong?" Steve Walker asked, puffing on his cigarette. "If I tell you we're gettin' on fine with Terry as our new lead guitar, it'll make me sound like a heartless bastard who never really cared about his mate Eddie. On the other hand, if I say that things are goin' really crappily, I won't be tellin' the truth."

"But you'll be ready for the big audition down in London the week after next?"

Walker nodded. "We'll be ready. Jack doesn't think that we will – but then Jack's not a musician."

"Meanin' he doesn't have any real idea of what it takes to get an act together?"

"Exactly," Steve Walker agreed. "Listen, there've been times – when one of us hasn't been able to play a gig for some reason – that we haven't found a replacement until five or ten minutes before we went on stage. But that's no problem for us. No problem at all. You bring me any guitarist in Liverpool, an' I'll guarantee that we'll know enough of the same songs to be able to put on a show."

"So you're sayin' that you'd only need to meet a new Seagulls guitarist five or ten minutes before you walked into the audition studio?"

Walker grinned. "No. I don't mean that at all. There's a big difference between playin' to a crowd of kids in some fifth-rate club and performin' in a studio in front of some record-company bosses. For the audition, we'd need two or three days to get ready. But we've got nearly two *weeks* – an' Jack's still so worried he's runnin' around like a headless chicken."

"He only wants you to do well," Woodend pointed out.

"What's that supposed to mean?" Walker asked, with a sudden, unexpected aggressiveness.

"It means exactly what it says. He's your manager. He wants to see the Seagulls doin' well."

Walker relaxed again. "Yeah, I suppose he does," he admitted. He looked at his watch. "Listen, I've got a rehearsal with the other lads in half an hour. Can I go now?"

"Yes, I think you an' me have talked enough for today," Woodend said. "Send me one of the others over, will you?"

From the sound of his rich baritone voice, Maria Rutter imagined the doctor to be somewhere between the ages of thirty and forty, and probably quite tall and slim. She also thought he was probably a kind man who had the best interests of his patients at heart. But how much easier it would have been to judge him if she could have seen the expression on his face.

"Do you have anyone waiting for you outside, Mrs Rutter?" the doctor asked softly.

That was a bad sign, Maria thought. A very bad sign. He was as good as saying that he didn't think she could cope with the news on her own.

"No, I've come alone," she said, trying her best to stop her voice from cracking.

"I see." The doctor paused for a few seconds, then he said, "Perhaps it might be better to leave the matter until tomorrow, when you can come back with your husband."

"My husband's away in Liverpool."

"A short business trip perhaps?"

"He's a policeman. He's investigating a murder."

"So you . . . er . . . don't know when he'll be coming back to London?"

"No, I don't. It could be tomorrow, or it could be three or four weeks from now."

There was another slight pause before the doctor said, "If you were to ring him and explain the situation . . ."

How could she do that? After she'd told him at least a dozen times that she wasn't a child and she wanted to be treated like any normal woman, how could she pick up the phone and ask him to come running back to London?

"My husband doesn't need to be here," she said. "I came for the results of my tests, and I'd be grateful if you'd give them to me."

The doctor sighed. "Very well. If you insist. They were positive."

Maria took a deep breath. "Yes," she said slowly. "Yes, I thought they might be."

"If you are to undergo the necessary surgical procedure – and that decision is entirely up to you and your husband – it would be best to have it as quickly as possible," the doctor told her. "You do understand that, don't you?"

"Yes, I understand," Maria replied, and she was thinking, I understand only too well.

"So if you could ring your husband . . ."

"I'll talk to him just as soon as the investigation is over," Maria said firmly. She took hold of her white stick, and rose to her feet. "Thank you for your time, doctor."

"If you'd like me to, I could ring up for an ambulance to take you back home."

Why had he suggested that? Because of what the tests had shown? Or because she was blind?

"I don't need you to call anyone," she said. "I arrived here under my own steam, and nothing has happened since then to prevent me going back the same way."

The boy in the battered leather jacket stood awkwardly in front of Woodend's rickety table, almost like a defiant – yet frightened – schoolboy who had been summoned to see the headmaster.

"I'm tellin' you right now, I don't know nothin' about Eddie's murder," he said.

"Why don't you take a seat, lad?" Woodend suggested.

"I'll stand."

"Oh, for heaven's sake sit down an' stop makin' the place look untidy," Woodend said exasperatedly.

Putting on a great show of his reluctance, the boy lowered himself on to the chair.

"I still don't know nothin'," he said sullenly.

"What's your name?" Woodend demanded.

"Tim O'Donnell."

Woodend looked down at the typewritten list Inspector Hopgood had given him, and put a tick by the boy's name.

"It says here you're a member of the Knockouts. Is that right?"

"I'm the *lead guitarist* of the Knockouts," O'Donnell said, as if he wished to make a clear distinction between himself and the rest of the group.

"That's interestin'. Did you happen to audition to fill Eddie Barnes's place in the Seagulls?"

The boy shook his head. "No, I certainly bloody didn't."

"Why not?"

"I'm already in a group – a good group."

That might be one of his reasons for not auditioning, Woodend thought, but he could see from the look on the lad's face that it wasn't his only reason.

"The Knockouts might be a good group," the chief inspector said, "but they're not a group which has the chance of gettin' a recording contract in the foreseeable future, whereas the Seagulls definitely have. Surely you must have at least considered tryin' out for them?"

"What? An' end up like Eddie?"

"So you think that the reason he was killed was because he was the lead guitarist, do you?"

"I don't know," O'Donnell admitted. "Nobody knows, do they? But I wasn't prepared to take the chance. Anyway, everybody knew the job would go to one of Steve Walker's mates."

Walker certainly seemed to have a reputation, Woodend thought.

"Let's get on to the night before Eddie died," he suggested. "You would have spent quite a lot of time backstage that night, wouldn't you?"

"A fair amount."

"So were you there when the fight broke out?"

It had been a guess – a shot in the dark – but from the shocked look which came to the young man's face, it had obviously been right on target.

"Well, were you there?" Woodend repeated.

"There wasn't any fight that I saw," O'Donnell said, weakly.

"Maybe you were in the bog when it happened, or had stepped out on to the street for a breath of fresh air," Woodend speculated. "But even if that were the case, you'd have heard all about it when you got back to the dressing room, now wouldn't you?"

"Nobody said anythin' about no fight to me," the guitarist replied unconvincingly.

Woodend leant forward slightly. "Do you really want to find yourself an accessory to murder, lad?" he asked.

A look of indecision flickered briefly across the young guitarist's face, but it was soon replaced by an expression of childlike stubbornness.

"I didn't hear nothin' about no fight – an' you can't prove that I did," O'Donnell told him.

Nor could he, Woodend thought regretfully.

"All right, you can go – at least for the moment," he said. "I'll see your bass guitarist next. Maybe he'll be a little bit more helpful. Maybe *he'll* want to see whoever murdered Eddie Barnes safely locked up."

If it was any appeal to make him change his mind, it had no effect on Tim O'Donnell. Instead of replying, the young man merely stood up, walked across the tunnel to the hard seats and tapped another lad – presumably the bassist – on the shoulder.

Woodend talked to them all – the drummers and the guitarists, the hangers-on and the managers. Yes, they had been in the dressing room at one time or another, they admitted. No, they hadn't seen anything unusual, and if there'd been a fight, they'd been somewhere else, and hadn't heard anything about it.

What about the girl who had gone behind the curtain for a quickie with Steve Walker? Woodend had asked.

They'd seen her around the club a few times, they agreed, but she hadn't put in an appearance since the place had re-opened after the murder. She was called Mavis – or it might have been Elaine – and her hair colouring was described as everything from nearly black to dark blonde.

By the time the chief inspector climbed the twenty steps which took him to street level, the pubs were already open – which was just as well because the way he was feeling, he would have battered down a closed pub's door if that was the only way to get a drink.

He had a pocket full of scribbled notes in his hairy sports coat, and a raging ache in his skull. He didn't understand these kids at all, he told himself, and if it had been revealed to him that they had all conspired together to kill Eddie Barnes *à la* Agatha Christie's *Murder on the Orient Express*, he would no longer have been the least bit surprised.

He entered the Grapes, negotiated his way past the shipping clerks who had just left off work, and ordered his first pint of the evening at the bar. He'd been intending to drink it standing up, but he suddenly felt so weary that he took it over to the nearest free table.

Would Bob Rutter, so much closer in age to the kids than he was, have been any more successful with the interrogations? Would it be better if Bob took over the whole investigation, while he contented himself with doing his sergeant's legwork?

But his legs were too old for that kind of work. He was the controlling brain – or he was nothing.

He took a grateful swig of his pint. It was still only half-past six in the evening, but he was already feeling ready for his bed. A cushy security job at probably twice the salary he was earning as a chief inspector was starting to look very appealing.

Thirteen

Night had fallen over the city. At first, the darkness was broken up by spots of twinkling light. But the later it grew, the more of those lights went out, so that by the time midnight had come and gone there were only the street lamps left to cast a watery glow over Liverpool.

There was a street lamp on the road where the bundle lay, but it wasn't working. The bundle itself, from a distance, could have been mistaken for a heap of old rags, thrown casually to the ground. Then it moved and groaned, and anyone watching would have realised that it was not rags at all, it was a man. But there was no one watching, because that part of the docklands, an hour after the pubs had closed, was as empty as a Lancashire mill town during Wakes Week.

The man climbed slowly and painfully to his feet. His ribs hurt with even the slightest movement, and his head felt as if it were being trampled underfoot by a herd of wild horses.

You've been a fool, he thought, when the pain retreated for long enough to allow him the luxury of thinking at all. A complete bloody fool! You could have been killed! Do your realise that? Right now, you could be bloody dead!

He was now standing as upright as his battered body would allow him to. He put one foot in front of the other, and a fresh wave of agony shot up his leg. He forced himself to take a step forward. Then another. Then another.

He could see the bright red telephone box at the end of the street. He could ring for help from there – if vandals hadn't ripped the phone out!

The road was swirling before his eyes. Even if the phone was still working, he was not sure that he had the strength left to get to it. It was then that he saw the figure turn the corner. At first he was afraid it was his attacker, come back to finish off the job, but as the figure got closer to the phone box, he could see that it was wearing a pointed blue helmet.

The injured man gasped with relief. "Help me!" he shouted, as loud as he could.

The constable heard no more than a croak, but that was enough to tell him that whoever had made it was in trouble. He sprinted towards the injured man, and reached him just in time to catch him as he collapsed.

Woodend's subconscious mind tried to ignore the sound of the shrill bell at first, but when it persisted he groaned, rolled over towards the bedside table, and switched on the light.

He glanced at the clock through bleary eyes. "You stupid bastard!" he growled. "What the bloody hell are you doin' ringin' now? Don't you know it's half-past one in the bloody morning!"

But it wasn't the clock making the noise, he realised – it was the phone.

The chief inspector picked it up. "Woodend," he barked into the offending instrument.

"I'm sorry to disturb you at this hour, sir," said the calm, soothing voice of the hotel switchboard operator, "but I have an Inspector Hopgood on the line, and he says it's important he speak to you right away."

"Then you'd better put him through," Woodend told her, as he reached automatically for his cigarettes.

"Sorry to disturb you, sir—" Hopgood began.

"Yes, yes, I've been through all that already with the operator," Woodend said impatiently. "Just tell me what's happened."

"I don't know whether this has anything to do your case or not," Inspector Hopgood said, "but I've just received a report from one of my lads that Jack Towers has been beaten up."

Bloody hell fire!

"How bad is it?" Woodend asked, remembering Towers' request for police protection – and fearing it could be very bad indeed.

"They're not sure of the extent of Mr Towers' injuries yet, but at least he's conscious."

"When, exactly, did this beatin' up occur?" demanded Woodend, now wide awake.

"About an hour ago. Down by Dukes' Dock."

"Where's the poor bugger now?"

"In the University Hospital."

"Send a car round to the hotel as soon as you can," Woodend said. "I think I'd better go an' pay our Mr Towers a bedside visit."

There was something about hospitals that was anathema to the northern working-class male, Woodend thought as he followed the pretty Jamaican nurse, who said her name was Sister Holmes, down the perfectly sterile, brightly lit corridor. He'd fought side by side in the war with men who'd never flinched in the face of a hail of German machine-gun bullets, yet had blanched at the idea of going in for a blood test. Fought with them? Hell, if he was going to be honest, he was a prime example of one himself. When he had a pain, his natural reaction – like that of his father before him – was simply to grimace and hope that, in time, it would go away.

Northern working-class women, on the other hand, were an entirely different story. For them, operations held more fascination than the FA Cup Final did for their husbands, and while talk of the surgeon's knife might put most men off their dinners, it only seemed to stimulate their wives' appetites – both for more food and more bloodthirsty details.

The sister came to a halt beside a door which looked just as anonymous as every other door they had passed.

"This is the doctors' lounge," she said. "Do you want me to come in with you?"

"Nay, lass," Woodend said, smiling. "I'm quite sure you've got much more important things to do with your time than shepherdin' me around."

The sister smiled back at him, giving him a brief glimpse of her perfect white teeth. "Ain't that the truth," she agreed. "Just knock on the door, and then go straight in. The doctors here are used to being interrupted."

Woodend watched her walk down the corridor. If he was ever sick, he decided, he could only hope he'd be looked after by someone as obviously caring as Sister Holmes. He knocked on the door, as instructed, and entered the lounge. The only person inside the room was reading a newspaper, and when he lowered it, Woodend was surprised to find that he already knew him.

"It's Doctor Atkinson, isn't it?" the chief inspector said. "We met this mornin', over at the *Mersey Sound* office."

"That's right, we did," the doctor agreed.

"Well, what a coincidence," Woodend said. "I'm in a strange city, an' twice, within a matter of hours, I run into the same man. What do you reckon are the chances of that?"

"In this job, you come across so many coincidences that you start to take them for granted," the doctor said tiredly. "I take it you're here to ask about Jack Towers."

"Yes, I am. How is he?"

"It could have turned out a lot worse than it has, to be honest. Some of the kicks he took in his ribs could just as easily have connected to his head – and if they had, I've no doubt they would have caused brain damage."

"So he'll be all right, will he?"

"He should be quite stiff for a few days," the doctor said, "but there's certainly no reason to keep him in here beyond tomorrow morning."

"If he's awake, I'd like to see him now," Woodend said. "As long as it wouldn't be disturbin' the other patients, that is."

"Oh, it won't disturb them," the doctor assured him. "I've put Mr Towers in a single room."

Jack Towers was sitting up in bed, and – from the ample evidence in his ashtray – chain-smoking. His right eye was discoloured, and there was a dark bruise on his jaw. Beneath his open pyjama jacket, Woodend could see the bandages wrapped tightly around his chest.

The chief inspector glanced quickly around the room. In comparison to the ward which his Joan had been in when she'd been operated on for her 'woman's problems', it was an absolute palace. For a start there was so much space – in Joan's ward the patients in adjacent beds could have held hands with no problem, whereas if Towers had been feeling up to it, he could have done gymnastics in this room. Then there was the decoration – the walls were not painted in the usual depressing institutional cream, but in a pleasant, soothing pastel blue. There was a bowl of cut flowers on the table, and – bloody hell! – the man even had his own fourteen-inch television set.

Maybe if I was workin' in private security, I could afford this kind of luxury for *my* family, Woodend thought.

He turned his attention to Jack Towers. "Well, you've certainly been in the wars, haven't you?" he said.

"I suppose you could say that, Mr Woodend," the Seagulls' manager agreed weakly.

Woodend pulled up a chair, placed it next to the bed, and straddled it. "Do you want to tell me what you were doin' down at the docks at well past midnight?" he asked.

Towers frowned. "If it's really necessary, I will. But I've already given all the details to that other policeman."

"What other policeman?"

"Quite a short, thin man. I think he said that his name was Inspector Hopgood."

"Oh aye," Woodend said. "An' just when exactly did you have this cosy little chat of yours with the good inspector?"

"I haven't exactly been keeping track of time, but I think it must have been about an hour ago."

Or to put it another way, a good half an hour before Hopgood phoned me at the hotel, Woodend thought – and found himself wondering just what the little shit of an inspector was up to.

"Maybe you have given all the details to Inspector Hopgood," he said to the Seagulls' manager, "but you should have seen enough of the way I work by now to know that I never like to hear things second hand. So why don't you go through your story again, tellin' me exactly what you told him?"

"I was at home," Towers said.

"Alone?"

"Yes, I was alone. My wife . . . my wife . . ."

Your wife ran off with the coal man, Woodend thought, but aloud, to save Towers any further embarrassment, he said, "The details don't matter. We've established that you were on your own. What happened next?"

"I was just making a hot cocoa to take to bed with me, when I got this phone call."

"Oh, you've got a private phone, have you?" Woodend asked. "I'm impressed."

"I'm the Seagulls' manager, don't forget," Towers said. "I need it for business."

Woodend suppressed a smile. Needed it for business! Well, he supposed there was no harm in being optimistic – and if the Seagulls did get their recording contract, he probably really would need it.

"Who was the caller?" he asked.

"He wouldn't give his name, even though I asked several times, but he said that he knew who'd killed Eddie, and if I'd agree to meet him, he'd give me all the evidence I needed."

"You should have told him to call the police," Woodend said sternly. "It's our job to handle things like that."

"I would have done, but for the fact that he sounded so frightened," Towers told him. "You see, I was worried that if I didn't do exactly what he wanted, he'd hang up and never ring again."

"You might have been right about that," Woodend agreed. "Carry on with your story, lad."

"He said we had to meet somewhere private – somewhere there would be absolutely no chance that anyone else would see us. As I told you, he seemed scared out of his wits."

"Who suggested meeting down by docks? You?"

Towers shook his head, then winced at the pain it caused him. "He was the one who suggested it. But I saw no reason to object. It's almost home ground to me, because that's where my office is."

Woodend nodded. "So you arranged to meet each other. How did you get there?"

"I was just in time to catch the last bus. I was going to take a taxi back. It never occurred to me I'd be making my next journey in an ambulance. Anyway, the place we'd agreed to meet was an alley near the dock – he said it would be safer for him that way."

"An' you weren't in the least bit suspicious?"

"No. I never thought he'd turn violent. On the phone he'd seemed too scared to hurt a fly."

"So you walked into it like a lamb to the slaughter?"

"He was waiting for me half-way down the alley. He was standing under a lamppost, but the light wasn't on."

"No," Woodend said dryly. "It wouldn't have been. He'd probably taken care of that before you arrived."

"He had a cap pulled down over his eyes. He wasn't much more than a black shape, really. I walked straight up to him, and I said, 'I'm Jack Towers. Are you the man that called me?'"

"Is that when he hit you?"

"Yes. He punched me in the face."

"An' you went down?"

"No," Towers said. "Not at first. I did a fair bit of boxing when I was at school, so I'm not completely useless in a fight. The moment he'd hit me, I swung back at him. I must have got a couple of good punches in myself before he knocked me to the ground."

"Did he say anythin' while he was doin' his best to kick the livin' crap out of you?"

Towers laughed, but there was not much amusement behind it. "Oh yes, he said something all right. He said that this was no more than a friendly warning, and that if I didn't get the Seagulls out of Liverpool by the end of the week, he'd kill another of them."

"You're sure those were his exact words," Woodend asked. "He'd kill *another* of them."

"It's hard to be sure of anything at all when someone's trying to break all your ribs," Jack Towers said bitterly. "But yes, I think that those were the exact words he used."

"What can you tell me about him, Mr Towers?"

"That's about it," the manager said helplessly.

"No," Woodend said. "There has to be more. I know it's difficult to think under these circumstances, but please try. Can you remember what his voice was like, for example?"

Towers pursed his brow. "That's hard to say. On the phone it sounded panicked – and a little high-pitched – but I know now that was just an act. When he was threatening me in the alley, it was much gruffer, but I think that might have been put on, too."

"Close your eyes an' try to imagine the voice if it wasn't pretendin' to be frightened or gruff," Woodend suggested.

Towers did as he'd been told, but after a couple of seconds he said, "This isn't helping."

"You can hear the voice in your head, can you?"

"Oh yes."

"But it still doesn't remind you of anyone you know? It doesn't even sound vaguely familiar?"

"I'm afraid not."

"Well, at least you tried, lad," Woodend said. "Let's go on to something else. How tall was he?"

"I couldn't say exactly," Towers said, opening his eyes again, "but I'd guess that he was five feet nine or five feet ten."

"Build?"

Towers gave a twisted grin. "I would say he was heavily built. His fist certainly felt like it had some weight behind it."

Woodend looked at his watch. Bloody hell, it was already nearly three o'clock in the morning.

"I'll leave you in peace now, Mr Towers," he said. "I don't expect I'll be seeing you again for a day or two."

Towers seemed surprised by the statement. "Won't see me for a day or two? Why?" he asked. "Are you going away, Chief Inspector? At this stage of the investigation – when the killer's actually threatened to murder another one of the Seagulls by the end of the week?"

"No, I'm not goin' away," Woodend replied. "But I would have thought that you might feel the need to take a bit of a rest."

"A rest!" Towers repeated. "I can't afford a rest, Chief Inspector. It's only ten days to the audition. The boys are going to need me."

Doctor Atkinson was standing in the corridor, holding a mug of coffee in his hand. He looked a little anxious, Woodend thought, then decided that the expression on Atkinson's face was probably nothing more than exhaustion.

"Did he say anything?" the doctor asked.

Woodend gave him a quizzical look. "He answered my questions, if that's what you mean," he said. He took out his cigarettes, then noticed the large, boldly printed no-smoking sign on the wall and slipped them back into the pocket of his hairy sports jacket. "It's a nice room you've put Mr Towers in," he commented. "They reckon it's grim up north, but I don't think we have anythin' as luxurious as that down in London."

"Yes, you do," Doctor Atkinson countered. "As long as you've got the money to pay for it."

"So it's a private room, is it?"

"That's right."

"An' how does a shippin' clerk manage to get enough money together to afford a private room?"

145

The doctor smiled. "He doesn't, of course. But there was one available, and I thought that, since he was only going to be here for a short time, we might as well give him all the comfort we could."

"If you're like that with everybody, I must remember to come here myself the next time I'm sick," Woodend said, then, noticing the doctor was looking a little sheepish, he added, "but it's *not* like that with everybody, is it?"

"No," the doctor admitted. "It isn't."

"So what has humble Jack Towers done to merit gettin' such special treatment?"

Doctor Atkinson smiled defensively. "I know all doctors are supposed to be as square as anything in their choice of music," he said, "but the fact is, I happen to be a really big fan of the Seagulls. So, naturally, when someone told me that Mr Towers was their manager, I took that extra bit of care. It was the least I could do after all the pleasure they've given me. And who knows – when they finally hit the big time, Mr Towers might just remember me and send me a front-row ticket for one of their concerts."

"Aye, maybe he will," Woodend agreed. "I can see why you're so enthusiastic about them – I've become a bit of a fan myself over the last couple of days. I like most of the stuff they do. But do you know what my favourite song of theirs is? Would you like to have a guess?"

The doctor smiled weakly. "I've worked far too many hours on this shift to have any brain left for playing guessing games," he said.

"All right, I'll tell you," Woodend said genially. He took a deep breath, like a compère who is just about to announce the winner of a beauty contest. "My absolute favourite is 'Lime Street Rock'."

"It's one of my favourites, too," the doctor agreed.

"You've got to hand it to that Steve Walker, he certainly does know how to put a song together, doesn't he?" Woodend asked.

"Yes, he certainly does," Atkinson agreed.

Woodend gave the other man a second questioning look. "Well, I'll wish you good night, then, doctor," he said, "though I've no doubt we'll be seein' each other again."

Woodend gave a parting smile to the pretty sister, and stepped through the main entrance out into the night air. There was a slight chill in the atmosphere, and even though it was nearly the middle of April, he suspected that there might be a ground frost the next morning.

The police car which had brought him to the hospital was still parked down the road where he'd left it, but now there was a uniformed officer standing beside the bonnet.

Bloody Hopgood! Woodend thought. What's that bugger doin' out at this time of night?

The chief inspector stopped to light a cigarette and collect his thoughts. Hopgood's appearance on the scene might have brought some helpful information, but Woodend very much doubted it. What was much more likely, especially after the stroke he had pulled earlier, was that the local inspector was about to stick his nose just where it wasn't wanted.

Woodend took a deep drag on his Capstan Full Strength, and walked up to the car.

"Good evenin', Inspector Hopgood," he said. "Or maybe it would be more accurate to say, good mornin'. What can I do for you?"

Hopgood smirked. "I think that it's more a case of what I can do for you, sir," he said complacently. "While *you've* been in there talking to Jack Towers, *I've* been very busy out on the street. I've already cleared up the little matter of who assaulted Mr Towers, and I think it's also highly likely that I'm about to hand you your murderer on a plate."

"Tell me more," Woodend said.

"The way I see it is this. The murder could have been carried out by anybody who knew a little about electrical wiring, so it could have been committed by a woman, or even an old-aged

pensioner. But . . ." he held up his right index finger " . . . the
attack on Jack Towers had to be carried out by a man – a very
strong, very violent man. Are you following me?"

"Aye," Woodend said. "By some miracle, I do seem to be
keepin' up with you."

"So the question I asked myself was, 'Who amongst Towers'
acquaintances has a reputation for violence?'"

"An' the name you came up with was Steve Walker's?"

Inspector Hopgood's grin broadened. "No, the name I came
up with was Rick Johnson's. In case you've forgotten, sir, he
attacked Eddie Barnes in a pub just a few weeks before the
murder."

"I hadn't forgotten actually," Woodend told him. "Even my
ale-soaked brain cells are capable of retainin' a *few* facts."

"Anyway, having worked that out, I took a couple of my lads,
and we went to pay young Master Johnson a call," Hopgood
continued enthusiastically. "It was after one o'clock when we
got there—"

"Which would make it about half an hour before you got
round to phonin' me, wouldn't it?" Woodend said pointedly.

"Yes, sorry about that," Hopgood replied, not meaning a
word of it. "I had actually intended to ring you earlier, but with
everything else which was going on, it slipped my mind."

"I'm sure it did," Woodend said dryly. "So, you took a couple
of your lads round Rick Johnson's house just after one o'clock.
An' what did you find when you got there?"

"The rest of the street was in darkness, as you might have
expected, but there was still a light on in Johnson's kitchen. I
sent one of the lads round the back, in case he made a run for
it when I knocked on the front door, but as it turned out there
was no need. As bold as brass, Johnson answered the front door
himself."

"Hardly the act of a guilty man."

"You'd never have said that if you'd seen the state of him."

"Why? What was the matter with him?"

"He had a black eye, and there were a couple of bruises on

148

his face." Hopgood wagged his index finger again, as if he were giving Woodend a lesson in criminology. "Now this is the point. Did Jack Towers say anything to you about getting in a few punches himself before he went down?"

"Aye," Woodend said. "That's another fact I amazin'ly seem to have retained in this thick skull of mine."

"Well, then, we're forced to the obvious conclusion that that it was Johnson who attacked Towers."

"Why?" Woodend asked.

"Why what, sir?"

"Why on earth would Rick Johnson ever want to beat the crap out of Jack Towers?"

For the first time, Inspector Hopgood looked a little uncomfortable. "I don't know that, yet," he admitted. "But I've got him sweating it out in the cells even as we speak, and it can only be a matter of time before he comes clean and tells me everything I want to know."

"There's lots of ways that a feller can get himself a black eye," Woodend pointed out. "He could simply have been in a fight in a pub. As you so kindly reminded me a few minutes ago, Inspector, it wouldn't be the first time that's happened. He's got a record of violence."

"That's very true," Hopgood agreed, the complacent smile returning to his face. "But if he'd been in a fight in a pub, he would have admitted it when I made it plain that I was arresting him for the attack down by the docks – because that would have been his alibi."

"An' what did he *actually* say?"

Hopgood sniggered. "He claimed that he'd walked into a door. I told him I didn't believe him – not unless the door's name was Jack Towers. Anyway, we've got him now, and I'm confident that by breakfast time he'll have confessed to beating up Jack Towers. Then I'll hand him over to you – and you can get him to confess to killing Eddie Barnes as well."

"It's not his style," Woodend said.

"What isn't?"

"Ringin' up somebody an' pretendin' to be a frightened man with some important information. Lurin' people into dark alleys, then attackin' them without warnin'. Rick Johnson's the kind of feller who wants you to know exactly who it is who's duffin' you up. Bloody hell, he nearly took a pop at me in the Cellar Club – in front of half a dozen witnesses. I just can't see him havin' either the inclination or the patience to lay a trap."

Hopgood frowned. "I wonder if you'd be saying that if you'd been the one who arrested him," he said, almost under his breath.

"Just what are you suggestin' by that remark, Inspector?" Woodend asked, lighting up another Capstan Full Strength.

"Nothing, sir. I'm just saying."

"Cards on the table," Woodend said. "Tell me what's on your mind, an' I promise you there'll be no comeback."

Hopgood hesitated for a second. "With respect, sir," he said in a tone which suggested that he had very little respect at all, "I think you resent the fact that we might have caught your murderer for you."

Woodend's eyes narrowed. "Is that right?" he asked.

"Yes, sir. It is. I'd even go so far as to say that I think you'd rather have no murderer under arrest at all than have one who you've got to through the Liverpool Police."

The chief inspector took a deep drag on his cigarette. "So that's how you see me, is it?" he asked. "In your eyes I'm the sort of feller who's so bloody self-important that he wants all the credit for solvin' every crime he investigates – whether or not he deserves it?"

"You asked me for my opinion, and I gave it to you."

Woodend shook his head slowly from one side to the other. "You really are a bloody fool, aren't you, Inspector Hopgood?"

Fourteen

The next morning, the people of Liverpool woke up to find that frost had formed a shimmering sheen on the early-morning pavements. Everyone took the usual precautions. Drivers drove to work slower than usual. Old people, fearing a fall, took cautious footsteps. And children, their satchels on their backs, attempted to slide all the way to school. Then the sun rose from behind the high civic buildings, and quickly vanquished its old foe.

Woodend and Rutter sat in the cafe near Lime Street Station, the chief inspector munching his way through an egg-and-bacon buttie, the sergeant contenting himself with a lightly boiled egg.

"The problem with this whole bloody case is that while I can see a logical solution, I somehow can't bring myself to accept it," Woodend said. "You know what I mean, lad?"

Rutter shook his head. "No, sir, I'm not sure that I do."

"Right," Woodend said. "Let me talk you through it. The note Jack Towers found on his doormat said, 'Which one will die next? Get out of Liverpool while you have the chance.' The feller who attacked Towers down at the docks last night said virtually the same thing. So it seems to me that the same man was responsible for both the letter an' the attack."

"Agreed."

"An' that fact turns the whole investigation on its head. You see, up until now, we weren't sure whether the letter-writer was a crank or not. But once we've found out he's not just full of piss an' wind, we have to accept that he was probably also the man who killed Eddie Barnes."

"Go on," Rutter said encouragingly.

"Which means that Barnes was killed because he was a Seagull, not because he was Eddie. An' the only reason I can come up with for anybody wantin' to hurt the Seagulls is jealousy. Somebody else wants what they've got. An' that's where I have my problem – because they haven't got a lot. Certainly not enough for anybody to risk life imprisonment tryin' to get it off them."

"Maybe the attack on Towers had no other purpose than to create an elaborate smokescreen," Rutter suggested.

Woodend stopped munching, and looked intently at his sergeant. "Go on," he said. "I'm listenin'."

"Say the theory that Steve Walker killed Eddie Barnes because he felt betrayed by him is actually what really happened," Rutter argued. "Now Walker's not stupid, is he?"

"Far from it."

"And because he's not stupid, he'll have realised that we were bound to find out about Eddie's plans to leave the group eventually, isn't he?"

"Very probably."

"And where does that leave him? As a prime suspect! So he needs to put us off the track, and he does it by writing a note to Jack Towers which he hopes will lead us to think that *all* the Seagulls are in danger. But even then he's not entirely happy, because he's still not sure we're convinced about the threat to the group. That's why he beats up Towers. To convince us."

"He's big enough an' hard enough to have hurt Towers," Woodend said thoughtfully. "An' he could certainly have carried off that 'scared feller on the telephone' act. But I still don't see him as our murderer."

"I think that part of your problem in that may be that you like the lad," Rutter asked cautiously.

For a second, the notion astounded Woodend, and then he began to see that his sergeant was right. Almost without noticing it, he *had* come to like the abrasive, kind-hearted Steve Walker. But he mustn't let that influence the way he carried out his investigation.

"If your instinct tells you Walker's our man, we'll go for him with both barrels blazin'," he told his sergeant.

"You're misunderstanding me, sir," Rutter replied. "I only used Walker as an example. I could have used Pete Foster or even Billie Simmons just as easily. The fact is that anyone in the club that night could have done what I just suggested Steve Walker might have done. The main point I was trying to make is that we should be looking for a man who killed for a personal motive, not a potential serial killer driven by jealousy."

Woodend shook his head. "No," he said. "You're wrong about that. The real main point is that three days into the case, we still don't know enough to rule out *any* possibility, however wild it might seem." He glanced down at his wrist-watch. "Speakin' of which, it's about time you set out on your quest to find Eddie Barnes's girlfriend."

"What about you, sir?"

"Me?" Woodend repeated. "I think I'll go down to the club an' see if I can sniff out any new leads."

Mrs Pollard had generously given the Seagulls her permission to rehearse in the Cellar Club that morning, and for once Steve Walker had dragged himself out of bed at the same time as everyone else got up. Now he stood on the stage, the sleeves of his jumper rolled up to his elbows, a Park Drive cigarette dangling from the corner of his mouth.

"OK, let's try it again," he said wearily.

Terry Garner stepped forward and played the opening bars of 'Roll Over Beethoven'. Woodend, occupying his usual position just next to the bar, lit a Capstan Full Strength, and wondered whether this would be any more successful than the last three attempts.

They were half-way through the song when Pete Foster suddenly lashed out angrily with his foot and sent his microphone flying off the stage. The mike hit the floor hard, and sent the amplified sound of its own downfall bouncing around the vaulted roof of the empty club.

Paboom, paboom, paboom.

The other two guitarists stopped playing, and Billie Simmons gave his drum one last, lonely pound.

Steve Walker glared at Pete Foster. "What's the bloody hell's the matter with you this mornin'?" he demanded.

"Him," Pete replied, pointing an angry finger at Terry Garner. "He's what's the matter. He's crap useless!"

"Come on Pete, you can't expect miracles – we've only just started playin' together," Steve Walker said, slipping into the unaccustomed role of conciliator. "When we've had a bit more practice, it'll all work out."

"It'll *never* work out, because he's just not good enough to be one of the Seagulls," Pete Foster raged. "So you can say goodbye to any record contract we might have got. We'll never make a hit. We'll be playin' in grotty little clubs like this for the rest of our lives. An' all because you insisted on havin' a mate of yours in the bloody group."

"It's all right for you lot!" Terry Garner said, speaking for the first time. "You're all safe enough!"

For a moment there was a shocked silence, and then Pete Foster said, "What's that supposed to mean?"

"You try concentratin' on playin' when you know that by this time tomorrow you could be bloody well dead!"

Woodend felt the hairs on his neck tingle. The lad might not actually be in any danger, he thought, but there was no doubt in his mind that Terry Garner really believed that he was

By eleven o'clock, Bob Rutter had five cups of coffee swilling around inside him, and his feet were already starting to ache. And he'd still only scratched the surface, he told himself. There were countless more coffee bars to visit, and after he'd covered that ground, there were the pubs and the cinemas to check out. And the worst thing was, it might all turn out to be a waste of effort. Because perhaps Steve Walker was right, and Eddie Barnes's mum was wrong. Perhaps the young guitarist had indeed gone to his grave as a virgin.

As he tramped the streets, crossing yet another coffee bar off his list, Rutter found his mind turning to his own problems. He was very concerned about Maria, yet he didn't know what he could do about it. She had made it pretty plain that she was not going to be molly-coddled by him, and however hard it was, he'd have to learn to restrain his natural inclination to help her every step of the way.

But stopping worrying was another matter entirely, especially when he was away from London. Anything could happen to her when she was home alone. She might fall over. She might be suddenly taken ill. She'd admitted feeling dizzy a couple of mornings earlier. What if she had an even worse attack, and fainted? Of course, he knew all these things could happen to a sighted person, but the fact that she was blind seemed to make them all the more dangerous.

It was at a quarter past eleven that he entered Gino's Coffee Bar on Everton Road. Like several of the other bars he had visited, the booths were separated by bamboo poles, around which someone had winsomely entwined strands of plastic ivy. Rutter glanced at the shiny Italian coffee machine bubbling away behind the counter, and felt slightly nauseous. This time he would order a cup of coffee, he thought, but he'd make sure he didn't drink any of it.

The waitress who came across to take his order was well over thirty, but wore much the same kind of make-up as the girls applied to their faces while they were queuing up outside the Cellar Club. She gave Rutter a wide smile that came very close to being flirtatious, and asked him, with some ambiguity, what he fancied. The smile stayed in place even when he produced his warrant card and showed her the photograph he was carrying with him.

"Who is he?" she asked, as she peered at the picture in a way which told Rutter she should wear glasses, but was probably too vain.

"His name is – or rather was – Eddie Barnes."

"That guitarist who got himself murdered?"

"That's right."

"You know, when I saw his picture in the papers I thought that it reminded me of somebody," the waitress said, "but it was so grainy I couldn't quite say who. This is a much better likeness."

"So you knew him, did you?" Rutter asked, his pulse racing as it always did when he sensed he was about to make a breakthrough in the case.

"I wouldn't say I knew him," the waitress replied. "But I've served him several times, poor little thing."

"And was he usually alone?"

"No, as a matter of fact, he wasn't."

"He came with his mates, did he?" Rutter asked, avoiding the temptation to lead her towards the answer he really wanted.

"Not his mates, no. He always came with a girl. It was the same girl every time."

So Eddie's mother had been right – and Steve Walker had been wrong. Eddie had had a girlfriend!

Rutter's pulse went into overdrive. "Could you describe this girl for me?" he asked.

The waitress laughed throatily. "It's the boys that I notice, sweetheart, not the girls," she told him. "Especially when it's a lad as good-lookin' as that poor kid was."

"But surely you must have *some* idea of what this girl looked like," Rutter urged.

"I think her hair was black," the waitress said uncertainly. "Either that, or very dark brown."

"That's not really very much help."

"An' she was young," the waitress said. "I do remember that. She was very, very young."

It was nearly noon when Doctor Trevor Atkinson finally

got off duty. He had been working practically non-stop for almost eighteen hours. His back ached, his eyes smarted and his head was pounding. On top of that, his nerves had been jangled by unexpectedly meeting that policeman from London in the *Mersey Sound* office. And it had been even worse when Woodend had come to the hospital. Even though he'd been expecting the big man to turn up once he'd been told Jack Towers had been admitted, it had still taken all his will-power not to make a dash for freedom when the chief inspector walked through the door.

What should he do now that his shift was finally over? he wondered. Go home and get the rest he so obviously needed? Or do what he always referred to in his head as *the other thing*?

He stood in front of the hospital, wracked with indecision. There was no doubt what the wisest thing – the safest thing – was. He could not get into trouble while he was lying in his own bed. And yet . . .

And yet he knew from experience that once the craving was in him, it didn't matter how tired he was, because he would get no rest unless he had at least *attempted* to satisfy it.

You spent seven years in medical school, he reminded himself. Seven long hard years when sometimes it seemed almost impossible to go on. But you did go on, are now you're a doctor. Are you really prepared to risk all you've worked for – all you've achieved?

He was horrified to find himself nodding that, yes, that was exactly what he was prepared to do.

You're a fool, he thought. A complete bloody idiot.

To reach his flat, where safety lay, he had only to turn to his left. With a sigh, he turned to the right and headed for St John's Garden.

Steve Walker had offered soothing words and promises to Pete Foster, the microphone Pete had kicked off the stage been retrieved, and the Seagulls were once again attempting to get 'Roll Over Beethoven' right. And they were making some progress, Woodend thought – even to his untutored ear there was no doubt about that – but there was also no doubt that Terry Garner was still so nervous that if someone had tapped him lightly on the shoulder, he'd have jumped a mile.

There was a sound of clicking heels on the stairs, then Mrs Pollard appeared in the archway. She saw Woodend immediately, and without even a word to the group, she strode purposefully over to join him.

She did not look good, the chief inspector thought. Her brassy blonde hair seemed to have lost most of its sheen, her shoulders drooped slightly, and her eyes were red, as if she'd been crying.

"Do you know that they've gone and arrested Rick?" she said, without preamble.

"Yes, I do know," Woodend replied.

"He didn't do it."

"Didn't do what? Didn't kill Eddie Barnes? Or didn't attack Jack Towers down by the docks?"

"He didn't do either of them things."

"He's got a history of violence, you know," the chief inspector said, playing devil's advocate.

"He's had a bit of trouble in the past through being hot-headed," the club owner conceded. "But now that he's older, and he's got a wife to look after, he's calmed down a lot."

"Interestin' phrase that – 'in the past'," Woodend said reflectively. "When does the past end an' the present begin, Mrs Pollard? As far as you're concerned, the dividin' line would seem to be about a month ago, when he attacked Eddie Barnes in a pub."

The club owner bit her bottom lip. "Maybe he had his own good reasons, for that."

"For example?"

"I don't know," Mrs Pollard said – and Woodend was almost sure she was lying. "But my . . . but Rick wouldn't just have gone at him without cause. I'm sure of that."

On the stage, the Seagulls had finally laid Beethoven to rest.

"Right, the pubs must be open by now," Steve Walker said, unstrapping his guitar. "Let's go an' get a drink."

"We need to practice some more," Pete Foster protested.

"Then we can come back this afternoon, can't we?" Steve said, leaning his guitar against the wall.

For a moment, it looked as if Pete Foster would continue to argue, then he shrugged his shoulders as if to say: What the hell? It doesn't matter how long we rehearse, we're not going to get any better.

The four young men headed for the exit, with Steve Walker and Terry Garner leading the way.

Mrs Pollard watched them go, then put her hand imploringly on Woodend's arm. "You have to get Rick released," she said.

"I'm here to investigate the murder of Eddie Barnes," Woodend told her. "Rick Johnson's been arrested for an assault on Jack Towers. That's a matter for the Liverpool Police to deal with."

"But there must be *something* you could do about it? Isn't there?" Mrs Pollard begged him. "After all, you're from Scotland Yard, and that makes you important. They'll *have* to listen to you."

After their exchange the night before, Woodend thought it unlikely that Inspector Hopgood would ever listen to anything he had to say again, but there was something pathetically touching about the brassy blonde's pleading, and he didn't have the heart to turn her down outright.

"Make me a nice strong cup of tea, Mrs Pollard, an' we'll talk it over," he said.

The club owner ducked under the counter flap. "He really is a good lad," she said. "I know he doesn't always show it, but underneath all that scowlin', there's a heart of gold."

"How did he meet his wife?" Woodend asked.

Mrs Pollard shrugged her shoulders. "How do any young couple meet? I don't see either of them as regular church-goers, so it was probably at a dance or in some pub."

"I notice you call them a young couple," Woodend said,

"but he must be at least eight years older than her."

"Seven and a half," Mrs Pollard replied defensively.

"Still, she was very young to be gettin' herself married. I'm surprised her parents allowed it, given that they must have known about Rick Johnson's reputation as a trouble-maker."

"What's Rick's marriage to Lucy got to do with anythin'?" Mrs Pollard demanded.

"Probably nothin'," Woodend conceded. "I was just curious about it, that's all."

Mrs Pollard put her hand on her hip. "Look," she said, "you'll probably find out about it from somebody else, so you might as well get it from me. They had to get married. They found out Lucy was pregnant, and Rick did the decent and proper thing and stood by her."

"So they have a baby?"

Mrs Pollard shook her head sadly. "No, Lucy lost it when she was four months gone."

"I'm sorry about that," Woodend said.

The club owner sighed. "These things happen, I suppose. Will you see what you can do about Rick?"

"I can't do anythin' to help him directly," Woodend told her, "but I will have a talk to him an' see if I can persuade him to help himself." He leant slightly forward. "If you really want to do what's best for him, you could start by not messin' up his marriage."

"Messing up his marriage? And what exactly do you mean by that?" Mrs Pollard demanded.

"I'm sure you know exactly what I mean, but if you like, I'll spell it out for you. If I was you, I'd give serious thought to gettin' myself a boyfriend closer to my own age."

The club owner looked shocked. "Is that what you think? That Rick an' me are havin' it off?"

"That's certainly the way it looks from where I'm standin'," the chief inspector told her.

Mrs Pollard shook her head disbelievingly. "You couldn't be more wrong if you tried."

"So why don't you put me right on the matter?"

For a moment, it looked as if the brassy blonde was about to do just that. Then she shook her head again, even more vigorously this time.

"No," she said. "I couldn't do that. It just wouldn't be fair."

"Fair to who?"

"I've said enough," Mrs Pollard told him. "If truth be told, perhaps I've said too much."

The Duke of Wellington public house was no more than a stone's throw from the coffee bar where the waitress had seen Eddie Barnes with a young woman, and therefore, Bob Rutter reasoned, it was a pretty good bet as the place to which the young lovers went when they felt like something a little stronger than a cup of cappuccino.

The landlord was a middle-aged man with very short hair and a clipped military moustache. He wore a regimental tie, and when he took the picture of Eddie Barnes over to the window to examine it in better light, he walked as if he were just coming off parade.

The pub he ran reflected the man, and was as neat and orderly as a barrack room awaiting inspection. Rutter got the impression he was the sort of person who would go around rearranging all the beer mats, until their edges were precisely parallel to the bar.

"Maybe," the landlord said, when he'd closely examined the picture for a full minute and a half.

"Maybe?" Bob Rutter repeated quizzically.

"Well, let me put it like this. If he ever has been in here – and I'm not sayin' he has, mind – then it was only the once."

"If he's only been in the once, you've got a remarkable memory even to think you recognise him," Rutter said sceptically.

"It's all part of the trainin' I've had," the landlord told him.

"Both in the army *an'* in the pub business. Besides, I always remember the faces of the people I have to bar. No good barrin' them if you can't recognise them the next time they try to come, is it now?"

Rutter held up the photograph again. "You barred him?" he asked, finding it hard to believe, from the picture he and Woodend had built up of Eddie Barnes, that the dead guitarist could ever have done anything which would have got him thrown out of a public house.

"Well, it wasn't so much him I barred as the girl he was with," the landlord admitted. "She said she was eighteen – well, she would, wouldn't she? – but she wasn't even close. An' I wasn't goin' to risk my licence for the profit I make on half a pint of shandy."

Steve Walker, Terry Garner and Billie Simmons sat huddled over their half-pints of bitter at a table in a corner of the Grapes public bar. There was no sign at all of Pete Foster, but then, Woodend thought, it was more than likely that he had gone off in a sulk.

The chief inspector walked over to the Seagulls' table. "I'd like to have a private word with Mr Garner," he said, in answer to Steve Walker's questioning expression.

"Can't you see that we're havin' a business meetin'?" Walker said aggressively.

"Is that what you call it?" Woodend asked mildly. "Well, I'd still like a word. Course, if he doesn't want to do it now, we can always postpone it till later – down at the local nick."

"What is this? Has England suddenly turned into some kind of police state?" Walker demanded.

But Terry Garner was already rising to his feet. "It's all right, Steve," he said. "I don't mind answerin' his questions."

Woodend led the Seagulls' new guitarist to a table out of earshot of the other members of the group, and signalled the waiter for two pints.

Now that they were sitting opposite each other, Woodend

took his first really close look at the young man. He was, the chief inspector guessed, somewhere around twenty, which put him midway, in age, between Steve Walker and the late Eddie Barnes. He had wide, candid eyes, and a few freckles just above his upper lip.

He was the kind of lad, Woodend thought, that he wouldn't have minded his daughter Annie bringing home for Sunday afternoon tea. Wouldn't have minded *too much*, he corrected himself, because no father likes to admit that his darling daughter is finally old enough to be going out with boys.

"So what's all this about?" Terry Garner asked, but without any of the hostility which Steve Walker would probably have displayed if he'd found himself in the same situation.

"Let's just say I'm interested in talkin' to anybody who might have inadvertently strayed into the middle of a murder inquiry," Woodend told him. "You did stray into it, didn't you? I mean, you weren't in the club the night before Eddie Barnes got electrocuted?"

"No, I wasn't," Garner said. "I was playin' with a group called Count Dracula an' the Vampires that night. We had a gig at a workin' men's club up in St Helens. We came off stage at closin' time, but we had difficulty startin' the van – well, it is on its last legs – an' the result was that we didn't get back to the 'Pool until after three o'clock in the mornin'."

"Well, assumin' your alibi checks out . . ."

"It will."

" . . . then that pretty much puts you in the clear. Why don't you tell me about you an' Steve Walker?"

"Is Steve a suspect?"

"Everybody who was in the club that night is a suspect," Woodend told him. "But I'm not askin' you to point the finger directly at your mate."

"Then why . . .?"

"My job is about collectin' details," Woodend explained. "Most of them turn out to be of no use to me, but I can't know that for sure until I've scooped them all in. An' right now, because you're the closest thing I can find to an expert on Steve Walker, I'd like to know what your impression is of him."

Terry Garner nodded, as if, now it had been explained to him, it seemed like a reasonable request.

"Where would you like me to begin?" he asked.

And again, Woodend thought how open and straightforward this particular young man seemed to be.

"Why don't you start with the first time that you met him?" he suggested.

"That would be when we were at school. Steve was the feller everybody else wanted to be like. You could tell that he wasn't gettin' properly looked after at home – his buttons were always hangin' on his blazer by a thread – but somehow he acted as if that didn't matter. He was so *cool*. Everythin' about him – the way he walked, the way he brushed his hair – was calculated to make an impression. You could see what he was doin' – it was as plain as the nose on your face – yet somehow you still couldn't help bein' impressed. Even the teachers were affected by it. Steve could be a right bugger in class sometimes, but I don't reckon he got caned half as much as the rest of us did."

"An' you were a big mate of his?"

"I would have liked to be," Garner confessed, "but I was never any more than a reserve-team mate – somebody to hang around with when Eddie Barnes was off school with the 'flu. But even that was considered somethin' of a privilege, an' other kids sucked up to me like mad, because they thought that was a way of getting closer to Steve."

"What about the other side of his nature?" Woodend asked. "The violent side?"

"You have to understand how that comes about," Garner said. "Steve likes to be the centre of attention – *needs* to be the centre of attention, I suppose. Most of the time he can get what he wants through words or his music, but when that fails he's quite prepared to make a scene, an', yes, there've been times when that's ended up in a fight."

"You're a very bright young man," Woodend said admiringly.

"I know that," Garner replied, without bravado. "If me mam an' dad could have afforded to let me stay on at school until I was eighteen, I might have ended up at university. As it is, I scrape by on what I can earn from doin' odd jobs, an' what I make playin' in groups."

"Do you still live with your parents?" Woodend asked.

"No, they emigrated to New Zealand a couple of years back. They asked me to go with them, but I didn't want to. I've got my own bedsit now. It's a bit pokey, but I get by."

"An' what about the future? You'd like to be a professional musician, I expect."

Terry Garner nodded. "If I can get my playin' up to the standard of the others, I would."

"So given that everybody seems to think they'll be goin' places, joinin' the Seagulls was a real opportunity for you?"

"I'll not deny it."

Woodend took a sip of his pint. "Yet from the way you were talkin' earlier, I got the distinct impression that you think you've stepped into a very dangerous situation."

"Eddie Barnes was the Seagulls' lead guitarist, an' now I am," Terry Garner said. "An' the only reason I got the job is because Eddie's dead."

"Steppin' into dead men's shoes is the only reason a lot of us get jobs," Woodend pointed out.

"I'm sure that somebody followed me home yesterday," Terry said in a sudden burst.

"Who?"

"I don't know," the young guitarist admitted. "I didn't see him. But I could feel his eyes on me. I could feel the look of . . . the look of . . ."

"Hatred?" Woodend suggested.

"No, it wasn't as intense as that. It was more like annoyance. It's hard to explain."

"I think you're doin' rather well," Woodend told him.

"It's like when you see a fly buzzin' around the larder window," Garner said. "You're annoyed because you know

165

you're goin' to have to do somethin' about it. I mean, there's nothin' personal in it, but you're still goin' to have to swat that little bugger before he lands on the meat. That's how I feel — like a fly that's goin' to have to be swatted before he does any damage."

Fifteen

It was late afternoon, and the sun, which had been smiling down benevolently on the city for most of the day, was covered with thick grey cloud.

Steve Walker shivered – but it had nothing to do with the fall in temperature. He had been standing on the street corner, watching the terraced house with the royal-blue front door, for over half an hour.

He knew he must stick out like a sore thumb – the strange looks he'd been given by passers-by had made that plain enough to him – but there was no help for it. He was there on a mission, and he was determined to stick with that mission to the bitter end.

He glanced quickly up the street, then returned his gaze to the blue front door. The father of the house was out at work, the son was still boozing with his mates in the Grapes the last time that Steve had seen him, but the mother – the bloody buggering mother! – was still inside the house and seemed to have no interest at all in coming out.

Didn't she need to go out to the shops? Steve asked himself. Weren't there any neighbours who she felt like dropping in on, for a cup of a tea and a mid-afternoon gossip?

Apparently not. In the time he'd been standing there, he'd seen her polishing the furniture in the front room and cleaning the upstairs sash window – two things his own mother would never have thought of doing. How he wished that this woman were more like his own mother now. How he wished she would feel the craving for a drink, and raid her son's piggy bank in order to obtain the price of a bottle of milk stout and a whisky chaser.

"Is there anythin' I can do to help you, son?" asked a voice immediately to his left.

He turned to see a grey-haired man in a three-quarter-length khaki coat standing there. Sod it!

"Are you deaf or summat?" the man said impatiently. "I asked if you needed any help."

"No thanks very much."

The grey-haired man frowned. "The thing is, you see, I've got the shop across the road," he said, indicating towards the corner grocery store with his right thumb. "I've got a good view of the street from there, an' I couldn't help noticin' that you've been hangin' around here for quite some time."

Why don't you mind your own business, you nosy old bastard? Steve Walker thought.

But aloud he merely said, "You're right. I have been here for a while. I'm waitin' for somebody."

The grocer's frown deepened, and suspicion clouded his eyes as much as the dark shapes overhead had clouded the sun.

"Somebody local?" he asked.

"Yeah."

"Well, as it happens I know most of the people who live around here," the shop keeper said, "an' I'd feel a lot happier in my own mind if you'd tell me who exactly it is that you're waitin' for?"

There was nothing for it but to be at least half-way honest. "Mike Finn," Steve Walker said. "I'm waitin' for Mike Finn. He promised to meet me here on the corner half an hour ago." He gave the shop keeper what he hoped looked like a rueful grin. "But you know what Mike's like. I mean, reliability's hardly his middle name, now is it?"

"He's probably just about as reliable as the rest of you kids – which means not at all," the grocer said, but the answer seemed to have satisfied him and he turned and crossed the road back to his shop.

The grey-haired man would remember the encounter later, Steve thought, and when it came to a police line-up he'd have no difficulty at all in picking out the lad he'd seen loitering on the corner. But that didn't really matter. Nothing in the future really mattered. The only thing which was important was for the bloody woman to come out of the bloody house and give him a chance to get inside!

The interview room was painted institutional chocolate brown up to about waist height, and in a kind of muddy cream from there up to the ceiling. The battered wooden chairs squeaked with even the slightest movement, as in almost every other interview room Woodend had ever used, and the chief inspector found himself wondering if there was a special factory which produced them with just that intention.

The man sitting opposite him didn't appear to wondering about anything. All his energy was channelled into an expression of defiance which already filled his entire face and still seemed to be looking for space to expand.

"Mrs Pollard asked me to come an' see you," Woodend said.

"So what?"

"I think she's worried about you."

"I've told the other flatfeet, and now I'm tellin' you – I didn't beat up Jack Towers, an' I didn't kill Eddie Barnes," Rick Johnson replied, as if the chief inspector had never spoken.

"If that's true, why won't you tell us how you got that black eye?" Woodend asked.

"Because it's none of your bloody business."

Woodend shook his head, almost sadly. "Inspector Hopgood wants to pin somethin' – *anythin'* – on you. He has to do that, you see. Otherwise he'll end up lookin' like a right bloody idiot for arrestin' you in the first place. Now I can probably talk him out of bringin' any charges, but before that, you've got to play your part by tellin' me what happened to you."

"I've said all I'm goin' to say," Johnson told him, folding his arms across his chest.

169

"Do you have any idea of just how upset Mrs Pollard is about you bein' in police custody?" Woodend asked.

"You leave her out of it!" Johnson shouted.

"Touchy on the subject of Mrs Pollard, aren't you. An' you know somethin' else? She's touchy on the subject of you, an' all. Strange that, isn't it, considerin' that all you are to her is an employee?"

"You're a bloody bastard!" Johnson said vehemently.

"I've been called worse things in my time," Woodend replied. He stood up. "Much worse – an' by experts. If you decide to behave sensibly, Mr Johnson, just tell the custody sergeant you'd like to see me again."

He opened the door and stepped out into the corridor. Two men were standing there, just as they had been when he'd started the interview with Johnson. One of them was a uniformed constable, the other a decidedly frosty Inspector Hopgood.

"You've finished with him, have you . . . sir?" Hopgood asked.

"That's right," Woodend agreed.

Hopgood turned to the constable. "Go and keep the toe-rag company until *I* can find the time to talk to him," he said.

The constable entered the interview room. Hopgood waited until the door was closed behind him, then said, "I don't suppose you had any luck with Johnson, did you . . . sir?"

"If you find it such a strain to keep callin' me 'sir', then drop the bloody title altogether," Woodend said.

The expression on Hopgood's face said he thought he'd probably gone too far. "Sorry, sir," he said.

"An' in answer to your question," Woodend continued, "no, I didn't have any luck with Johnson."

A triumphant sneer replaced the look of mild apprehension on Hopgood's face.

"With respect, sir, the trouble with bobbies like you – bobbies who've left the sharp edge of policing very far behind them – is that you forget what things are like in the real world," he said. "You'll get nothing out of a hard case like Johnson by holding

170

his hand, and offering him a cup of tea. Firmness is the only language his kind understand."

It would serve him right if he was left to stew in his own juice, Woodend thought, but when all was said and done, the man was a colleague, and it was perhaps worth making one more effort to show him the error of his ways.

"Why don't you let Johnson go?" he suggested. "You'll never be able to pin the attack on Jack Towers on him, even if he did it – an' I'm almost sure that he didn't."

"He'll crack," Hopgood said stubbornly. "Sooner or later, he'll crack. They all do. And now, if you don't have any more business here, sir, I'll escort you to the door."

They walked in chilly silence down the long corridor which led to the lobby. From beyond the door at the end of the corridor there was suddenly the sound of loud voices. Inspector Hopgood tut-tutted disapprovingly, but seemed in no particular hurry to find out what was going on.

They entered the lobby and saw the cause of the disturbance for themselves. Two uniformed constables were struggling to restrain a man in a smart blue suit who seemed to be on the verge of hysteria.

"This is outrageous!" the man screamed, as he fought to free himself from the policemen's grip. "I'm not some kind of common criminal! I'm a physician, for God's sake!"

"I don't give a toss what you do for a livin', sunshine," one of the constables grunted as he twisted the prisoner's arm firmly behind his back. "You've been arrested an' charged, all in accordance with the law, an' you'd save us all a lot of trouble if you'd come quietly."

Suddenly, the prisoner stopped resisting – perhaps because he finally realised how undignified he must look, perhaps because he saw the pointlessness of struggling any longer. The two officers, still keeping a firm grip, led him, unprotesting, towards the custody cells.

"He really is a doctor, you know," Woodend said. "His name's Atkinson, an' he works at the University Hospital. You probably saw him yourself. Last night. When you went to the hospital without rememberin' to ring me first."

"We get all sorts in here," Hopgood replied, indifferently. "Anyway, it's nothin' to do with me."

You've no curiosity, lad, Woodend thought – an' without curiosity you'll never make a really good bobby.

They had reached the main desk. A white-haired sergeant sat behind it, writing in a ledger.

"That feller they've just brought in? What's he charged with?" Woodend asked.

The sergeant looked up from his work.

"Him?" he said in disgust. "One of our lads in plain clothes caught him solicitin' outside the public lavatories in St John's Gardens. Bloody queers – I bloody hate them."

"A homosexual, is he?" Woodend mused. "An' not a pink handbag or a powder puff in sight. Well, it only goes to show – you never can tell just by lookin' at them, can you?"

"When he goes to court, he'll probably get no more than a six-month sentence," the desk sergeant growled. "As if that'll do any good! In my opinion, if the courts are too squeamish to hang 'em, they should at least lock 'em up an' throw away the key."

"Tolerance has always been a quality I've admired in a man," Woodend said mildly.

"I beg your pardon, sir?"

"Well, I think you should certain beg somebody's," Woodend told him.

Hopgood coughed. "If there's nothing more, I'll see you to the door, Mr Woodend."

He's like a pub landlord at closin' time, Woodend thought, with mild amusement. He's got to show a certain amount of civility, but he just can't wait to get me off the premises.

The inspector held the door open, and Woodend stepped out on to the street. It had been cloudy when he'd entered the police station, but now the sun was shining brightly again, and the people walking past seemed to have developed an optimistic spring in their steps.

Woodend turned round. Inspector Hopgood was still standing there, as if he wanted to make absolutely sure that the troublesome bobby from London was actually leaving.

"I really would let Rick Johnson go if I was you," Woodend told Hopgood, knowing, as he spoke, that he was probably wasting his time. "He had nothing to do with the attack on Jack Towers. I guarantee it."

"You sound a lot more sure of yourself than you did a few minutes back," Hopgood said.

"I am."

"In that case, I suppose you imagine that you know who *did* attack him, as well."

"No, I don't," Woodend admitted. "That's something we'll probably never know. But I do think I know *why* he was attacked."

Mike Finn's mother, a string shopping bag on her arm, closed the royal-blue front door behind and set off down the street. Finally! Steve Walker, puffing nervously on a Woodbine, waited until she'd turned the corner, then he threw the cigarette away and made his move.

He sprinted down the alley which ran at the back of the houses, counting off the numbers until he reached the one he'd just watched the woman leave. He lifted the latch on the back gate and pushed. The door gave a little, but not much, and he realised that the bloody thing was bolted from the inside.

"Shit!" he said, louder than he had intended.

A locked gate just about doubled his chances of getting caught, he thought, but there nothing else for it – he was going to have to go over the wall.

He stepped back and took a running jump. His hands connected with the crumbling brickwork on the top of the wall, and he pulled himself up and over, landing heavily next to the outside lavatory. He paused there for a moment – partly to listen for anyone raising the alarm, partly to let his galloping heart slow down. He had never done anything like this before, and it was turning out to be harder – and far more frightening – than he'd ever imagined.

He moved quickly past the coal shed to the back door. Once there, he pulled the jemmy out of his jacket and inserted it between the door and the jamb. When he'd planned the job, he'd pictured the door flying open immediately, but all his initial efforts succeeded in doing was splintering the wood.

Sweat was dripping down the back of his neck. He forced himself to pull the jemmy free, and insert it closer to the keyhole. He levered again, and the door groaned. He tried once more, and felt the lock give.

He was in the back kitchen now, but what he was looking for wouldn't be there.

Perhaps it wouldn't be in the house at all, he told himself.

It was more than possible, now he thought about it, that Mike Finn had realised how incriminating it would be, and had got rid of it – which meant he was putting himself through all this gut-wrenching terror for nothing.

Now wasn't the time for thinking, his mind screamed. Now was the time for action.

He made his way into the hallway and up the stairs. There were three bedroom doors, but only one them had a poster of the Knockouts pinned to it. He turned the handle and stepped inside.

The room was a mess. Clothes lay strewn all over the floor, bits of old amplifiers were spread out haphazardly on the table. But it was the corner of the room which caught Steve Walker's attention, because lying there, amid a pile of other miscellaneous junk, was what he'd come for.

He picked up his precious trophies and rushed downstairs again. Once in the hall, he was faced with two choices. It would be quicker to leave through the front door – and anything which was quicker had to be very tempting – but there was more chance of being spotted by some passer-by. Better, then, to take a little while longer and leave, as he had arrived, through the back gate.

He retraced his steps through the back kitchen and across the yard past the coal shed and lavvy. No need to climb over the wall this time. All he had to do was draw back the bolt. He did, but before he had time to open the door, it swung open of its own accord.

A volcano of nausea erupted in Steve Walker's stomach as he realised that the gate had not swung, it had been pushed – and that the pushing had been done by the man in a blue serge uniform who was standing in the alley.

"Looks like that shop keeper was right," the constable said. "You *were* up to no good, weren't you, son?"

Steve Walker glanced longingly over his shoulder at the open back door. "Listen . . ." he said.

"No, *you* listen," the constable said commandingly. "You're in a lot of trouble, kid. It's a very serious charge, breakin' and enterin'. An' if I was you, I wouldn't make things worse for myself by tryin' to make a run for it, because there's another officer posted outside the front door."

Steve bowed his head, acknowledging defeat. "I'll come quietly," he promised. "But I've got to speak to Chief Inspector Woodend right away."

"*Got* to, have you?" the constable asked. "Well, we'll see about that when we're back at the station."

The Grapes had only just opened its door for business again, so Woodend was not more than a third of the way down his first pint of bitter when Bob Rutter walked into the bar.

Rutter sat down opposite his boss. "First the good news," he said. "Eddie Barnes did have a girlfriend."

"You're sure of that?"

The sergeant nodded. "I've turned up three witnesses – a waitress in a coffee bar where they used to go, the landlord of a pub who wouldn't serve them, and a cinema usherette who says she noticed them because they sat through two complete showings of *Spartacus*."

"So what's the bad news?" Woodend asked.

"None of them could give me anything like a clear description of her, so while we now know she does exist, we're no closer to finding her than we ever were."

"Well, we've at least made some progress anyway," Woodend said encouragingly.

"But not enough," the sergeant countered. "I'll grab a bite to eat, then hit the streets again. There's usually a different crowd of people around at night to the ones who are out in the day, so who knows, I might just get lucky."

But he didn't sound very hopeful, Woodend thought. "There's one thing that's not clear to me," he said.

"And what's that, sir?"

"You say the landlord you talked to barred them from his pub. But from all we've learned about Eddie Barnes, he just doesn't seem like the kind of lad who'd cause enough trouble to get himself barred."

"That was my first thought as well," Rutter said, "but it turns out his getting barred had nothing to do with causing trouble. The landlord just decided that the girl was too young to serve. Come to think of it, that's the one thing they all said about her – that she was very, very young."

Woodend slapped his forehead with the palm of his hand. "I can be so bloody stupid sometimes," he said.

"What do you mean, sir?"

"You said your witnesses weren't able to give you much of a description, but did any of them happen to notice the colour of this girl's hair?"

"The waitress and the landlord did."

"An' did they describe it as dark brown – almost black?"

"Yes," Rutter gasped. "As a matter of fact, they did. How on earth did you know that?"

"Oh, I'm a dab-hand at spottin' the bloody obvious, if it's held right under my nose," Woodend said.

Sixteen

In less than two hours, the Cellar Club would be full of teenagers, gyrating to the latest records which the stewards who worked on the transatlantic liners had brought back hot from the United States, but for the moment Woodend and Mrs Pollard had the place to themselves.

Woodend, standing on one side of the bar counter, was smoking a Capstan Full Strength with all the concentration of a man who took his regular shot of nicotine very seriously indeed. The club owner was sitting on a tall stool at the other side and was apparently going through her accounts ledgers. But from the number of times she stopped to glance up at the policeman, it was clear that her mind was not really on the job in hand.

It was the woman who finally broke the silence. "I realise that bein' deliberately mysterious is part of your charm," she said, "but I really would appreciate it if you'd tell me what all this is about."

Woodend chuckled. "Do you know, there's a lot of people – includin' some young, green detectives – who think that solvin' a murder is like doin' a jigsaw puzzle?" he said.

"A jigsaw puzzle?"

"That's right. But it's much more complicated than that. When you're startin' out in my game, you see all the pieces of the puzzle lyin' on the table in front of you, an' you assume that all you have to do is slot them together. But you soon find out you're wrong – at least, I did – because what you learn is that although all the bits of your puzzle *are* there, there's also bits of other puzzles mixed in with them. An' sometimes, in order to

177

make sure that all you've got is the pieces which will help you make the big picture you're interested in, it's necessary to put some of the smaller puzzles together first."

"Well, thanks for that," Mrs Pollard said. "Now that you've explained it to me, it's as clear as mud."

"Exercise a bit of patience, an' it should soon be as clear as a newly polished window," Woodend promised her.

There was a sound of two sets of footsteps coming down the stairs. One was heavy and masculine, the other had the click-click quality of a woman wearing high heels.

"Who the hell's that?" Mrs Pollard asked.

"That," Woodend replied, "is the young lady who's goin' to help us find out which pieces belong where."

The man and woman had reached the bottom of the stairs, and now Mrs Pollard could see that they were Bob Rutter and Lucy Johnson.

"You know all about it, don't you?" the club owner said to Woodend.

"Well, let's just say that I've got a pretty fair idea," the chief inspector told her.

Lucy Johnson advanced across the room, stopping a few feet from them.

"Why did you tell him to bring me here?" she asked, pointing her thumb over her shoulder at Rutter. "Is this anythin' to with Rick?"

"In a way," Woodend said. "Your husband doesn't treat you very well, does he, Mrs Johnson?"

"You've got it all wrong. He's—"

"In fact, he's a proper domestic tyrant, if the truth be told. Even knocks you about from time to time, doesn't he?"

Lucy Johnson looked down at the brick floor. "He does have a bit of a temper on him," she admitted.

"You'd never have got married to him if you hadn't been pregnant, would you?"

Lucy Johnson looked to Alice Pollard for guidance, and when the older woman nodded her head, as if to say she should tell the truth, she said, "No, I wouldn't have. To be honest, I was just about to break it off with him when I realised I'd missed my period."

"So when another a man – a much *gentler* man – started to pay attention to you, you were naturally flattered. Then it got to be more than that, an' you actually fell in love with him."

"We didn't do anythin' we shouldn't have done," Lucy Johnson said passionately. "All we used to do was go to places where nobody knew us, an' sit around an' talk."

"Like the back seats in the cinema?" Woodend suggested. "Did you enjoy *Spartacus*, Mrs Johnson? He's a very good actor, that Kirk Douglas, isn't he? Well worth sittin' through the film twice!"

The girl's jaw dropped. "All right," she said reluctantly. "Maybe we did go in for a bit of kissin' and cuddlin'– but it was never any more than that. Eddie was very insistent about it. He said that it wouldn't be right to go all the way – not until I'd divorced Rick an' married him."

"So it was *almost* innocent," Woodend said. "But your husband was furious when he found out about it, wasn't he? That's why he attacked Eddie Barnes in the pub. An' the reason Eddie didn't press charges when he had the chance was because he was feelin' guilty."

"Yes," the girl said.

"Which, of course, explains why Rick likes to have you by his side wherever he is – because now he's found out what was goin' on, he doesn't trust you anymore." Woodend lit a fresh Capstan Full Strength. "Now think very carefully about these next few questions, Mrs Johnson. You an' Rick were the last two people to leave the club the night before Eddie Barnes died, weren't you?"

"Yes."

"Did Rick go into the dressin' room at any point – even for just a few seconds?"

"No," Lucy Johnson said firmly.

"You know what you're tellin' me by sayin' that, don't you?"

Woodend asked. "You're tellin' me that your husband, Rick, couldn't possibly have murdered your boyfriend, Eddie."

The girl looked the chief inspector straight in the eyes. "I still love Eddie even though he's dead," she said, "an' if my husband had killed him, I'd want him to pay for it. But he didn't. Rick kept me close to him all evenin', and he never once went anywhere near that dressin' room."

"One more question," Woodend said. "More for curiosity than for anythin' else. It's about the feller who did such a good job of beatin' your husband up." He closed his eyes, and pictured the man who he'd seen arguing with Rick Johnson outside the Cellar Club's entrance. "Am I right – he had brown hair, was aged around twenty-three or twenty-four an' couldn't have stood much more than five foot six in his stockinged feet?"

"Yes, you're right," Lucy Johnson said.

"An' who might he have been?"

"Martin, my big brother," Lucy said. "He'd warned Rick a couple of times that if he knocked me about any more, he'd give him a seein' to. An' that's exactly what he did."

Woodend allowed a light smile to play on his lips. "Your husband must have a good four or five inches on your brother," he said.

Lucy Johnson smiled back. "He does," she agreed. "But Martin's always been a tough little sod."

So Rick Johnson had allowed himself to be locked up in gaol, rather than admit he'd been given a beating by someone who was smaller than he was. It was crazy, Woodend thought, but given what he'd learned about Rick Johnson's character during the course of the investigation, he couldn't honestly say that it surprised him.

"Thank you for all your help, Mrs Johnson," he said. "You can go back home now."

"Will you be lettin' Rick out of jail?" the girl asked.

"Yes," Woodend said. "I'm sorry, but given what you've just told me, I'm rather afraid that we'll have to."

Lucy smiled again. "There's no need to be sorry," she said.

"Violence is one thing that Rick does understand, an' after the pastin' that our Martin gave him, he won't dare lay a hand on me from now on."

"You're sure about that?"

The girl's smile acquired a sad tinge. "Oh yes, I'm sure. I know exactly what my future's goin' to be like. Would you like to hear about it?"

"If you want to tell me."

"I'll get pregnant again, an' this time I know I'll manage to keep the baby. Rick'll work hard to put food on the table, an' we'll end up happy enough – in our own way."

But nowhere near as happy as if you'd run away with Eddie Barnes, Woodend thought, feeling another surge of the anger which he knew was so unprofessional but which he could do nothing about.

"Good luck, Mrs Johnson," he said, realising, as he spoke, that he had never meant anything more sincerely in his entire life.

"Thanks," Lucy said, "but I don't think I'll need it now."

Woodend waited until the girl had begun climbing the stairs, then turned his attention back on Mrs Pollard.

"There was a time when I thought I understood exactly how you fitted into all this, but now I'm not so sure," he confessed. "Would you care to enlighten me?"

"I don't think that I want to talk about it right now," Alice Pollard said, looking meaningfully at Rutter.

Woodend glanced down at his watch. "This shouldn't take very much longer," he said. "Do me a favour, Bob. Nip across to the Grapes an' get a couple of pints in so that mine'll be waitin' for me when I get there."

Rutter nodded to show he understood, and followed Lucy Johnson up the stairs.

"Rick Johnson's not your lover, is he?" Woodend asked the club owner, as he heard the door bang shut at the top of the stairs.

"No, he isn't."

"So what the bloody hell is he?"

181

"When I wasn't much older than Lucy is now, I was already on the game," Alice Pollard said, matter-of-factly.

"I know," Woodend replied.

"Who told you?"

"I've seen all the details on your sheet down at the station – or, at least, my sergeant has."

Alice Pollard nodded sadly. "Of course you have. You can never tear up your past, can you? However much you might try – an' however much you want to?"

"I wouldn't be so sure of that if I was you," Woodend told her. "My sergeant's a bit on the careless side, you see, an' we might find, when we get back to London, that he's still got your charge sheet tucked in his pocket. Course, what with the shockin' price of postage these days, he won't want to send it back to Liverpool, so he'll probably just throw it away."

Mrs Pollard smiled gratefully. "You're a nice man," she said.

"There's a lot of folk who'd disagree with you," Woodend told her. "Anyroad, carry on with your story."

"I knew nothing about nothing in them days," Alice Pollard said, "and I hadn't been walking the streets for more than a few months when I found out I was goin' to have a baby. I didn't know where to turn. There were people who said they could get it fixed for me, but when I asked them what it involved they started talking about drinking a bottle of gin while you were sitting in a hot bath. There were even a few who said it was amazing what you could do with a knitting needle." She shivered involuntarily. "Well, I didn't fancy doing either of them things, so I went ahead and had the baby. But I knew I couldn't keep him, and the minute he was born, I offered him up for adoption. Then, over twenty years later – though I can't say in all honesty I deserved it – that kid looked me up."

"Rick Johnson."

"Yes, my tiny, helpless baby was adopted by a family called Johnson," Alice Pollard agreed. "And he still goes to see them regularly. But as far as he's concerned, *I'm* his mother. And though he's got his faults – God knows he has – I love him with all my heart."

The sound of heavy footfalls came from the stairs. Mrs Pollard looked questioningly at the chief inspector.

"Size-nine police-issue boots, at a guess," Woodend said. "Well, whatever else the Liverpool Police might say about me – an' I imagine they say quite a lot – they can't complain that I'm not keepin' them busy."

A uniformed constable appeared at the foot of the stairs. He strode across to the snack bar, came to a halt, and saluted.

"Inspector Hopgood sends his compliments, sir," he said. "The inspector thought you might like to know that about an hour ago I arrested Steven Henry Walker."

"On what charge?"

The constable took out his notebook, licked the end of his finger and turned a couple of pages.

"Walker was arrested on suspicion of burglary as he was leavin' the home of a Mr an' Mrs Walter Finn," he said, as if he were in the witness stand being cross-examined by a hostile barrister.

"Would they be Mike Finn's parents?" Woodend asked.

"As to that, sir, I have no details about the rest of the family, so I couldn't possibly comment."

But though coincidences did happen in life, this was highly unlikely to have been one of them, Woodend thought. So what, in heaven's name, would have motivated Steve Walker to break into Mike Finn's home?

And then it came to him in a sudden flash of inspiration! Walker wanted to find Eddie Barnes's killer. Walker suspected that the killer was Mike Finn. Seeing it from that angle it was obvious what he'd been looking for!

"Did he actually steal anythin' from the house?" the chief inspector asked the constable.

"Yes, sir," the other man replied. "It wasn't actually worth very much, but stealin' is stealin'. What he'd taken was—"

Woodend held up his hand to silence the constable. "Don't tell me, let me guess," he said. "What he had under his arm when you caught him was a stack of magazines."

"That's . . . that's right, sir," the constable said, looking very much as he might have done if he'd been standing on a stage and a magician had pulled an egg out of his ear.

"Do you know somethin', Constable?" Woodend said. "There's more than a fair chance that by this time tomorrow I'll be on a train speedin' back to the bosom of my family."

Inspector Hopgood sat behind his desk, staring at the man in the hairy sports jacket who was sitting opposite him. He did not look at all pleased to see Woodend back in the station so soon after the chief inspector's last visit.

"I only let you know about Steve Walker's arrest out of professional courtesy, sir," he said across his desk.

Professional courtesy? Woodend thought. Professional bollocks was more like it! The bastard was just playing it very carefully and making sure that he'd covered his own back.

"But I never for a moment imagined that you'd have any real interest in the arrest," the inspector continued. "After all, it was just a common-or-garden burglary which can't possibly have anything to do with your case."

Woodend sighed, and wondered whether any of these provincial police forces would ever assign him a man he could work with as well as he worked with Bob Rutter.

"What magazines did Walker steal?" he asked.

Hopgood consulted the file which was lying on his desk.

"Let me see now," he said. "There was a *Woman's Weekly*, a *Ladies' Home Journal*, a copy of *John Bull* . . ."

"It's hardly the sort of readin' material you'd think would interest a teenage rock'n'roll singer, is it now?" Woodend asked.

Hopgood laughed patronisingly. "We're assuming for the purposes of our investigation that the magazines in question were the property of Mr an' Mrs Finn, and not of their son," he said.

"Yes, I should imagine the *Ladies' Home Journal* would be very popular with workin'-class folk livin' in a terraced house," Woodend said. "Tell me, Inspector, have you asked yourself if it was just a coincidence that Steve Walker should choose to break into the house of a lad he knew well?"

"Not really, but—"

"An' have you stopped for a second to wonder why he should risk goin' to prison just to steal a few magazines?"

"Kids today! Who knows what makes them tick?" Hopgood said, as if he'd provided a watertight and all-encompassing answer.

"There was a stage in this investigation when I might well have agreed with you on that point," Woodend told him. "For a couple of days, I couldn't understand them either. But do you know what? They might dress differently, they might talk differently an' they might have more money to spend than we did when we were young, but once you get under the surface they're just the same as we are. Steve Walker's taught me that."

"He has?" Hopgood asked, as if it were the most outrageous statement he'd ever heard.

"Aye," Woodend said. "An' he did it by actin' just like I would have done at his age."

"You'd have committed a criminal act! You'd have forced your way into someone else's house!"

"Aye, maybe I would have done – if that's what it took," Woodend said. "But what I really mean is that if the police didn't seem to be gettin' anywhere with their inquiries, I'd have gone out lookin' for justice myself."

"I'm afraid I'm not following you, sir," Hopgood confessed.

"No, I didn't think you would," the chief inspector said. "Where are these magazines that Steve Walker stole?"

"They've all been placed in the evidence cupboard, just like they're supposed to be."

Woodend lit up a Capstan Full Strength. "Good. Well, send somebody to fetch them for me, will you?"

185

The idea seemed to deeply shock Inspector Hopgood. "But they've already been classified and filed."

Woodend sighed again. "Don't make me go above your head, lad," he said. "That won't make either of us look particularly good – an' you know that as well as I do."

Hopgood hesitated for a second, then picked up the phone and barked an order into it. For perhaps two minutes the men sat opposite each other in uncomfortable silence, then a female clerk entered the room with the magazines in a plastic wallet.

Woodend opened the wallet, and took the magazines out. "Be careful of the prints, sir!" Hopgood warned.

"Bugger the prints!" Woodend told him cheerfully. "They'll be so smudged they'll be no good as evidence anyway." He flipped through the copy of *Woman's Weekly*. "There it is," he cried triumphantly. "Or rather, to be more accurate, there it isn't."

"I'm afraid that I don't know what you're talking about, sir," Inspector Hopgood said.

"Well, that's nothin' new, is it?" Woodend countered. He placed the magazine back on the desk. "I know there's not a great deal of love lost between you an' me, Inspector Hopgood, but in view of what he's done to assist my inquiries, I'd consider it a personal favour if you let Steve Walker go."

"But he's already been charged!"

Woodend shrugged. "Lose the paperwork – it wouldn't be the first time it's happened."

"An' there's the Finn family to consider. They'll want to see the man who broke into their house brought to justice."

"I'll send my sergeant to sort them out," Woodend said. "He's such a smooth young bugger he could talk an Eskimo into buyin' a fridge. Besides, the Finns will have a lot more to worry about than a busted back door."

"You've lost me again," Hopgood confessed.

"If I was them, I'd be more concerned about the fact that my son had been arrested on suspicion of murder," Woodend told him.

Seventeen

They were sitting the same cream and brown interview room in which Woodend had talked to Rick Johnson only a few hours earlier, but the whole atmosphere was very different this time. Johnson had been aggressive and defiant. Mike Finn, on the other hand, was cowed, and even from across the table it was possible to catch the stink of his fear.

"The sooner you've got all the dirty water off your chest, the sooner you're goin' to start feelin' better," Woodend told Finn. "It might not seem like that from where you're sittin', but believe me, it's perfectly true. I've seen it a hundred times. So why don't you just come clean now, lad?"

Finn twisted nervously in his seat. The chair creaked in protest. "Can I go to the toilet?" he asked.

"Of course you can, lad," Woodend said benignly. "Just as soon as we've got a statement from you."

"But I really need to go now."

"No, you don't," the chief inspector assured him. "It's just your nerves that make you think you do. An' like I was just tellin', you'll feel much better once you've confessed."

"But I've got nothin' to confess *to*," Mike Finn protested. "Honestly I haven't."

"Do you think I'm totally thick, lad?" Woodend asked. "Do you think I'd pull you in if I couldn't make it stick?"

Mike Finn bowed his head. "I don't know," he muttered into his chest. "I don't know anythin' anymore."

"Well, let's look at the evidence. For a start, Inspector Hopgood's got the names of half a dozen witnesses who saw

a lad with long blond hair hangin' around near Jack Towers'
house the night somebody posted that threatenin' letter through
his box," Woodend lied.

"It wasn't me."

"We'll soon see about that, won't we? There'll be a line-up,
as you must realise, an' I don't reckon that the witnesses will
have much trouble pickin' you out." He paused for effect. "An'
even if they did, we don't really need them because there's all
the forensic evidence."

"What forensic evidence?"

"It's all so scientific an' complicated that I don't understand
half of what the boffins can do myself," Woodend admitted.
"But I do know that you can't handle a dead rat – especially
when you go to all the trouble of puttin' a string noose around
its neck – without leavin' some traces of yourself behind. An'
then there's your poisonous little *billet doux* to Jack Towers.
Do you imagine, even for a second, that you can put together an
anonymous letter without some of the sweat from your fingers
stickin' to it?"

"But I was wearin' . . ." Finn began, then dried up as he
suddenly realised his blunder.

"But you were wearin' gloves," Woodend supplied. "Yes,
I thought that you might have been. So we won't get any
sweat samples. But who needs them, when we've got the
magazines?"

"You can't use them," Mike Finn said. "Not unless you had
a search warrant to go into my house."

"Proper little barrack-room lawyer, aren't you?" Woodend
said unconcernedly. "An' you'd be quite right if we *had* gone
into your house too look for them. But we didn't. Steve Walker
removed them, we merely took them off him when he was
arrested."

The chief inspector opened the *Woman's Weekly*. "Bet
you got some funny looks from your newsagent when you
bought this lot. Or perhaps you didn't buy them from your
own newsagent. Maybe you were just smart enough to go

somewhere else to buy them. Doesn't really matter. We'll find whichever newsagent you did use, an' I've no doubt he'll remember the transaction well enough."

Mike Finn licked his dry lips. "I didn't buy no magazines," he said, but with a total lack of conviction which showed that he'd all but given up trying to defend himself.

Ignoring the comment completely, Woodend continued to flick through the *Woman's Weekly*.

"Here we are," he said. "Under fashion. The headline reads, ' . . . season's frocks'. Funny that, isn't it?"

Mike Finn said nothing.

"Of course, what it should say is '*Next* season's frocks'," Woodend continued. "Only the 'next' has been cut out, because you needed it for the sentence, 'Which one will die next?' As bobbies are always supposed to say at this point: Give it up, lad. I've got you bang to rights."

"We really wanted the dinnertime spot at the Cellar Club," Finn said. "It was our big chance to get noticed."

"So in order to drive the Seagulls out of Liverpool, you rang up a couple of clubs to cancel their bookin's, you slashed the tyres on their van an' you sent them the dead rat with a noose around its neck? Isn't that right?"

Mike Finn nodded his head despairingly. "I thought it would be all over when Eddie Barnes died," he said. "An' then the bloody Seagulls went an' got themselves a new guitarist. He wasn't nearly as good as Eddie, but that didn't matter. They'd still have got their dinnertime spot at the Cellar Club back. Mrs Pollard told me as much. So I posted that letter through Jack Towers' box in the hope they'd pack up their things an' move to London."

"We're gettin' a bit ahead of ourselves, aren't we?" Woodend suggested. "Let's go back to the night Eddie died. You'd tried everythin' you could to get rid of the Seagulls, but nothin' had worked. You were feelin' pretty desperate. Then there was a disturbance after the Cellar Club had closed down for the evenin' – it was a fight, wasn't it . . .?"

"Yes, it was a fight."

" . . . when everybody else's attention was distracted – and that's when you saw your chance to re-wire Eddie Barnes's amplifier."

"No!" Mike Finn gasped, almost sobbing. "I couldn't have done it – because I was one of the people who was fightin'."

Terry Garner was pacing the floor of his small bedsit, as he had been doing since the moment he had double-locked himself safely inside. He had smoked the last of his cigarettes over half an hour earlier, and though he desperately wanted the soothing sensation of nicotine, he knew he wasn't brave enough to leave his refuge in order to buy some more.

He was out there. Terry knew he was. Watching. Waiting. And while he had no idea who the Watcher was, he was convinced that the man would not be content until the Seagulls had lost another lead guitarist.

All kinds of crazy plans passed through his head. He would put on a disguise, slip out of the city and never return. He would place an advertisement in the *Mersey Sound* which would say that he promised never to play with the Seagulls again, so could whoever was stalking him please leave him alone now. He would commit a crime so the police would lock him somewhere safely away from the menacing presence he felt everywhere he turned.

He heard the sound of heavy footsteps, coming up the stairs. The Watcher? Dear God, let it not be the Watcher!

Why should it be? he asked himself. Why couldn't it be one of the other tenants instead?

He rummaged around in the overflowing ashtray, found a stub and – with trembling hands – placed it in his mouth. He could taste the harsh cigarette ash on his tongue, but that didn't matter because what he needed right at the moment – above anything else in the whole wide world – was the reassuring feeling of smoke curling around his lungs.

The footfalls were getting louder, as the man making them

drew ever nearer. Terry opened his box of matches, fumbled them, and watched helplessly as they spilled on to the floor.

"Oh Christ!" he moaned softly, as he bent down and clawed at one of the matches.

There was now only silence outside the bedsit. Terry struck the match, and lit the cigarette. He coughed as the acrid smoke hit the back of his mouth, and wished that at that moment he was somewhere else. Anywhere else!

The loud knock on the door made his heart leap into his throat. "Who . . . who is it?" he gasped.

"It's only me," said a voice.

Terry gasped again, this time with relief. He walked over to the door, drew back the bolt, turned the key in the lock and opened the door.

The visitor had a reassuring grin on his face. "I thought we should have a little talk," he said. He held up a bottle of scotch. "And I've brought this to keep us company."

Bob Rutter stood by the duty sergeant's desk, the black Bakelite telephone clenched tightly in his hand.

"How are you feeling?" he asked, trying to mask his concern and make it seem as if it were no more than a casual enquiry.

"I'm fine," Maria said.

She didn't sound fine, Rutter thought. She sounded anything but fine.

"What's the weather like down there?" he asked, cursing himself for talking in clichés, yet unable to think of anything else to say.

"I heard it raining about an hour ago," Maria told him. "When are you coming home, Bob?"

"Cloggin'-it Charlie thinks we're getting pretty close to solving the case. In fact, he's interrogating a suspect right now. With any luck, we could be back in London in the next two or three days."

"That long!"

Alarm bells started to ring inside Bob Rutter's head. He'd
offered to go home a couple of days earlier, and that had only
served to make his wife angry. Now, though she was trying
to sound as casual as he was, it seemed to him that she was
practically begging him to catch the next train.

"Are you sure you're all right, darling?" he asked. "Maybe
you should go and see a doctor."

"I've already seen one."

She'd already seen one! Rutter felt the panic rising in his
throat. "And what did he say?"

Maria laughed, though she didn't sound very amused. "I'm
not dying, if that's what you're worried about," she said. "But
we really need to talk."

"Talk? Talk about what?"

"I can't say over the phone."

"At least give me a hint," Rutter pleaded.

"I . . . no, I can't. Tell me you love me."

"You know I love you."

"And I love you. I love you perhaps more than you can ever
imagine."

Then the line went dead.

"You'd better tell me how the fight between you an' Steve
Walker started," Woodend said to Mike Finn. "An' don't rush
it, lad. I want details, an' I've got all the time in the world."

"I suppose it all goes back to Hamburg," Finn told him.

Woodend nodded. "I rather suspected it might."

"When we were there, we were gettin' maybe three or four
hours' sleep a day," Mike Finn continued, confirming what
Billie Simmons had already said to Woodend in the Grapes.
"We needed somethin' to keep us goin' when we were on
stage. There were these German slimmin' pills . . . an' . . .
an' . . ."

"Yes? Spit it out!"

"Preludin was their proper name, but we called them
Prellies. They'd keep you awake, all right. We used to eat

tubes of the bloody things every night. They made us all feel really great."

Woodend already had a sense where this story was going. "But you can't get them in England, can you?"

"No, you can't," Finn agreed. "But Steve had some. I don't know how he got his hands on them – maybe he smuggled them in when he came back after the last time the Seagulls played in Germany. He was dead tight with them. I asked for some – just a few – more than once, but he always said no."

"An' why do you think that was?"

"His excuse was that if he gave them to me, he'd have to give them to everybody who'd tried them in Hamburg."

"Go on," Woodend said.

"The night before Eddie Barnes was killed, I knew Steve had some Prellies on him, because I'd seen him takin' them in the bog. Then, just before he went on stage, he took his jacket off. I waited till the Seagulls had started playin', then I went through his pockets an' found the pills. Leavin' them around like that, he was askin' for it, wasn't he?"

"Of course he was," Woodend agreed, not even trying to sound convincing. "Make a habit of stealin' other people's property, do you?"

"It wasn't stealin'. I'd have paid him back in the end. Anyway, after the club had closed down for the night, and we were just messin' about – playin' our guitars an' stuff like that – he checked in his jacket an' realised the pills were missin'. He must have remembered I'd asked him for some, because he accused me right away of pinchin' them."

"An' that's when the fight broke out?"

"No, there wasn't really the space in the dressin' room. We went into the dancin' area. Pete Foster an' a couple of the others tried to calm things down, but Steve was really angry, an' I'd been lookin' for an excuse to take a poke at him for months."

"How long did this fight last?"

"It couldn't have been more than a couple of minutes. Then

Steve got a lucky punch in, an' I went down. He asked me if I'd had enough, I said I had, an' that was it."

"Why hasn't anybody told me this before?" Woodend demanded, just managing to keep his anger under control.

"We all talked it over, an' there didn't seem to be much point," Mike Finn said. "I mean, everybody who was there in the club was watchin' the fight, weren't they? Any re-wiring must have been done after we'd gone. Besides," he continued sheepishly, "we couldn't really tell you about the fight without tellin' you what caused it, an' as far as I know, Prellies are illegal over here."

"So to save yourselves bein' booked on a minor drugs charge, you were willin' to let a murderer get away scot-free."

"We were worried you'd close the club down if you knew about the drugs. An' even if you didn't, once Mrs Pollard had found out, she'd have made sure that none of us ever worked there again. But if we'd really thought that tellin' you about it would help catch Eddie's killer, we'd have come clean right away."

"Bollocks!" Woodend said.

"Am I goin' to be charged with anythin'?" Mike Finn asked.

"There's a lot I *could* charge you with – vandalism, threatenin' behaviour, obstruction of justice – an' that's just the start."

"But you're not goin' to, are you?" Finn asked, with the first signs of hope in his voice since the interview began.

"No, to tell you the truth, I can't be bothered with all the paperwork," Woodend said. Then, seeing the look of relief on Finn's face, he added, "But what I will do is tell everybody at the club what a louse you've been. By this time tomorrow, I'd be surprised if even your fellow members of the Knockouts will want to have anythin' to do with you."

Eighteen

There was a thick air of gloom hanging over the corner table in the public bar of the Grapes where the two London detectives were sitting.

"For a while back there, I was so sure Mike Finn was our man," Woodend said. "Everythin' seemed to be pointin' to him. Maybe *that* should have alerted me to the fact I was on the wrong track – murders hardly ever come in neat packages."

"Hmm," Rutter said abstractly.

"But there's no doubt he was involved in the fight," Woodend continued. "I had a talk with Billie Simmons and Pete Foster ten minutes ago. They weren't exactly eager to come clean about it, but when they realised I knew the story already, they told me exactly the same as Finn did."

"Hmm," Rutter said, for a second time, as he stared down at his half-pint of bitter.

Woodend put his pint down on the table. "Is somethin' the matter with you, lad?"

Rutter looked up. "I'm worried about Maria," the sergeant confessed. "She didn't sound right when I talked to her on the phone. Actually, she's not sounded right all the time we've been in Liverpool. I really think that she might be ill."

"Then you'd better get yourself off back home right away."

"I've thought about doing just that. But if I rush back to London every time we have a minor domestic crisis, how will I ever be able to do my job properly?"

"It's a problem," Woodend agreed. "Why don't you put in for a desk job? I'd be sorry to lose you, but at least

195

that way you could be back home by six o'clock every night."

"I've thought about that, too. But doing this particular job has become part of what I am. I'd be a different person if I became a pencil-pusher who never left his office – and that wouldn't be the person Maria married." Rutter lit a cork-tipped cigarette. "How do you manage it, sir?"

Woodend sighed. "I'm from a completely different generation to you, lad," he said. "Young women were brought up to expect their men when they saw them, back then. An', of course, there was the war – a lot of us were away for five or six years. Still, it hasn't always been easy. I was on a case up in Northumberland the day our Annie was born. I've managed to miss most of her birthday parties an' all." He paused, to light a cigarette himself. "How does that Gilbert an' Sullivan song go? 'A policeman's lot is not a happy one'? Isn't that it? But somebody's got to do the job, an' I flatter myself I'm not bad at it."

Someone coughed discreetly, and looking up they saw Steve Walker standing there, looking uncharacteristically deferential.

"I hear you got that Inspector Hopgood to drop the charges against me," he said.

"That's right, I did," Woodend agreed.

"Thank you."

"It was the least I could do for you, after all you'd done to help me. What put you on to Finn in the first place?"

Walker shrugged. "It was just a feelin' at first. I've known Mike for a long time, an' I could tell from the way he looked at me that he was up to somethin'. Then this mornin' I noticed a stain on his jeans. It looked like the kind of stain we used to get when we did glue an' paper work in school. So I reckoned he must have sent that letter to Jack – which meant that he'd killed Eddie."

"But he didn't, you know," Woodend said gently. "The only real chance he'd have to do that was durin' the fight – an' he was too busy gettin' knocked on the floor by you to do it then."

Walker grinned, but only for a second. "I suppose you're right," he agreed. "I suppose I've always known it, really. Even when I was tellin' myself that it had to be him, there was a small part of me that couldn't see him havin' enough guts to go through with it." He reached into his pocket, took out a crumpled piece of paper, and flattened it out on the table. "That's the name an' address of the girl I was with behind the curtain on the night before Eddie died. She'll tell you I never went anywhere near the amp."

Woodend glanced at the paper. "How did you get this?" he asked.

"I've always known who she was. I just wanted to keep her out of it. But I was wrong to try an' do that. If you're goin' to catch Eddie's killer, you're goin' to need every bit of information you can get."

"Let me get this straight," Woodend said suspiciously. "You knew that I suspected you, but you still wouldn't give me the name of the girl who could clear you?"

"Yeah, that's right."

"Why?"

Walker was beginning to look uncomfortable. "She might be a bit of a scrubber," he said, "but I didn't want her mum an' dad findin' out what she'd been up to."

Sitting slumped in one of the bedsit's two battered armchairs, Terry Garner tried to focus his eyes on the whisky bottle. It looked to him as if only a couple of shots had been poured from it, but if he'd had such a small amount to drink, why was he feeling so queasy?

He turned his attention back to the man sitting opposite him. The visitor's face had seemed perfectly normal only a few minutes earlier, but now his features appeared to be constantly changing, so that one moment his nose would be long and thin, and the next it was as round and flat as a squashed tomato. His voice had altered, too. Hearing him talk was like listening to a tape recorder which wasn't playing at quite the right speed.

"I'll poom yooo another drrwink, Twerry," the visitor said, reaching for the bottle.

But he didn't pour himself another one, Terry Garner's fuzzy thoughts told him. In fact, as far as he could tell, the visitor didn't even appear to have touched his first drink.

A glass of water might help, the young guitarist decided. Water might do just the trick. All he had to do was stand up, and walk over to the sink. It was such an easy thing to do, he told himself. Get up and go over to the sink. Get *up* and go over to the sink. Yet when he tried to rise from his chair, his legs felt as if they were being held down by lead weights.

"It bwon't be long now, Twerry," said the visitor. "Bwany second now you're going to bwack out."

Woodend ordered another pint, and took a rumpled copy of the previous Tuesday's *Mersey Sound* out of his jacket pocket.

"Might as well see if flickin' through this gives me any inspiration," he told his sergeant.

But after all the disappointment earlier in the day, he couldn't really summon much enthusiasm. It looked like this one of those cases he'd told Geoff Platt about, the kind you either solved quickly or not at all. And right at that moment, 'not at all' seemed like being by far the most probable outcome.

With a sigh, he opened up the *Mersey Sound*. Even a first sweeping glance told him that the newspaper was considerably better organised than Geoff Platt's office had been. True, some of the photographs had come out a little grainy, and occasionally the print was slightly unaligned, but on the whole, it promised to be a clear, informative read.

Woodend, being the man he was, had soon left his despondency behind him, and was plunging headlong into the world of the Liverpool music scene. He learned, among other things, that the Fantastics were soon to follow the Beatles and the Seagulls and play in the Star Club in Hamburg, that Johnny and the Deltas had split up, and that a big bash was being organised in three weeks time at the New Brighton Tower Ballroom.

Woodend reached the classified advertisements at the back of the paper, and a gentle smile of anticipation came to his lips. He'd always loved the classifieds, because to him they weren't just about buying and selling goods and services, they were also about needs and desires – which were not the same things at all.

'BSA 250 cc. motorbike, 1954, 50,000 miles on the clock,' he read. 'Will swap for Fender bass guitar in good condition.'

The chief inspector's smile broadened. Despite what Geoff Platt might say about most of the kids in Liverpool joining groups for fun, there were still enough Steve Walkers around, and here was one of them – a young hopeful willing to give up what was probably his most prized possession on the off-chance that it might help him to find fame and fortune.

'Band needs singer,' said another. 'Must be tall, good looking and have his own van.'

But Woodend was willing to bet that if the singer who applied could satisfy the third requirement, the group would be more than willing to overlook the need for the first two.

'The Seagulls, one of Liverpool's premier groups, are looking for a new lead guitarist,' said a third advertisement.

The Seagulls, one of Liverpool's premier groups, are looking for a new lead guitarist.

Jesus!

Woodend involuntarily scrunched up the paper in his big hands. "I want Terry Garner found!" he said urgently to Rutter. "Now! Get on to Inspector Hopgood. Tell him to put as many men as he can spare out on the streets lookin' for the lad. An' make sure he sends a couple of bobbies to Terry's home."

"What's happened, sir?" Rutter asked.

"Never mind that," the chief inspector said. "Just get on

199

the bloody phone to that prat Hopgood." He glanced across at the bar. Steve Walker was still there, nursing a half-pint of bitter.

Thank God!

"Steve! Do you know where Terry Garner lives?" the chief inspector shouted.

Walker turned round. "Yeah. I've been round to his place a few times. We done a couple of jam sessions, an'—"

"I'm not interested in your bloody social life," Woodend interrupted. "Take me round to Terry's now – before the poor lad ends up like Eddie Barnes."

Nineteen

The black Liverpool taxi hurtled down the road – its headlights flashing, its horn blaring. It wove its way dangerously between Austin Cambridges and Ford Anglias, leaving their drivers pale and shaking. It narrowly missed buses and came perilously close to scraping against the sides of high lorries. And still, wedged as he was against the back door of the vehicle, Woodend fretted that they weren't going fast enough and would arrive too late.

If only we had a proper siren! the chief inspector thought. If only this was a proper police car!

But there just hadn't been the time to wait for one of *them* to turn up outside the Grapes.

The taxi shot tightly round a sharp corner, and the tyres screamed out in protest.

"We're hardly movin'," Woodend yelled through the glass partition at the cabbie. "You're drivin' like an old woman. Get your bloody clog down, man!"

"You're sure that Terry Garner's in real danger, are you, sir?" Bob Rutter asked, as the taxi swung again, and he was cannoned into his boss.

"Of course I'm bloody sure," Woodend said. "I wouldn't be riskin' life an' limb if I wasn't!"

"If anything's happened to Terry, I'll never forgive myself," Steve Walked moaned from the other side of Rutter.

"It's not your fault," Woodend told him. "Always remember that. Whatever happens, it's not your fault!"

But in a way, it was. It was Steve Walker's fault because

he was Steve Walker – the cool kid who everybody wanted to get close to.

The taxi turned on to a side street lined with dilapidated three-storey terraced houses.

"Fifth door down!" Steve Walker shouted to the cabbie.

The taxi screeched to a halt, but even before it had finally finished moving, Woodend had his door open. "Wait here," he ordered the driver. "We might be needin' you again."

The chief inspector dashed across the pavement to the front door, with Steve Walker close on his heels.

"The place is all bedsits," Walker explained. "Terry lives up on the top floor."

Woodend stabbed the two top bells, and, without waiting for a response, punched all the others for good measure. There was the sound of footsteps in the hallway. Then the door swung open to reveal a youngish woman with her hair already in night-time curlers and a Park Drive hanging lethargically from the corner of her mouth.

"Police! Emergency!" Woodend said, barging straight past her and heading for the stairs.

He took the steep stairs three at time. Behind him he could hear the pounding feet of the others. Even from only half-way up the last flight, Woodend could smell the gas which had managed to insinuate its way under Terry Garner's door.

He reached the top floor. There were two doors on the landing. "Which one is it?" he called down the stairs. "The left or right?"

"The right!" Steve Walker gasped.

Woodend hammered furiously on the right-hand door, then immediately turned the handle. The door was locked – but he was prepared to wager that they would find no key inside.

The chief inspector stepped back, braced himself against the wall, and lashed out with his right leg. His foot made contact with the lock, but though the door groaned, it did not give. He swung his leg again, and this time the door splintered, and swung open.

Woodend rushed into the room, the other two men now close behind him. The smell inside was almost overpowering, and its source was easily identified. The fire set into the far wall was hissing like an angry snake, but there was no flame to burn off the gas.

Terry Garner, the young man the chief inspector would have considered suitable dating material for his own daughter, was lying directly in front of the fire, his head resting on a pillow – as if all this had really been his own choice.

"Open the bloody window!" Woodend shouted over his shoulder to Rutter. "And turn the bloody gas off."

Garner was lying on his stomach. Woodend turned him over and placed his index finger against the young guitarist's neck, hoping against hope that he would find some evidence of a pulse.

It was drizzling slightly as Woodend walked down the cobbled street towards the Grapes. On the other side of the road, in front of the Cellar Club, stood a muscular man sheltering under an umbrella – Rick Johnson, newly released from the cells and already attending to his mother's business.

Woodend crossed the street. "I wouldn't have thought a hard man like you would be bothered by a bit of rain," he said, looking first at Johnson and then up at his brolley.

"I've given up bein' hard," Johnson told him, and though his tone could not have been called exactly friendly, perhaps some of his customary aggressiveness was missing.

"Good for you," Woodend said. "Any particular reason?"

"I don't want the kids me an' Lucy plan to have only seein' me on visitin' day. I don't want them to grow up thinkin' I belong behind bars."

An' maybe you just can't allow yourself to value hardness any more, Woodend thought – not after you've been beaten up by your runt of a brother-in-law.

"I'm goin' into the club," he said. "Is that all right with you?"

Johnson shrugged. "I can't stop you, can I? You're the law."
As he opened the door, he bit his lower lip. "I'd still have been
in the nick if it hadn't been for you. Thanks."

He'd been thanked twice in the same day, Woodend told
himself. That had to be some kind of record. If this went on,
he'd probably start thinking he was the bloody Lone Ranger.

He made his way down the narrow stairs, the noise level
increasing with every step he took. He didn't recognise the
group who were performing on the stage, but it certainly
wasn't one of those which had been playing in the club the
night before Eddie Barnes died.

The chief inspector took what he knew would be his last
look round the Cellar Club – at the hard chairs which faced
the stage, at the girls dancing in the far tunnel – and wondered
why he always found it so hard to leave the scene of the crime
behind him.

He crossed the tunnel, stopping at the edge of it so he was
still some distance from the snack bar, and found himself
looking across at some faces which had become all too
familiar. There was Alice Pollard, her brassy hair having
regained some of its springiness now that Rick had been
released. There was Ron Clarke, the mild, unassuming man
who could be so powerful when he was just a disembodied
voice coming through the tannoy system.

Two of the Seagulls were by the bar, too. Pete Foster, who
was following his mother's dream while trying to tell himself
that it was his own, was talking to a girl he might later persuade
to go behind the curtain with him. And Billie Simmons, who
seemed to have reduced all life's complexities into the single
act of banging the drum skins, was smoking a cigarette and
waving occasionally to girls who had waved to him first.

The fifth familiar face belonged to Jack Towers, who was
standing just as he must have been when Steve Walker first
noticed him – watching the stage yet totally unmoved by
the music.

Though the music was too loud for Woodend to hear their

words, he could not fail to notice the sudden reaction of the teenagers closest to the entrance. With surprised – or perhaps apprehensive – expressions on their faces, they were looking up the stairs at the two pairs of legs, clad in blue serge, which had just appeared there.

The legs continued their downward path, blue tunics became visible, and now there could be no doubt that two uniformed policemen were entering the club. Word of their arrival was travelling rapidly up the tunnels. Girls stopped dancing, boys stopped trying to chat them up, and finally the group playing on stage fell silent.

An eerie silence followed, in which no one said a word, yet the music continued to ring in everyone's ears.

The two constables made their way over to where Woodend was standing. The one who was leading saluted. "Inspector Hopgood told us that you had a job for us, sir," he said.

Woodend nodded. "That's right," he agreed.

It was only a few steps to the snack bar, but as he took them Woodend was aware of five pairs of eyes which were looking at him so intently that they were almost burning holes in him.

He came to halt in front of the Seagulls' manager. "It's all over, Mr Towers," he said.

Twenty

After a brief pause, it had started to rain again. Woodend stood by the window of the brown and cream interview room, watching as the drops of water spattered against the pane, then slid slowly down to the sill. They made the same sort of noise on impact as might be made by a small timid animal which was begging to let in out of the cold, he thought fancifully.

He turned from the window to face the man who had been out in the cold for most of his life. Jack Towers was sitting at the table, his head in his hands. He no longer looked like the tall, gangly clown who had nervously tried to talk Steve Walker into seeing things his way. Now, even through his despair, it was possible to gain some sense of the ruthlessness which had led him to cast away human life without a second's thought.

"You'd probably been planning to get rid of Eddie Barnes for quite some time, but it was the audition with the record company in London which really spurred you into immediate action," Woodend said.

Towers looked up, peering through his outstretched fingers as if he were already in gaol. "Eddie would have let the Seagulls down," he said. "He just wasn't good enough to play with them."

"So why didn't you, as their manager – as the guidin' force in their career – simply say that to the rest of the group?" the chief inspector asked.

Towers closed his fingers again, as if, by doing so, he could shut out the world.

206

"I'll tell you why, shall I?" Woodend said – but it was a rhetorical question, and he expected no response. "You weren't just afraid that Steve would ignore your suggestion – you were terrified that if you criticised his mate, he'd get rid of you. In other words, if he had to choose between you an' Eddie, he would have picked Eddie every time."

Even though Towers' hands still covered his face, it was obvious from the way his body slumped even more that the barb had hit home – just as Woodend had intended it to. The chief inspector lit up a Capstan Full Strength, and felt the harsh smoke rasp against the back of his throat. He was getting old, he thought, and the years of heavy drinking, smoking and fried food were starting to catch up on him. Maybe it was time he switched to the kind of poncy cigarettes his sergeant smoked.

"So you decided that the only way out was to kill Eddie," he continued. "An' you had to kill him *quickly*, because you thought that his replacement needed to get plenty of practice in with the group before you went down to London for the audition." He took another drag on the cigarette. It still irritated his throat. "I don't know exactly what method of murderin' him you were workin' on," he continued, "but when the fight broke out between Mike Finn and Steve Walker, it seemed like fate had dropped the perfect opportunity right into your lap, didn't it?"

The manager sighed, but said nothing.

"Only it didn't quite work out like that, did it, Mr Towers? Because Steve's the sort of feller who needs to have his mates around him, an' so he brought in Terry Garner, who was a far worse guitarist all the time than Eddie was even on his worst day. But again, you didn't dare complain, so you soon realised you were goin' to have to kill for a second time. It was almost too easy, wasn't it? Terry would have been frightened to let most people into his flat, but he trusted *you*. An' you took advantage of that trust to feed him doped whisky an' fake a suicide attempt. That should add another ten or fifteen years to your sentence."

207

"It doesn't matter," Towers mumbled from behind his hands. "Nothing matters now that Steve knows I killed Eddie."

"You lied about what happened to you down at the docks, didn't you?" Woodend said.

"I *was* beaten up."

"Of course you were. But there was no mysterious phone call from a man who claimed to know something about Eddie's death. You were down there on the pick-up, lookin' for a bit of rough trade. Only you picked the wrong sailor, an' instead of him givin' you what you wanted, he worked you over."

"It could have been worse," Jack Towers said. "I've got friends who've had bones broken."

"Geoff Platt over at the *Mersey Sound* will be one of those friends of yours, will he?" Woodend asked.

"Yes."

"An' Doctor Atkinson from the Royal Liverpool University Hospital?"

"Yes." Towers spread his fingers a little, as if he wanted to see Woodend's reaction to what he had to say next. "You must be delighted the killer's turned out to be a raving queer," he continued.

"I'm not one of those fellers who goes around thinkin' homosexuals should be strung up by their thumbs," Woodend said, and anyone who knew him would have been able to detect an edge of anger slipping into his voice.

"Of course you're not," Towers said cynically. "At least, you're not one of those fellers who'd ever say so *in public*."

Woodend slammed his fist down hard on the table, his anger almost full-blown by now. "Listen, one of my best mates in the army was a homo," he said. "He was a brave soldier, an' a good comrade. He was killed just outside El Alamein, an' I still miss him, even now. So you see, as far as I'm concerned it doesn't really matter who you end up in bed with – it's how you live your life that counts. An' neither me nor the homo lad I served with have ever been cold-blooded killers."

Woodend's head was pounding. If he stayed in the same

room with this man much longer, he'd beat him to a pulp.

"Eddie Barnes didn't deserve to die," he said. "You had no right to take his life away from him." He stubbed his cigarette viciously in the ashtray. "Is there anythin' else you'd like to say before we draw up your statement?"

Towers lifted his hands away from his face, and looked Woodend squarely in the eyes. "The only thing I'd care to add is that I love Steve Walker," he said defiantly.

"What do you think that is?" Woodend demanded. "Some kind of mitigatin' circumstance?"

"I love him, but I've never touched him," Towers said dreamily, as if he hadn't heard Woodend's words at all. "And never *would* have touched him. He doesn't feel the same towards his own sex as I do. I've always known that. But sometimes you just can't help who you fall in love with, can you?"

"I don't need to hear all this crap," Woodend said harshly.

But once again, Towers acted as if he hadn't heard him. "All I ever wanted was for the Seagulls to be successful, because I knew that that was what Steve wanted more than anything else in the world. And I was prepared to do whatever was necessary to see that he achieved his ambition."

Woodend put both his big hands flat on the table, and leant forward towards Towers. He had only one ambition at that moment – to hurt the other man as much as he could.

"So you took one young life, an' nearly took another," he said. "An' what have you got out of it?"

"Nothing," Towers said.

"*Less* than nothin'," Woodend told him. "Steve Walker never loved you like you love him, but at least he was very fond of you." He paused, to make sure the effect of his final words really sank in. "I'm willin' to bet that now, if they were goin' to hang you for this, he'd be elbowin' his way to the front of the queue for the chance to put the rope around your neck."

*   *   *

It was almost closing time in the Grapes, but in Woodend's book, until the towels were actually over the pumps, there was time for one last pint.

The chief inspector took a sip of best bitter and smacked his lips contentedly. "I'm doin' my best to wash the taste of this case out of my mouth," he explained to his sergeant.

"How long have you known that Towers is a homosexual?" Rutter asked.

"A while," Woodend replied. "I'd have mentioned it to you before, but it didn't seem relevant."

"What put you on to him? Was it just a gut feeling?"

The chief inspector shook his head. "Not at all. I've never been one of those fellers who think that just because a man's a bit effeminate he has to be queer. An' by the same token, I don't assume that because he's built like a brick shithouse, he must automatically chase every bit of skirt he sees. Like you heard me say to Towers, I fought in the army with homos."

"So what did tip you off?"

"Doctor Atkinson gave Jack Towers special treatment when he was admitted to the hospital after the attack at the docks. A private room, his own telly – the works. Now why should he have done that? I asked Atkinson that very question, an' he claimed it was because Towers was the Seagulls' manager, and he himself was a big fan. Which was, of course, a complete bloody lie."

"How do you know that?"

"I told him I thought that 'Lime Street Rock' was one of the best songs Steve Walker had ever written, an' he agreed with me."

"So what?"

"Think back to the auditions, lad," Woodend said. "One of the young hopefuls wanted to play 'Lime Street Rock', an' Steve Walker absolutely hit the roof because he said he wasn't goin' to have anybody else playin' one of the songs that Eddie Barnes wrote. Now if Atkinson had really been a fan of the group, as he claimed he was, he'd have known it was Eddie's song."

"I see," Rutter said. "I should have spotted that."

"So we're back to the question of why Atkinson gave Towers special treatment," Woodend continued. "Remember what I said at the start of this case – when we were on the ferry comin' across the Mersey – about not all villages bein' geographical?"

"Yes?"

"The only reason Atkinson could have had for lookin' after Towers so well was that they were friends – from the same non-geographical village. But what kind of village would it be that could accommodate both a successful doctor an' a humble shippin' clerk? As soon as I learned that Doctor Atkinson was a homosexual, I had my answer."

"Very smart," Rutter admitted.

"Aye," Woodend agreed, almost complacently. "I do have my moments now an' again."

Rutter took a sip of his drink, and wondered whether he had better order another round before last orders were called. "And now you're going to tell me how you knew that Jack Towers was the killer?" he asked.

"It was timin' again," Woodend replied. "When I went to see Geoff Platt over at the *Mersey Sound*, he told me he'd heard Eddie Barnes was leavin' the Seagulls, but he also said he couldn't remember who'd told him. But he *did* remember. He'd got the information from Jack Towers."

"So why did he lie? Was he deliberately shielding a murderer?"

Woodend absent-mindedly reached across and helped himself to one of his sergeant's cork-tipped cigarettes.

"I'm sure it never occurred to Geoff Platt for an instant that Towers might have killed Eddie Barnes," he said, "but you're right when you say he was shieldin' him from somethin'. He didn't want to give us a reason to take a closer look at Towers – in case we found out he was a homo. It was simply a case of one villager doin' all he could to protect another."

211

"That makes sense," Rutter agreed.

Woodend smiled, almost mischievously. "But you've still not asked the important question, which is: why did Towers lie to Platt about Eddie leavin' the group in the first place?"

"Why did Towers lie about Eddie leaving the group in the first place?" Rutter asked deadpan, slipping effortlessly into the role of comedian's dupe again.

"Because he didn't have any choice," Woodend replied. "Look, he'd convinced himself that the Seagulls needed lots of time to practise with their new guitarist before the audition, an' that meant he had to be available even before Eddie Barnes was cold. On the other hand—"

"On the other hand," Rutter interrupted, "the Mersey *Sound*, which was the best place to advertise for a replacement, went to press before Towers had had a chance to murder Eddie!"

"Exactly," Woodend agreed. "Even if Eddie Barnes had been plannin' to leave the group – an' he'd have been a fool to do that when things were just startin' to happen for them – he'd have told Steve Walker long before he told Jack Towers. An' Steve said he didn't know anythin' about it. So when I saw that advert in the *Mersey Sound*, it told me that Towers knew Barnes was goin' to die days before it happened – an' that could only mean he was the killer."

Steve Walker entered the pub and made a beeline for them. "I've just heard you've charged Jack Towers with Eddie's murder," he said.

"That's right," Woodend agreed.

A lopsided, ironic grin came to Walker's face. "Well, at least now you won't have to question the lovely Mavis, an' ruin her chances of becomin' a Mother Superior someday," he said.

"You knew Jack Towers was a homosexual, didn't you?" Woodend asked.

"Yeah, I knew he was queer," said Steve Walker. "Once you'd knocked around with him for a while, it became pretty obvious."

Of course he'd known. But he had hidden that knowledge

212

from the police – not because he was a fellow villager as Geoff Platt was, but because protecting people more vulnerable than himself was just part of his nature.

"An' did you also know that he had a big crush on you?" the chief inspector said.

"Yes, I knew Jack had a bit of a thing for me," Steve Walker said, shrugging awkwardly. "So what? He never tried anythin' on. There was no real harm in it."

No, Woodend thought. No harm at all. Except that it had resulted in the death of Eddie Barnes – and had almost cost Terry Garner his life, too.

Tears were forming in Steve Walker's eyes. "Why did Jack do it?" he asked, pleadingly.

"He wanted to be rich," Woodend lied, "an' he thought he'd never make money out of the group as long as Eddie was in it."

"You're not makin' any sense. How would Eddie have stopped him makin' money?"

"Jack didn't think Eddie was good enough to play with the Seagulls. He thought he'd hold the rest of you back."

A look of deep sadness came into Steve Walker's eyes. "Do you want to hear somethin' funny?" he said. "Or is the word I'm really lookin' for 'ironic'?"

"I won't know till I've heard it," Woodend said softly.

"The *Mersey Sound* had a poll last month. All the readers got the chance to vote on who they thought was the best lead guitarist in the whole of Liverpool. Eddie came top by a mile." Steve Walker wiped a tear from his eye with his shirt cuff. "Thank you for savin' Terry's life," he said, and then, without another word, he turned and walked away.

"That was a nice thing you did there, sir – lying about Towers' real motive," Rutter told his boss.

Woodend's shrug was almost as awkward as Walker's had been earlier. "The lad's had enough tough breaks in his time without havin' to live with the knowledge that, however indirectly, he's responsible for Eddie's death," he said. "But

213

even though I'm a good liar when I want to be, I don't know if, deep down, he was really fooled." The chief inspector sighed. "It's a funny thing, is love. Jack Towers has convinced himself that he killed Eddie because he wasn't a good guitarist, but it wasn't that at all, was it?"

"No," Rutter agreed. "It was jealousy. He killed him – and he would have killed Terry – because they could get closer to Steve Walker than he could."

Woodend glanced down at his watch. "Well, there'll be some paperwork to do in the mornin', but with any luck we should both be back in London by this time tomorrow night."

"Yes, sir, it'll be good to be home," Rutter said, though the thought of seeing Maria and hearing whatever it was that she had to tell him was already starting to churn his stomach up.

Epilogue

J ack Towers had been in custody for over twenty-four hours
when Bob Rutter paid off his taxi and opened his own front
gate for the first time in days. There were no welcoming lights
shining in the windows of his home, but that didn't necessarily
mean Maria had gone to bed, he reminded himself, because –
day or night – his wife's world was one of total darkness.

He inserted the key in the lock, turned it as quietly as he
could, and eased the front door open.

"Is that you, Bob?" asked a voice from the front parlour.

"It's me," Rutter said, putting down his suitcase in the
hallway and reaching for the light switch.

Maria was sitting on the sofa, her hands sedately folded
on her lap. Rutter hadn't been away long, but after all the
tense phone calls he had been half expecting some incredible
transformation to have taken place in his wife during his
absence. He need not have worried. If anything, she looked
even more beautiful than he remembered her.

He knelt down in front of her, and took her hands in his.
"I missed you," he said. "And I know you don't want to hear
me say this, but I was worried about you, as well."

She didn't get angry, as she might have done. Instead she
smiled the most beautiful smile he thought he had ever seen.

"You're going to have more to worry about than me in
future," she said. The smile suddenly faded, and was replaced
by a look of deep concern – perhaps even of fear. "At least,
you are if we decide to go ahead with it."

"Go ahead with what?"

"Because we don't have to if we don't want to, you know," Maria continued, speaking faster than he'd ever heard her speak before. "The doctor said that for a woman in my position it would be perfectly possible to argue that the psychological pressure would be too great and I could have the . . . the operation." She stopped – breathless and exhausted.

"Psychological pressure?" Rutter repeated. "Have the operation? I don't have a clue what you're talking about."

Maria squeezed his hands, very, very tightly. "I'm pregnant," she said. "The doctor confirmed it yesterday afternoon. If it's what you want, you could be a father in a few months' time."

Rutter felt as if he'd been hit squarely in the chest with a sledgehammer. Maria – his beautiful blind wife – was expecting a baby! It wasn't something they'd planned. It wasn't even something they'd discussed. And it still didn't have to happen if they decided they didn't want it to.

Bob took a deep breath and tried to decide how he felt about the bombshell his wife had just dropped.

It was in the kitchen where Joan Woodend was at her most comfortable, and it was in the kitchen that she was waiting for her husband when he returned from his rock'n'roll murder in Liverpool.

Woodend pecked his wife on the cheek, and lowered himself into the chair opposite her. "Well, that's another one wrapped up," he said.

"Yes, I expect I'll be readin' all about your exploits in the paper tomorrow," Joan replied.

"I shouldn't be surprised," Woodend agreed, though the thrill of seeing his name in print had long since faded away.

Joan stood up. "I'll make you some grub, Charlie," she said. "Will a fry-up do you?"

"I don't feel like eatin' right now."

"You don't! You're not ill, are you?"

Woodend shook his head. "No, I'm not ill. I just seem to

have lost my appetite for quite a lot of things lately." He forced a tired smile to his face. "If I feel like some food later, I'll let you know. Right now, I'd like to talk."

With a puzzled look on her face, Joan sank back into her seat. "What's this all about, Charlie?" she asked.

"I had this discussion with Bob last night about the difficulty of balancin' home an' work, an' it got me thinkin'. We've been married for over twenty years. How much of that time do you think we've actually spent together?"

"Well, it wasn't always *possible* to be together," Joan said, slightly awkwardly. "There was the war for a start, an' . . . ."

"Forget the war," Woodend told her. "How much time have we spent together since I got demobbed?"

"Not a great deal," Joan admitted, "but your work takes you away from London a lot."

"Aye, that's the point," Woodend agreed. "Neither of us are gettin' any younger—"

"It'd be a miracle if we were," Joan interrupted. "But you're still a fine figure of a man, Charlie Woodend, an' even though I'm a bit heavier than I used to be, I can manage to turn the occasional head on the street."

Woodend grinned. "I've no doubt about that. But the fact is, I've been wonderin' whether I might take the same advice I gave Bob, an' get a job that will keep me in town."

Joan frowned. "Is that what you want?"

"I'm not sure."

"Well, I'm sure what I want," Joan said. "Or should I say, I'm sure of what I don't want."

"You are?"

"Most definitely. What I *don't* want is to have a great lollopin' brute like you hangin' around the house all the time, forever gettin' under feet when I'm tryin' to do the housework."

"You don't?"

"I do not. The reason this marriage of ours has lasted so long, Charlie Woodend, is that we spend just enough time apart for us to be able to appreciate each other when we get the chance."

"Are you sayin' that I should stick to the job I've got?"

Joan stood up again. "Indeed I am. An' now we've got that sorted out, I'll go an' make you that food I promised you."

Woodend's stomach rumbled just at the thought of it. He could murder a fry-up, he decided. As he reached into his pocket for his cigarettes, he felt a great sense of relief surge through him, and realised that even the prospect of a desk job had weighed on him like a prison sentence.

He lit up a Capstan Full Strength and inhaled deeply. Capstans were such a bloody lovely smoke. And to think that just the day before he'd actually been contemplating switching to his sergeant's cork-tipped. He must have gone temporarily insane.

Joan, her back to him as she melted the lard over the stove, finally allowed herself the luxury of the amused smile she'd been holding back for the previous couple of minutes. Men! she thought affectionately. Most of the time they were nothin' but big soft kids.

The telephone rang in the hallway. Woodend sighed theatrically and rose to his feet.

"I'll get it," he said. "At this time of night it could only be the Super, tellin' me to pack my bags an' ship out to some Godforsaken hole in the middle of nowhere as soon as possible."

But he did not seem displeased at the prospect, Joan noted.

When Woodend returned to the kitchen a couple of minutes later, there was a broad smile on his face. "That wasn't the Super after all," he said. "It was that sergeant of mine."

Joan looked up from her cooking. "What's Bob doin' ringin' at this time of night? I'd have thought that after the last few days, you'd both be sick of the sound of each other's voices."

"An' so we are," Woodend agreed. "But he's just had a bit of good news, an' he wanted us to be the first ones to hear about it."